TOXIC

T0346934

NATASHA DEVON

Toxic

uclanpublishing

This is a work of fiction. All the names, characters, businesses, places, events and incidents in this book are either a product of the author's imagination or used in a fictitious manner. Any resemblance to actual persons, living or dead, or actual events is purely coincidental.

Toxic is a uclanpublishing book

First Published in Great Britain in 2022 by uclanpublishing
University of Central Lancashire
Preston, PR1 2HE, UK

978-1-912979-89-9

1 3 5 7 9 10 8 6 4 2

Set in 10/16pt Kingfisher by Amy Cooper.

A CIP catalogue record for this book is available from the British Library.

Printed and bound in Great Britain by Clays Ltd, Elcograf S.p.A.

To Shahroo, Karen and Amy,
thank you for being my Olivias

A note from the author

Please be aware that the following story contains vivid descriptions of panic attacks, as well as references to eating disordered behaviour. However, I have ensured there are no mentions of specific weights, sizes or calories. I hope the result is that this novel is honest in conveying the nature of mental health issues, without being gratuitous or triggering.

Prologue

Summoning every scrap of defiance I had left, I pulled my knees up to my chin and met her eyes. I repeated the line from Labyrinth, my favourite film, in my head. Y*ou have no power over me.*

She might be my therapist, but she couldn't make me talk. Not if I refused.

'I don't want to talk about it.'

'I know you don't. But if we're really going to work through this, we're going to have to talk about it. There's no other way.'

'But I'm fine now! I haven't had a panic attack in weeks. My grades are back to where they were before . . .the *thing* happened. I've done what I came here to do. I'm cured!'

'You are functioning much better than when you first came here, that's true. But functioning is not the same as cured, Llewella. You know that, don't you?'

'I'm . . . not ready. I don't want to go there. I'm scared the panic will come back. I can't go through that again. I'd rather just carry on as I am.'

'OK. It's your call. I can't force you to do anything you don't want to do. But remember this – our traumas are like bags of poison we carry around inside of us. In this room, you can lance them safely and it'll be painful for a bit, but I'll be here to help you deal with it. If you leave here today with that bag of poison intact, something else will burst it, one day. Probably when you least expect it . . .'

Two years later . . .

Autumn Term

'All that glitters is not gold;
Often have you heard that told'

The Merchant of Venice
Act 2, Scene 7

Chapter 1

It was one of those days when the clouds hung low and the air felt dense and heavy as I sweated my way up the long hill towards St Edith's High School for Girls. I hated it when the weather was like this.

It wasn't just the atmosphere which felt oppressive. Despite having spent the summer avoiding this part of town in a futile attempt to get into the 'holiday spirit', everything remained spookily unchanged. The square, grey facade of the bus station still blighted even the sunniest of skies. The green paint was still peeling from the front gate of the first house on the left at the bottom of the hill. An untamed tree still spilled on to the pavement halfway up, requiring even the tiniest of pupils to dart into the road to go around it. In about twenty minutes, the street would fill with SUVs as mums with huge sunglasses, designer handbags and faces frozen with Botox – or else their identical-but-younger au pairs – dropped off pupils who didn't live within walking distance. After attending St Edith's for six of my seventeen years on this planet, everything I saw, heard and felt was depressingly predictable.

Chiddingwell, the suburban Surrey town where I'd lived since I was five, was one of those places where everyone knew everyone's business. You could obtain a reputation in Chiddy merely by existing. Some residents chose to stay here after their education, getting jobs as office assistants in one of the solicitors or estate agents we seemed to have in abundance, but I couldn't think of anything worse. There was only one acceptable way to be a young human woman in Chiddy – white, slender, glamorous and conforming. I was none of those things. I'd spent my life here feeling alien, dreaming of being unleashed into the vibrant, diverse world I'd read about in books and seen in films; to finally find my tribe.

I took in an impatient, raggedy breath, reminding myself that right now, everything was fine. I tried to 'consciously count my blessings', like my therapist had taught me. I was safe. I was healthy. I was on target for all As in my exams. I practised the technique I'd learned to calm my mind – breathe in for a slow count of five, out for a slow count of seven. To make sure I didn't rush, I counted three of my rapid footsteps for each 'beat'. It helped, but I still felt irritable.

I heard someone running behind me and turned to see it was Olivia. A fellow oddball, Olivia and I had bonded in Year 7 over a mutual love of acting. Whenever I got overwhelmed by the sense of being a fish out of water, it was Olivia I sought out. She could usually help me make sense of life at St Edith's, or at least laugh at it with me.

'Hey!' she gasped, putting her hand on my shoulder, forcing me to stand still. I wondered if she could feel that I was damp with perspiration and resisted the strong urge to shrug her off. 'I was calling you but I don't think you heard. You walk so fast!' She put her hands on her thighs for a few seconds, breathing heavily.

I studied her for a moment, thinking how unfair it was that she was this unfit, apparently survived on a diet of Haribo and cheesy Wotsits and yet remained enviably thin. I immediately felt self-conscious, my hands travelling to my stomach which I could feel straining against the waistband of my trousers.

About three years ago I'd promised myself I'd lose weight by the time I left sixth form. But then I'd think that going on a diet made me a traitor to the body-positivity movement and I would tear into tubes of Pringles with new-found zeal. As a result, I was thought of as the 'pudgy' girl at school and I wasn't sure I wanted to spend three years at university wearing the same label.

I'd once overheard one of the Botox Mums saying, as she swiped a Twix out of her daughter's grasp, 'a fat girl will only ever be seen as a fat girl, no matter what else she achieves.' I was appalled by what she said, but somehow it also stuck with me. I found myself wondering how I looked, through that woman's eyes. It's weird how you can despise everything a person stands for, but still want them to like you at the same time.

Together, Olivia and I started back up the hill, me making a conscious effort to slow my footsteps.

'So, who do you think got in?' Olivia asked without preamble, as soon as she'd got her breath back.

There was no need to ask her what she meant. Just before summer break, we had auditioned for our school's annual Shakespeare production. This year, it was going to be *The Merchant of Venice*. The plays were a big deal at St Edith's. They were directed by Professor Coleman – a huge, booming, eccentric man with a penchant for flamboyant waistcoats, who swore within the context of beautifully constructed sentences and fashioned his bushy eyebrows into elaborate peaks.

He was in equal parts terrifying and inspiring and let it be known to anyone involved in his plays that he wouldn't let the trifling fact that we were teenage amateurs deter him from directing a masterpiece worthy of the Globe.

Anyone remotely interested in drama knew that to score a part in one of Professor Coleman's productions meant you had 'made it' and usually the main roles were given to Year 13s. Seeing as I was just over six feet tall and at an all-girls' school, I'd auditioned for two of the main male parts – Shylock and Antonio. Casting was supposedly a 'blind' process, but the taller pupils always somehow ended up cast in the male roles because, well – stereotypes and patriarchy, I supposed, and I wanted to maximise my chances.

Shylock, as the villain of the piece, would be fun, but it was Antonio I really wanted. The way I read it, Antonio was an outcast – outwardly confident but a misfit trapped in his own head and prone to bouts of low mood. All of which I could relate to.

Traditionally, auditions took place during the last week of the summer term and the cast was pinned up on the sixth-form notice board by the time school began again in September. Hence why Olivia and I were half an hour earlier than usual, along with a smattering of people doing theatre studies or from drama club, all huffing our way up the hill while trying (and failing) not to appear too eager. I had some ideas about who had been given which role, but I didn't want to say them out loud in answer to Olivia's question and jinx anything.

'I couldn't possibly speculate,' I told her.

'OK, so, one – you're not in a Shakespeare play now, so why are you using words like "speculate"?' Olivia retorted, but there was a smile on her face. She loved to tease me about my habit of using words she considered archaic, but I knew it came from a place of affection. 'And two – you know the list is already pinned up. There's nothing we can do to change it. So you don't have to worry about, like, tempting fate, or whatever.'

'Well, I think Charlotte's probably a shoo-in for Portia,' I replied, carefully. I didn't like Charlotte, but I couldn't decide whether it was because of her (lack of) personality or because I was jealous of her. Until I had worked that out, I had to try hard not to let my dislike show. After all, everyone knows fourth-wave feminists do not display envy; women should support other women unconditionally.

Charlotte was a quintessential PST (Perfect Surrey Teenager). She had blemish-free, porcelain skin; long silky blonde hair which naturally fell as though it had been carefully styled and a physique which was somehow both slender and curvy at the same time. She was a decent actor and had an OK singing voice, but seemed to be given opportunities over and above what her talent merited. Last year, she had played Rosalind in *As You Like It* and I didn't think she had done the Bard's brave, strong-willed heroine any justice with her two-dimensional performance. But that could have just been my bitterness talking. I would literally sever a limb for that part.

'Yeah,' Olivia replied, with what I thought might have been the subtlest of eye-rolls. 'I really hope I get Bassanio.'

I hoped so too. Olivia had been trying for a lead role for years and had always been given a chorus part. But last year she'd really dedicated herself to 'EMBODYING THE ESSENCE OF THE FUCKING CHARACTER' (as Professor Coleman was fond of saying) in drama club and I reckoned she stood a decent chance.

'Well. Here goes!' I said with a thin-lipped smile as the red-brick entrance to St Edith's loomed, ancient and imposing, ahead of us.

Kara, Head Girl and known as the school swot on account of her nothing-but-A*s record for absolutely everything, was sitting behind a desk in reception. I noticed she was wearing an immaculate black trouser suit and white shirt without a crease in sight, and wondered how she found the time to be so put-together.

'Ah, the drama crew!' Kara exclaimed as Olivia and I pushed through the heavy glass doors. 'I thought you'd be here early. You're ticked off,' she assured us, indicating a tablet in front of her on which, presumably, was a register. Kara loved doing this kind of extra-curricular school admin – it won her brownie points with teachers and, I was fairly certain, gave her a mildly thrilling power trip.

'Off you go.' She gestured in the direction of the notice board, just beyond her in our vast oak-and-brass-lined entrance hall, in a way that was borderline infuriating. She always acted like she was a teacher, giving us 'permission' to go about our day whenever the opportunity arose.

'Thanks. See you later,' I replied. I didn't bother to ask her about her summer. Other girls at school seemed to have a knack for pretending to like people. They had lengthy, small-talk-packed conversations with others, then bitched about them the moment their back was turned. I really didn't know how they found the requisite skill or energy.

6

Olivia and I practically sprinted to the board. I was surprised to notice we had gripped each other's hands at some point as we approached, although I didn't remember doing it. There, laminated as traditional and pinned at a precise angle, was the cast list. It might have been my imagination, but as the shiny surface caught the light from the chandelier overhead (donated to the school by an earl or a duke of somewhere in fifteen hundred and something-or-other) it looked as though it was actually glittering.

I could feel my heartbeat thundering in my ears as I scanned the list. Charlotte had, of course, got Portia. Shylock had gone to a girl in the year below called Rebecca who I didn't know that well but had absolutely smashed the minor role of Jaques the year before. Bassanio would be played by Olivia.

I caught her in a fierce embrace and jumped up and down, both of us squealing with delight. I was so happy for her.

'I'm so happy for you!' Olivia shrieked at a gazillion decibels and in a register probably more suited to dogs than humans.

'Wait, what?' I asked.

We broke apart, I ran my finger down the first few names and there I was.

Antonio: Llewella Williams.

Chapter 2

I felt euphoric all morning. I was practically skipping between lessons, a goofy smile plastered on my face. The first *Merchant* rehearsal was after school and I couldn't WAIT.

First, though, I had important business to attend to. At the end of last year, I'd been voted a member of the student council. That meant I could finally assemble a meaningful protest against our stupid school crest, which was so regressive it made my blood boil.

While our 'brother' school on the other side of Chiddy (which my actual brother Hugh attended) had *Credimus et Consequi* ('believe and achieve') stitched on to their blazer pockets and etched into their walls, St Edith's had *Mansuetudine et Oboedientia*, which means 'meekness and obedience'

Meekness and obedience! As Olivia would say – 'what in the actual fudge sticks?' It made a mockery of all the assemblies we'd sat through where we'd been told we could achieve anything and that we came from an academic lineage of proud feminist pioneers. Our motto evoked images of us learning needlecraft with books balanced on our heads in a bid to make us fit for marriage.

Of course, I'd brought this up before (numerous times, in fact) during my six years at the school and the response had always been the same: times had changed since the motto was created; it was appropriate for its era and it would be wrong to erase our history. Which I thought sounded suspiciously like 'it would be really expensive to replace all the crests and uniforms'.

Truth be told, this wasn't the first time I'd started a campaign which hadn't gone anywhere. There was the bitter winter I'd tried to persuade our head of year that forcing us to choose between wearing tights and socks (and not allowing us to wear both) contravened our human right to have simultaneously warm legs and feet. Then there was the petition I'd started to make our school adopt a neglected puppy from Battersea Dogs and Cats Home as a therapy animal. And the time I tried to get the librarian to remove all the novels by an author who'd been saying transphobic things on social media.

None of these projects had produced tangible results and a few had earned me a stern talking to from our long-suffering deputy head (who constantly bore the air of someone who'd 'had it up to here'), Mrs Tidwell.

'You have to pick your battles, Llewella,' she'd said, wearily removing her glasses and dangling them from one hand while rubbing her eyes with the other. 'You can't save the world.'

'Why can't I?' I'd fired back, churlishly.

Mrs Tidwell had sighed. 'Look, I think it's great that you are so passionate about social causes. But the truth is, change doesn't happen just because you've signed a petition, or done a speech in assembly. It takes sustained time and energy and a lot of boring admin, I'm afraid. And you're only one person. So, decide what change you'd most like to see, show me you can dedicate yourself to it and I'll see what I can do to support you.'

I'd left Mrs Tidwell's office huffing and stomping, in a rage at her implication that I wasn't prepared to put the effort in. Like all those hours I'd spent researching online, making posters, setting up stalls on the school field and shouting animatedly at people until they relented and agreed to add their signatures to petitions wasn't 'work'. Now, though, my shiny, shield-shaped student council badge gave me extra leverage. I was determined that by the time I left, our school motto would be something more befitting of the twenty-first century.

But what, though? That was the question I'd assembled a few members of the council that lunchtime to discuss.

'Shouldn't it have "diversity" in there somewhere?' asked Sophie, one of the very few people who occupied the centre of the popular crowd and student council Venn diagram.

'Not if we're being honest,' replied Isobel, a forthright but serious character who'd made her opponents in debating society actually weep on more than one occasion. 'I mean, take our year group. Llewella here' – she paused briefly to gesture in my direction – 'is the closest thing we have to an ethnic minority in fifty-five pupils. That's more than ninety-nine per cent white.'

I nodded. This wasn't news to me. Being of mixed heritage (Mum, white; Dad, of unknown brown origin), along with my height and the fact that I wasn't a stick insect meant I was as visually mismatched with most of my peers as it was possible to be. No one with eyes would ever describe us as diverse.

As we threw ideas back and forth, we passed around a box of Celebrations someone had bought along as a start-of-term treat. I'd been shoving the chocolates into my mouth absent-mindedly and was horrified to notice I'd managed to amass a small mountain of wrappers. Sugar helped me think – I regularly got through a whole family bag of Maltesers while writing an essay – but it was also one of the reasons I had to buy my clothes from plus size collections. Surreptitiously, I tried to scrunch the wrappers into a small ball, hoping no one else had noticed how I'd troughed my way through several handfuls.

By the time the bell rang to signal it was the end of lunch and time for us to scuttle back to our form rooms for afternoon register, we were no closer to agreeing and it was clear I'd lost control of the meeting. Sophie was singing 'Reach for the Stars' (a tune she'd discovered on YouTube by a 90s band called S Club 7) at the top of her voice, after someone had suggested '*Ad Siderum*'. Kara was correcting everyone's Latin grammar while Isobel lectured someone who'd submitted '*Carpe Diem*' on how predictable and unimaginative they were being.

I felt a familiar annoyance surge through my chest and thought of a phrase my mum sometimes used – 'a camel is a horse designed by committee'. I'd always thought the quickest way to get things done was by yourself and loathed group projects of any kind. Other people mucked about, slowed things down and made pointless objections for the sake of it.

Sighing, I suggested another meeting the following week. A mixture of chocolate and irritation made me feel slightly sick as I scooped up my satchel and lever-arch folder and stomped away.

What seemed like about twenty-five years later, we were partway through an unfathomably boring post-lunch 'induction' assembly. Why our head of year, Ms Trebor, felt we needed to be inducted when we were halfway through our A Levels and most of us had been at the same school since Year 7 was anyone's guess.

Ms Trebor was a PE teacher and constantly sported a combo of navy tracksuit trousers, neon trainers and a hoodie branded with the school crest, whatever the weather. She was also always bouncing. Today, she was hopping from foot to foot, making her dark glossy ponytail hop around maniacally. She was liberally peppering her speech with irritating colloquialisms, referring to us as 'guys' and punctuating her sentences with rhetorical 'yeah?'s.

I had always hated being referred to as 'guys' It was just another tool of the patriarchy, as far as I was concerned – referring to everyone in the room by a word associated with men. It had always seemed especially ludicrous to me when people used it at our all-girls' school. True, we had a few transgender boys, but that didn't seem a good enough reason to verbally erase all the women in the room. I even spoke to Mrs Tidwell about it once and received a lecture on how I need to 'pick my battles' and 'not read so much into everything'.

It was at least twenty-five degrees outside, yet because it was officially the autumn term, radiators had been switched on anyway. I winced as I felt a droplet of sweat trickle down my lower back towards the black, polyester-blend, boot-cut trousers I threw on virtually every morning. I sensed a familiar panic rising in my throat. What if we were only five minutes in and I was trapped here, all sweaty and uncomfortable? What if I started to sweat in visible places and people saw? There was no clock in the assembly hall and phones were prohibited, so I could only pray that the thirty minutes were nearly up and I could dash to the toilets to run my wrists under the cold tap, a strategy I'd learned to get my temperature back to normal.

I frantically scanned the hall for potential escape routes. I was suddenly very aware that my left elbow was touching Sam Cleathorn's right elbow. Sam hung around with the popular girls, but she wasn't one of the 'main ones' everyone (except me and maybe Kara) apparently aspired to be. Gossip was the collateral she traded to keep herself useful and relevant. I had no doubt that if I started 'being weird' now, rumours that I'd lost my mind again would have made their way around our school and probably to every other school in Surrey before the bell went.

I started to get that itchy feeling, where the effort of staying still becomes too much and it feels as though my insides are clawing to burst forth from my skin. I tried to do my breathing exercises without being too obvious. Breathe in for five, out for seven, in for five, out for seven.

They reckon when you're on the cusp of panic the best thing to snap you out of it is to be distracted. I was approaching the point of no return – the stage where I knew I'd have to stand up and run from the room in search of fresh air – when Aretha Jones mercifully provided that distraction.

'We have a new student joining us this year,' Ms Trebor declared. 'Her name is Aretha Jones and she's come to us from a stage school in London.' She gave the word 'London' a weird upward inflection, like it was some magical, faraway land where the streets are made of marshmallows and unicorns skip about leaving trails of glitter in their wake, as opposed to a place we could get to in half an hour on the train. 'I'll let her introduce herself.'

Usually when new students joined the school they'd have to be dragged reluctantly from where they'd been sitting in the audience to stand in front of us and mumble a few words about where they used to live, before slumping back into their seats with their chin tucked into their collars, cringing themselves inside out. In contrast, Aretha Jones emerged from where she had clearly been waiting behind one of the musty maroon drapes which served as a stage curtain for school performances. I felt Sam twist in her seat and glanced up to see she was looking at Grace, the alpha of her group, who was sat directly behind her, eyebrows raised and face set in a smirk. I couldn't blame Grace, really. I mean, who hides behind a curtain for twenty-five minutes just so they can make an entrance?

Someone started clapping and most of us joined in confusedly as Aretha emerged from 'backstage'. She was, I thought, probably the most attractive person I'd ever seen in real life. She wasn't what you'd call conventionally beautiful (or certainly not by Chiddy standards) – she was short and solidly built with a halo of tight curls, dyed platinum blonde and tied into two bunches. Yet, she had that thing that can't be bottled or bought – the indescribable quality which makes you want to look at someone forever. Until that day, I'd never really understood what people meant when they said that someone glows from within.

Aside from admiration, I felt something unfamiliar I couldn't quite put my finger on when I looked at Aretha.

Later I would identify it as kinship, with a side-order of hope. Aretha was another brown person, someone to help break up the sea of heads covered in centre-parted, poker-straight, light-brown and honey-blonde hair that was St Edith's. She was someone who must surely understand how it feels to be different; indeed, she seemed to emphasise and revel in her difference, wearing it proudly and unself-consciously. She might also reassure me that things *were* as different as I had imagined outside my claustrophobic little town.

Aretha was dressed in high-waisted jeans, a mint-green cropped top which showed just a hint of midriff and trainers, showing a flagrant disregard for our sixth form's 'business wear' policy. She also had a strictly-against-the-rules silver hoop in her left eyebrow, as well as a tattoo of a treble clef on her left wrist. I appreciated her style – I'd never really understood why we needed to dress like candidates in The Apprentice in order to learn, anyway. She was holding a microphone in one hand, using the other to wave at us. And not the kind of wave I would give in her situation (frenetic jazz hands which would make me look like an idiot, or a too-enthusiastic mime act); it was a slow, simple, confident half-circle accompanied by a wide, dazzling smile.

'Hey, guys!' she almost-shouted, as though she was walking on stage at the O2 and had to yell to be heard above the din of enthusiastic applause. When Aretha said the dreaded word, 'guys', I found I didn't mind.

'So, I'm Aretha,' she continued. Her accent was one of those difficult-to-place ones which gives the impression the person speaking has lived in lots of different countries.

She seemed like she was always on the verge of giggling but was having to contain herself. I wanted to be let in on whatever the joke was. 'My parents named me after their favourite musician – Aretha Franklin. I suppose that means I was destined to be a singer.' She laughed, letting us know that she was being ironic and didn't take herself so seriously as to actually believe in destiny. 'Actually, I spent the summer doing backing vocals for a band. You might have heard of them. They're called Brass Traps.' At this, a few of the girls gasped and I heard one of them whisper, 'no *way*!' They were clearly one of those bands who had a massive cult following, although I had no idea who they were. 'It was really exciting getting to perform at all the festivals, especially Glastonbury.' I watched as every torso in the room leaned infinitesimally forward – a sure sign that her audience were intrigued.

Grace, perhaps sensing that having performed at Glastonbury was popularity currency she couldn't compete with, stood up, cupped her hands around her mouth and yelled, 'GO ON, THEN – SING!'

Sam and a few other of Grace's cronies stood too, and, as though by instruction, began to chant, 'Sing! Sing! Sing! Sing!'

Ms Trebor flapped her hands. 'Guys! This is not how we welcome new people into our school! Grace! Samantha! Sit down!' she commanded.

They fell into an apologetic silence. Aretha, however, didn't seem fazed in the slightest. And then she did something both extraordinary and unexpected – she actually began to sing.

Her voice really was something else. Deep and soulful, it reminded me of the blues records Mum sometimes played on Sunday mornings. She was singing a song I recognised as 'Respect' by her namesake. It was difficult to interpret this song choice as anything other than a dig at Grace, which made me like Aretha even more. She was clearly not here to be messed with.

There wasn't a hint of a wobble in her voice – the assurance with which she sang made me feel at least ten per cent sexier, just watching. I was absorbing her confidence through osmosis and, for a good minute, I forgot I was Llewella Williams – try-hard, anxious, rotund – and was able to imagine myself as a girl who knew with absolute certainty that what you wanted, baby, she'd got it.

After one verse and a chorus, Aretha stopped as abruptly as she'd started and fell into a deep bow. There was a beat of stunned silence and then we applauded. Some of us even *woo*oed. Aretha stretched back upright and beamed at us. In three minutes we'd gone from *WTF* to newly converted fans.

I had one overwhelming thought.

I *must* be friends with this person.

Chapter 3

The problem was, you couldn't just walk up to someone and say, 'I believe passionately we're destined to be BFFs. Let us hang out continuously henceforth, please thank you.' That's how you'd enhance your reputation as a proper weirdo.

After assembly, I sat mapping out in my mind all the ways I could engineer a chance to hang out with Aretha while pretending to listen to Mr Copeland, our history teacher, hold forth about how Henry VIII was really misunderstood and wasn't actually a misogynistic wanker as pop history has painted him.

While one half of my brain worked on the problem of how to approach Aretha, the other was thinking about all the things I had to do later that day. I really needed to check on my blog – to go through and approve the comments on my last post.

For the past three years I'd been working on a blog called Loo Reviews. It involved me going to various public places – museums, libraries, restaurants, train stations – and reporting on the state of their toilets. I got the idea when an author came to give a talk at St Edith's at the end of Year 9. I've wanted to be a writer for as long as I could remember and I'd sidled up to her afterwards to ask what her advice would be for someone just starting out.

'Oh, the internet has made it much easier for people your age than it was for me,' she'd replied airily. 'You can just get your work straight out there.'

I wasn't sure I agreed with her on that, because while technically anyone can publish their own work, it also means there are a gazillion voices competing for attention in infinite cyberspace, making it much more likely yours will get lost.

I said as much.

'Well, what's your USP?' she asked. I looked at her blankly. 'Unique selling point,' she clarified. I had no idea. 'That's what you need to work out' she said. 'Like, for example, there are a million food writers out there. But say you're a food writer who is also a coeliac. Now, you're writing to an audience of other coeliacs and giving them advice on where they can find delicious, gluten-free options. That's what's going to get your blog traction. You need to find a perspective which will make you stand out from the crowd.'

So, I went home and I thought about it . . . and thought and thought and thought. What was my USP, as a human? I'm half-Welsh on my mum's side, but I wasn't sure I had much to say on the topic of Welshness. I knew even less about the other half of my heritage. I loved reading, but YouTube was already full of people my age doing book reviews and I wasn't confident I'd have anything fresh to say. I have a ginger cat called Fiona (named after the princess in *Shrek*) but I hardly thought the internet needed more feline content. And then, inspiration struck: toilets.

I have a thing about toilets. It started when I was twelve. Mum got a big promotion at work and took Hugh and me out to a fancy restaurant to celebrate. A waiter took us to our seat, then a different one poured us some water before a third recommended Mum the most expensive wine from what looked like an encyclopaedia. I could have sworn one of them was putting on a French accent to make himself seem fancier. Hugh and I kept giggling because the whole thing was so pretentious, but we enjoyed ourselves – especially when they brought out free mini plates of food between each course.

Right before we left, I told Mum I was going for a safety wee (the wee you don't really need but will also regret not having when you inevitably need one on the car journey home). And the toilets in that place . . . well, they were rank. It's not that they were particularly dirty, but they were cramped, dingy, the mirror was shattered, the taps were covered in limescale. The liquid soap had also run out.

All in all, the wee I had at the end of the meal tarnished my whole experience. That might sound over-dramatic, but I now know that one of my anxiety triggers is feeling claustrophobic and honestly, there wasn't even enough room to turn a circle on the spot in those cubicles. You had to sit down on the loo *then* close and lock the door. So there were about five seconds where you ran the risk of someone else opening the door right in your face to see you sitting there with your knickers around your ankles. When I sat on the loo, my bum cheek spilled over and touched the sanitary bin next to it. I have a thing about germs, so that freaked me out. And then of course there was no soap, which meant I had to wash my hands using just water and felt icky and close to panic for the whole forty-minute drive back home.

I figured I couldn't be the only one who thinks toilets are important and would take the state of them into account when calculating whether they were prepared to splurge on a meal. That was how Loo Reviews was born. My first review was of the public toilet in Chiddy town centre. It's one of those that looks like a TARDIS. You put a pound in and then you get two minutes to do your business before the automatic door opens. Which is all very well and good but, as I wrote in my blog, what if you're wearing a body with six poppers on the crotch and tights tucked into it? I showed it to my English teacher, who said my writing was hilarious and sent a link to our local newspaper. They did an article all about me and how I was turning my 'OCD into an opportunity'.

Anyway, it must have been a slow news day because a tabloid newspaper then picked up the story and a TV cleaning expert shared my blog on Twitter. That's when it really began to fly. Before I knew it, thousands of people were reading each post. Now, on a good week I get tens of thousands. I also get tickets for events and invited for free meals from venues confident their toilets will meet my standards.

The other reason the blog works is because my name is Loo. Well, not really. My name is Llewella, because my Mum is the Welshest woman who ever lived and wanted to stamp a bit of her culture on me. That would be fine, except we live in Surrey, where no one has ever heard the name 'Llewella'. They have, however, heard the name 'Louise'. So I started introducing myself to people as 'Loo' because it was easier than having to have endless conversations where I spell my actual name out and spend ages explaining that the Welsh are obsessed with the letter L for some reason and that technically two ls are supposed to be pronounced kind of like a c as said by someone with a really phlegmy cold and HAHAHA yes, aren't we a strange little nation and no, I don't know anyone who has actually shagged a sheep.

While my name's a little unusual I don't actually hate it. Plus, it could have been worse because apparently my Mum toyed with the idea of calling me Blodeuyn, which means 'white flower' in her native tongue. (And wouldn't it be cruelly incongruous to call your baby that when she isn't white?)

I've been doing a Loo Review every other week for a couple of years and, in addition to getting me out of the house, it's now making fairly decent money from ad revenue.

On the Friday after Aretha joined our year, I was going to the new Italian restaurant in Chiddy town centre. They'd offered me a free meal for two (maximum of two courses, not inclusive of alcohol) in return for a mention on Loo Reviews. I was going to take Hugh with me, but the last time I'd brought him to a restaurant he'd somehow got an olive wedged in his ear, which then broke in half when he tried to remove it and we resorted to having to coax the thing out with the handle of a teaspoon ... Which didn't exactly convey the kind of sophisticated vibe I was aiming for. Besides, I always took Hugh. He's three years younger than me and spends his life playing video games, so can always be relied upon to be in his bedroom, glued to his console, when I need a plus one for something.

Something – I couldn't put my finger on exactly what – stopped me from inviting Olivia. Other than her, I'd kind of given up on having friends my own age. No one in my year hated me enough to be actively unpleasant to me, but I wasn't popular either. My form tutor was always telling me I needed to work on my social skills. Apparently, my strident opinions were 'intimidating'.

I did try for a while, but engaging in conversation with my

fellow sixth formers about anything other than what we were studying was like trying to speak a foreign language when everyone else was fluent and I didn't even have a guidebook. I wasn't interested in endlessly second-guessing the inner machinations of the minds of boys, or fashion, or make-up.

I couldn't find it in myself to care about the things other girls did. Like when Mum said she'd 'treat' me to a 'lovely cut and colour' for my hair before sixth form began and I said I was too busy doing my required reading to go to the hairdresser. I think she thought I was being ungrateful, but when you have anxiety spending hours in a boiling-hot, cramped salon with a stranger touching your head in an intimate fashion while asking you invasive questions about your life is horrific enough, even when you're remotely bothered about what the result might look like. Which I wasn't.

If Instagram was any barometer, all the people in my year ever seemed to do for 'fun' was drive around aimlessly or drink cheap alcohol in deeply unglamorous locations, like the multi-storey car park after dark. A couple of the girls in my year had older boyfriends who'd take them clubbing in London, but even that sounded like more hassle than it was worth. Sometimes, I worried that I might be a psychopath because I just didn't see the appeal of socialising.

I wished I'd accepted some of the many invitations from Olivia to go and get a hot chocolate after drama rehearsals. But there had always been homework to do, or lines to learn, or a Loo Review to write up. Now I needed to impress someone and I had none of the necessary skills.

I snapped back to reality as Mr Copeland dropped a marker

23

on the floor, muttering crossly to himself as he bent to pick it up. Suddenly, it hit me – I would invite Aretha to my next blog mission.

That evening, I stood in front of the floor-to-ceiling mirror in my mum's walk-in wardrobe and studied myself. I tried to imagine how I looked from the viewpoint of a stranger.

I was big – that much I knew. I took up space, whether I wished to or not. While I'd never thought of myself as fat, I was what my Mum would call 'well covered'. My stomach was what a fitness influencer would deem to be my 'problem area'. I had long, slim arms and legs, but my torso was round and squishy.

If your fat distribution happened to land on your bum, there were any number of celebrities out there showing how to make that sexy. Ditto thighs. But no one had yet come to the rescue of us big-bellied girls and made our defining feature aspirational. You didn't hear about famous people getting tummy implants.

I poked the roll of flesh that sat above the waistband of my trousers. Then I grabbed it with both my hands and squeezed. If only I could just chop it off, or wish it away, the rest of my body wasn't so bad, I reflected.

I often had thoughts like this and they made me feel guilty. I knew that logically, beauty is a social construct, shifting between cultures and over the centuries. I understood that women's body insecurity is a tool in our oppression. I'd liked hundreds of posts on social media about owning our 'flaws' and celebrating our imperfections. Yet there were days where I just couldn't seem to apply those sentiments to myself.

Sighing, I renewed my promise to myself to shift a bit of weight. Whenever I spoke to Olivia about how not being thin might stop me from getting roles in school productions, she always said, 'but look at Lizzo!' But I wasn't Lizzo. Lizzo was insanely talented. She was also fat, defiant and beautiful. I was just a bit porky. My body didn't make any kind of statement to the world, other than 'can't really be arsed'.

I dragged my eyes away from my torso and looked at my head. My hair wasn't in anything you could describe as a 'style' It was naturally thick, wavy and dark brown but I could never get it to grow any longer than just below the tops of my shoulder blades, where it began to break off. I hadn't had it cut in years – I'd just let nature take its course and allowed it to break and fall wherever it liked, which had resulted in it looking slightly lopsided.

My complexion was light brown. If I stood in certain lights, it looked almost white. I had bushy brows, my eyes were large and brown, my lips full. I laughed, as it suddenly occurred to me I had a lot of the things reality-TV stars paid money for – the big boobs, eyebrows and lips – just not in the way they'd want them (i.e. attached to a very thin, white body).

I appeared to be a person too busy, or perhaps too feminist to expend energy worrying about how I looked. Certainly, that was the person I aspired to be. But on several occasions I'd laid awake at night stewing on how unfair it was that the beautiful people at school got attention just for existing, fantasising about a magical swimming pool where the water would melt away all my imperfections and I could emerge lithe, swishy-haired and stunning, like Charlotte.

I knew I could learn how to do make-up; get my hair cut; buy some new, more 'flattering' clothes; join a gym. None of the things I disliked about my appearance were theoretically unchangeable. But there was always a reason not to – a drama rehearsal, a piano recital, a looming exam, a feeling that I was betraying the sisterhood. Or the old fallback – I'll start exercising and eating clean on Monday.

Would my appearance repel Aretha? People who don't make any effort with how they look are by definition not popular and, for the new girl, popularity might be an important consideration.

I'd have to find common ground, I decided. Maybe offer to accompany her singing on piano in the music block one day after school and then tell her about my blog.

I'd have to convince her of all the invisible things of value I had to offer before my body put her off.

Chapter 4

It had been surprisingly easy, in the end.

I thought after her performance in assembly Aretha would have sixth formers literally queuing up to congratulate her and had reconciled myself to getting in line, but at lunch time the next day she was sitting on her own. I seized my chance and practically ran over to her, my tray laden with my usual lunch of a baked potato, a mountain of grated cheese and coleslaw and a can of Diet Coke, all wobbling precariously.

Ms Trebor was also making a beeline for Aretha and had apparently decided this was a great time to intervene and humiliate me utterly.

'Hey, guys! Aretha! Do you know Llewella here?' Ms Trebor enquired, before I'd even had a chance to open my mouth.

'No,' Aretha replied, but it wasn't harsh or dismissive. She beamed one of her huge smiles up at us both and used a tone which seemed to silently add 'but I'd like to'.

'Well,' said Ms Trebor, as I willed her to go away and let me make my own introduction, 'Llewella is the perfect person to help you get settled here. She is one of our best performing students. And she's on our student council, so she knows all the latest gossip. She's also the lead in this year's Shakespeare production. Oh, and an accomplished pianist! So maybe she could accompany your singing?'

Ms Trebor gestured between us as though she was a gracious

hostess introducing us at a party. I winced inwardly. This wasn't the meet-cute I had imagined. I mean, Ms Trebor and I both know I'm a massive overachiever and have to be involved in absolutely everything extracurricular (which is fine because I have no social life) but it's not necessarily the first thing I'd tell someone I was trying to impress.

'That's great!' Aretha replied, while I stood there wishing I could fold myself into a small shape and disappear. 'What kind of music do you play?'

Ms Trebor silently – but not subtly – motioned for me to sit opposite Aretha. I obeyed, banging my knee painfully on the long table as I did so. I ignored the discomfort, hoping that if I didn't acknowledge it Aretha wouldn't notice. Ms Trebor jogged away in that bouncy way she has and Aretha and I were left alone. The problem was, I couldn't in that moment recall one single song I knew on piano. So, I settled instead for saying, 'Loo'.

'Pardon?' Aretha was understandably confused.

'Oh, sorry,' I replied, flustered. 'Everyone calls me Loo. And I just wanted to say, your performance yesterday was incredible.'

Aretha's smile broadened and reached her eyes. In fact, her whole face seemed to light up with the compliment I'd just paid her. This was a good start, I decided, so I carried on showering her with praise.

'I mean, your range is just amazing. I thought the way you performed the song a capella and out of nowhere like that was brilliant. Just incredible.' I became aware that I was definitely gushing at this point and had also used the word 'incredible' twice.

These kinds of nerves were a new experience for me. I sometimes still got panicky talking to people outside of school, but St Edith's grounds were my turf. I'd been going there a long time and felt safe enough to be myself. But something about Aretha put me in a fluster. She didn't seem to mind. In fact, she reached across the table and covered my hand with hers, giving it a little squeeze.

'Thank you' she said, slowly and deliberately. 'That really means a lot'

She was being kind, but my anxiety whispered that I'd somehow disappointed her by not being more insightful. I chastised myself and made a mental note to command Alexa to play some obscure Aretha Franklin tracks that evening, so I could impress this Aretha with my knowledge the following day. I decided to get straight to the point before I did any more damage, making a conscious effort to sound like a normal person.

'So, I have this blog where I review toilets. It's not as weird as it sounds ... Actually, it is. But people have really responded to it well, for some reason. It gets lots of hits and I get sent invitations to things ...' I glanced up to check I still had Aretha's attention. I did. She definitely looked interested.

'Anyway, on Friday I'm doing this new restaurant in town and I thought, since you're new here, you might want to come with me so you can get to know the area. I thought it might be ... nice ...' I trailed off, lamely. Then I did a weird sort of wide-eyed, exhaling gesture because I wasn't sure what I was supposed to do with my face.

'I mean, YEAH!' Aretha replied, grinning, to my immense relief. 'I'd love that.' She took out her phone. It was new and sleek and the sort of thing Hugh would enthuse about. 'What's your number?' she asked, waving her phone in my face even though we aren't supposed to have them visible in the dining hall. 'I'll ring you now and then you'll have my number. You can WhatsApp me what time and where, otherwise I'll just forget. I'm terrible with remembering stuff.'

'Oh. Actually, can I text you? My phone is really old so I don't have WhatsApp.' I held my breath, knowing that if Aretha was at all concerned about me not being as cool as her, our friendship had just ended before it began.

'You're adorable,' she replied finally, grinning.

And just like that, I'd made a friend.

Aretha seemed happy to be taken under my wing. I dedicated a lot of thought to what wisdom I could impart to her about St Edith's. I gave her an 'alternative guided tour' of the school (letting her know which toilets to avoid and showing her the spot where Year 10s glued pound coins to the ground so they could shout 'SKANK' at you at lunchtime if you tried to pick them up . . . that sort of thing).

She'd come to watch one of our *Merchant* rehearsals and told me she thought my portrayal of Antonio was 'really authentic' She also agreed with me when I had confessed to thinking Charlotte's Portia was 'more style than substance'. Aretha had even made a joke of the professor's tendency to have hissy fits if we didn't say the lines with the correct inflection.

'RRRRREMEMBER THE RRRRHYTHM OF THE IAMBIC PENTAMETEEEEEEER!' Aretha roared, in a surprisingly accurate impression of Prof Coleman's mellifluous

30

roar, before collapsing into giggles. It was liberating to view the professor through her eyes. In our school bubble he was known as a genius and a maverick and we all went out of our way to impress him. But the way Aretha described him, he was a failed, ageing actor who made himself feel important by flouncing around and being intimidating to teenage girls. Aretha made it very clear his efforts didn't work on her. Her respect was harder to win.

I'd given Aretha advice on exactly what time to get to the rehearsal rooms in the music block to guarantee nabbing the one with the best acoustics and the most in-tune piano. We'd tried duetting together – me fumbling my way through an Adele song on keys while Aretha belted out the high notes with apparent ease.

When we found ourselves alone – walking between classes, or eating lunch – Aretha told me about her life before she came to Chiddy. Her parents had moved to Surrey in the summer because her mum, who was a teacher, had found a position as head of year in a local state school. Her dad, who was a firefighter, simply transferred to a different station. Before that, they'd lived in East London. The way Aretha told it, her former home was vibrant and fun-filled with just a hint of danger – the complete opposite to Chiddy, which was sleepy, suburban and dull.

Aretha had been studying at a college which specialised in performing arts. She wanted to be a professional musician, but had been frustrated by the way her tutors seemed to be preparing her for a life of entertaining at weddings and bar mitzvahs.

'I suppose they thought that was more realistic,' she told me. 'There were all these people in my year who thought they were the next Billie Eilish or Sam Smith and, you know, statistically that just wasn't going to happen, for them.'

Aretha told me what it had been like working as a backing singer during the summer holidays. How she'd travelled in a tour bus and played stages at V, Latitude and Isle of Wight before hanging out with famous musicians and journalists at afterparties. She'd met Lauren Laverne, Kendrick Lemar, George Ezra and Stormzy, she told me. They were all, according to her, 'amazing'.

'Oh my god, that's so cool!' I exclaimed, with a distinct lack of originality, because I wasn't sufficiently knowledgeable about the music industry to say anything more perceptive. 'Will you do it again next summer?'

'Maybe . . .' Aretha replied. 'Not with the Brass Traps boys, though. They weren't very nice to me, in the end.'

What followed was a long and convoluted tale involving the management of Brass Traps demanding Aretha stand closer to the front of the stage and giving her small vocal solos, which apparently caused resentment within the main band. Eventually they'd stopped talking to her, which made the last few weeks of the tour really awkward.

'I think, ultimately, there was a lot of jealousy there,' Aretha concluded. 'And I don't want to be one of those girls – you know, the ones who are like "everyone's jealous of me!"' – she put on a whiney, vaguely Essex-sounding accent as she said this, making me giggle – 'but sometimes that's the only explanation, you know?'

I nodded, lapping it up. Aretha's life sounded like a movie, complete with glamour, stardom and betrayal. I wondered if that was where the soulfulness in her voice had come from.

In turn, I shared some of my history with Aretha. 'I'm completely non-judgmental,' she assured me. 'All my friends from back home say that's my best quality'. This encouragement, and the feeling I got when I was around her – that life had been in shades of sepia and had suddenly been transformed into glorious technicolour – put me at ease.

I told Aretha about having an anxiety disorder. Everyone at school knew about it anyway and I wanted to reassure her I wasn't 'mad' before someone like Grace or Sam persuaded her otherwise. I showed her the small white pill I swallowed with a pint of water every day at lunchtime to regulate my serotonin levels. I confided in her about my GCSE results having not being as good as I'd hoped, because during Year 10 my anxiety had become so bad I was having several panic attacks a day. I assured her it was pretty-much under control now – I'd had a tonne of therapy and learned how to manage my mental health.

Aretha cocked her head to one side and nodded sympathetically. 'You know,' she mused, 'I could tell when I met you there was something . . . off. You clearly have a lot of pain going on in there, babes.' She tapped her temple.

This assessment surprised me. I knew I'd been a bit clumsy and socially awkward, but I'd never considered that I might give the impression of someone in emotional distress. It was unnerving to think that Aretha, intuitive as she was, was seeing something in me I wasn't ready to show. I tried to think of plausible reasons I could talk about, telling her my mum was a single parent who worked long hours.

'Mmmm,' Aretha replied, her eyes suddenly watery.

Had I made her cry? I didn't think my circumstances were that tragic or unusual. 'You know, I'm so lucky. My parents are so lovely and they devote a lot of time and energy to making sure I succeed, but I know lots of people who aren't in a position to be able to say that.'

I felt guilty then, like I had betrayed Mum. I hadn't meant to imply that she was negligent. I moved to safer ground, asking Aretha if she felt pressure to look a certain way, as a performer.

'Not that you aren't gorgeous. I mean, you are, clearly,' I backtracked, seeing her eyes widen slightly. 'But do you ever feel pressure? Or that if you put on a few pounds you wouldn't get the same opportunities?'

'You know,' Aretha leaned forward to catch my eye. 'I used to be a lot bigger.'

'Really?' I was intrigued.

'Yeah. I'm naturally a fat person, I think. But I realised a couple of years back I had to get fit if I wanted to perform and that the industry . . . well, it expects a certain aesthetic.'

I scanned Aretha's body. In complete contrast to me, she was small and solid. Her waist was miniscule and her limbs, while thick and short, didn't jiggle when she moved. If I had to describe her in one word, I'd say she was 'compact'

'How did you do it?' I asked.

'Mostly exercise,' she replied. 'I mean, I did stop eating fried chicken on the regs and made a few other changes to my diet, but the short answer is – I worked out.'

'Oh.' I was disheartened, hoping she'd say something like, 'I discovered a magic juice you can drink before you go to bed

34

and you miraculously drop three clothes sizes overnight with no adverse side-effects!'

'I can show you some of the things I do, if you want?' Aretha offered.

I was torn. I didn't want to work out. Mainly because I knew I'd be dreadful at it. The only form of physical activity I was even slightly good at was netball and I hadn't done that since Year 11. Visions of me trying and failing to do a single press-up while Aretha effortlessly vaulted over boxes, did chin-ups on high iron bars and battered punch bags with glove-clad hands filled my head. I couldn't imagine anything more humiliating. On the other hand, this was an opportunity to make good on my promise to myself to give my body an overhaul in time for university, as well as a chance to spend more time with Aretha.

'OK,' I replied, tentatively.

I always walked away from conversations with Aretha feeling elated. Being close to her was like being friends with a famous person. Everything she said and did was so . . . on purpose. By contrast, I felt like I'd just been stumbling through my existence, not achieving as much as I could or should have done. The excitement always outweighed the discombobulation. I'd been waiting for something to shake up my life and now, here she was.

Chapter 5

I was already seated by the time Aretha arrived at Giuseppe's, the cosy, family-run Italian where I'd arranged to do my Loo Review. As soon as she walked through the door, every head in the room turned. She looked stunning. Her afro, which I'd only ever seen tied into two Minnie Mouse-style bunches, was loose and enormous, the vivid blonde catching the light so it almost looked as though it was sparkling. Her eyes were made up with a glittery silver liner, making them look even more huge and dark than they already were. She was wearing a denim playsuit which was pulled in at the waist, emphasising her curves.

The waiter spotted her immediately (I'd had to hover awkwardly by the entrance for five full minutes before I'd managed to get his attention) and hastened over, at which point she turned the full force of her mega-watt smile in his direction. I saw him simper. Aretha said something and they both threw their heads back as they laughed. The eyes of other diners followed their trajectory as they made their way to my table.

After chatting to the waiter for an unfathomably long time – yes, she was new to the town; no, she'd never been to this restaurant before; yes, so far she liked it and would definitely consider coming back – Aretha slid into the seat opposite me and started fumbling in her leather rucksack.

'Babes!' she declared with excitement. 'I have news! So . . .' She glanced up from what she was rooting around for, it now transpired, her phone to gauge my reaction. I must have looked sufficiently captivated because she began swiping furiously at the screen while firing hyper, half-formed sentences in my direction.

'I've been chatting . . . hang on, wait . . . ah, there!' She turned the screen in my direction with a flourish to reveal a picture of what I could only describe as an excessively handsome boy. His face had that slightly-too-symmetrical-to-be-believable quality that preposterously good-looking people have. His cheekbones were high and protruding. His skin gleamed and his biceps bulged from beneath a tight white T-shirt. It was a professional headshot, I realised.

'This is my friend Oli from back home. He saw the selfie we took the other day. You know ' – more swiping – 'this one!' The screen revealed a strictly-against-the-rules picture Aretha had taken the day we rehearsed the Adele song in the music rooms. She was in the foreground, clutching a vintage, 1950s-style microphone she'd brought from home and looking up at the camera coquettishly from underneath her eyelashes. I was sat at the piano behind her, balancing one buttock on the stool and leaning over to get in shot, smiling without showing any teeth. The sun streaming through the window behind me concealed most of my features, although not so much you couldn't make out the frizz ball my hair had turned into because of the heat. I looked like a nervous mess.

I'd felt that way, too, I remembered. It wasn't that I was averse to breaking school rules – I had a reputation for being outspoken on the student council and openly contradicting teachers when I thought they weren't being fair, which often got me into trouble. But I also wasn't the sort of person who did something forbidden I couldn't justify, simply because I felt like it. I'd been worried that a teacher might walk in and see us using the phone. I had a suspicion if that happened I was more likely to be blamed than Aretha, who was still settling in.

Plus, if I was being honest, I'd been worried I didn't really look good enough to be photographed. So, as Aretha had counted us down to her taking the shot, I'd settled on a kind of goofy grin – mouth closed, eyebrows slightly raised – an expression I'd hoped conveyed that I wasn't trying to look attractive and also that the taking of the selfie hadn't been my idea.

Aretha, perhaps sensing that my mind was wandering, snatched the phone from under my nose while working up to the headline of her announcement, namely that Oli apparently thought I was 'really pretty'.

'So . . . what do you think?' Aretha asked, flicking back to the picture of her friend and leaning across the table to wave it in my face in what I assumed was meant to be a tantalising manner.

This was completely unchartered territory for me. No one, to my knowledge, had ever described me as 'really pretty' before. (Except perhaps my nain back in Wales, who thought both Hugh and I were the best-looking humans who had ever lived, despite – or perhaps because of – being so short-sighted as to be almost blind.) Certainly, no one as attractive as Oli had ever paid me any romantic attention. I was incredibly flattered, but didn't want to make an idiot of myself by making it obvious. I didn't know what the protocol was.

'He's really good looking,' I said, in a way I hoped didn't sound too desperate. 'What's he like?'

'Oh, he's amazing,' Aretha cooed, 'and I can totally see you two as a couple. This is so exciting. I'll tell him you're interested.'

She began typing, clearly not willing to lose a second in communicating my enthusiasm back to Oli.

'I'm just . . . hang on . . . I'm just saying that you think he is hot too and . . . wait a sec.' She twisted sharply round in her chair, held her hand aloft and snapped another selfie. This time, she didn't give me any warning, meaning I had a breadstick hanging out the side of my mouth, like an asymmetrical walrus. 'No, that's crap. Also' – Aretha snatched the breadstick from my mouth – 'we have discussed empty calories and carbs. You're doing so well this week, don't spoil it.'

It turned out, despite Aretha's insistence that she 'just worked out', there were quite a lot of rules involved in her weight-loss regime. For this first couple of weeks, I wasn't allowed chocolate or sweets (killer), fizzy drinks (not ideal, but do-able) or 'simple carbs' (bread, basically). I'd be able to introduce them back into my diet later, but I was currently in what was called the 'detox phase' where I was ridding my body of 'toxins' and my mind of bad habits. Or something. Either way, breadsticks were apparently contraband.

'Smile, babes!' Aretha instructed. I did. 'Ooooh, Juno is totally your filter. You look gorgeous in this one,' she declared, her fingers moving so fast they began to blur.

I giggled, bashfully.

Aretha didn't show me the photo, or what she had typed, she simply threw her phone back into her rucksack and leaned on to her elbows, looking expectant. I understood that it was now my turn to carry the conversation.

'You can order whatever you like,' I said, gesturing at the menu, 'well, within two courses. And then afterwards I just need five minutes or so to go to the bathroom, to take some photos and notes.'

'Can I come with you when you go?' Aretha asked. 'I want to see what you do, behind the scenes.'

'Errr . . . sure. Although, there's not much to it. You might be disappointed!'

'Babe! You're always putting yourself down!' Aretha was suddenly looking me dead in the eye, unflinching and earnest. 'You've done so well to build your blog up and you get so many hits. I know we haven't known each other long and it's a bit weird to say, but I'm really proud of you.'

At that moment, the waiter appeared, brandishing two glasses of amber liquid in tall flutes, garnished with raspberries and mint leaves.

'Bellinis for the beautiful ladies,' he declared, with what appeared to be a genuine Italian twang. This was presumably addressed to both of us, although he looked only at Aretha. 'On the house, of course. Enjoy! Also, I talk to the chef and he say if you tell him about any allergies or dietary requirements, he will make you something special, off menu.'

I opened and closed my mouth a couple of times, like a goldfish. First, Aretha with all her celebrity connections, being impressed by my little blog. And now, free cocktails. Nothing like this had ever happened to me before and I wasn't sure how to respond.

'Thank you!' Aretha and I chorused in unison, as she swiped both glasses from the tray, taking a large gulp of one and passing the other to me in one synchronised movement.

This presented quite the dilemma. I could count the number of alcoholic beverages I'd drunk up until this point on one hand. Mum had taken a 'if you're going to drink, I'd rather you did it in the house' approach and had a metaphorically (and literally) unlocked liquor-cabinet policy. In spite of this, it had just never really appealed to me. While most of my year group had taken to frequenting any local pub which didn't ask for ID, I rarely touched booze. The few times I had, it had made me feel woozy, like my head was full of cotton wool. I'd found myself grasping for words, half-remembering names, before feeling the overwhelming desire to slump in a corner somewhere to sleep it off.

Nonetheless, I didn't want to appear either ungrateful for the cocktail or unsophisticated in front of Aretha. I took a tentative sip and made a noncommittal 'mmm' sound.

'I saw him pouring these from behind the bar,' Aretha stage-whispered. 'It's quite cheap, this stuff. Not really how prosecco is supposed to be. That's why they've put the raspberries in. To mask the taste. Also, they've served it in the wrong glass.' On she went, explaining about coupes and bubbles and surface areas and how if you want the best prosecco you really have to go to the Amalfi Coast.

I was agog. Sure, some people at school were well-travelled but all they ever seemed to come back to Britain with were STIs. Aretha was a mine of sophisticated information. I felt as though I was floating outside of my body, watching myself drink free prosecco with a glamorous, knowledgeable companion who inexplicably thought I was worthy of her attention.

And Aretha's expertise wasn't limited to beverages, either.

She skilfully took apart her share of the whole king prawns we were served as a starter, depriving them of their head and sucking out their insides with little moans of pleasure. I was both fascinated and appalled. She chuckled when I said I couldn't eat anything with a face and thought the prawns were looking at me accusingly.

Between courses, I told Aretha about the ongoing saga of the school crest.

'Eurgh!' Aretha replied, waving her drink in the air, 'that is just the worst. You know, we had a similar thing back in my old college where we found out that female musicians on average get paid' – she held her finger aloft, as though trying to recall the exact figure – 'something like forty per cent less than men and we started up an online campaign. Paloma Faith came in and presented us with an award.'

'No way!' I said, spilling my prosecco slightly in my enthusiasm, even though I wasn't entirely sure who Paloma Faith was. 'What was that like?'

'The day itself was great. Paloma watched me perform one of my compositions and was really positive. She even took my details afterwards so she could keep an eye on what I was up to. But afterwards, some people got salty . . . you know, the people who Paloma hadn't singled out for praise. It caused quite a lot of tension and I lost some people who I thought were friends, which was sad.'

'That is really sad.' I felt so sorry for Aretha – many people, it appeared, had tried to dull her shine. I made a mental promise I'd be a different sort of friend to the ones who had let her down in the past. I'd always be happy when she succeeded and do anything I could to help.

The waiter unceremoniously plonked a whole fish in front

of me for my main course, barely casting a glance in my direction. I'd definitely detected a hint of disapproval when I'd told him I was pescatarian and couldn't eat pasta (Aretha's weight-loss orders).

'I'm sorry,' I told him, lightly touching his sleeve. 'Would you mind . . . ah . . . taking the head off for me? I can't eat it like this.'

'Babes, no! You can't ask him to do that!' Aretha interjected, aghast. 'I'm so sorry,' she told the waiter.

The waiter strode away, shaking his head slightly. I didn't really understand what I had done wrong. Aretha took my plate from me, smiling.

'It's OK, I'll deal with this guy for you,' she said, proceeding to debone the fish and put its head on her plate before handing it back, cut into bitesize pieces.

When the meal was over and the waiter had presented us with vivid yellow shots tasting suspiciously like washing up liquid (but which he assured us were a 'traditional delicacy') it was time for the Loo Review.

I was a little unsteady by that point, but focused on putting one foot in front of the other and eventually made it down the wrought-iron spiral staircase leading to the toilets. There was a water feature at the bottom of the stairs, a heavy stone structure with a mermaid at the centre, water cascading down her (in my opinion, unnecessarily hyper-sexualised) body and into a shallow pool below. Some people had thrown coins into it. It was quite a nice touch and I snapped a photo.

There were two doors indicating gender neutral toilet cubicles, which I added to my notes as a plus. Having individual cubicles afforded a pleasing amount of privacy; they were usually bigger than stalls and it certainly saves a lot of argument about who is allowed in which toilet. The loos themselves were the 'cheeky', novelty type I'd seen on a couple of occasions before. Above the cistern in the left cubicle was a picture of former President Obama, clearly Photoshopped, sitting on the toilet with his stars and stripes boxers around his ankles, holding a copy of *The New York Times* and smiling at the camera in that enigmatic way he has. On the right was a similar image of the Queen.

I checked the width of each cubicle and perfunctorily assessed them for cleanliness. I was pleased to discover individual hand towels, rolled up in a small wicker basket next to the sinks. The liquid soaps were a posh brand I recognised and smelled of lavender. I described all of this into the little, old-fashioned Dictaphone my taid had given me years before when I'd first decided I wanted to be a writer. I was concentrating hard on not slurring too much.

Aretha stood next to the fountain, watching the process with her chin resting on her fist, her eyeliner glinting in the half-light. When I was satisfied I'd observed and noted everything these toilets had to offer and went to head back up the stairs, she put her hand on my forearm and looked me in the eye. I tried to look away, conscious that my vision was bleary with the alcohol intake which had apparently left Aretha completely unaffected.

'Hey, take my picture. Then you can post it on your blog!' she commanded, striking a pose next to the sexy mermaid.

Chapter 6

'Loo's got a girlfriend!' Hugh chirruped gleefully though a mouthful of baked beans, a few nights later. His eyes were scrunched into slits and there was bean juice dribbling down his chin. He looked even more disgusting than usual.

It was Tuesday evening, the night which – come hell, high water or a particularly 'difficult' artist flouncing about having a tantrum while demanding six white kittens dipped in glitter as he brushed cow urine on the floor of Mum's gallery in the name of creativity – we all sat down and had a proper, family meal together.

As soon as they tumbled out of his bean-filled gob, I knew the impact Hugh's words would have on Mum – she'd be absolutely beside herself with delight. She's started badgering me about when I was going to start my sexual experimentation since my sixteenth birthday. The fact that my apparent love interest was a girl would only add to her excitement. She really wants at least one of her children to be somewhere within the LGBTQ+ spectrum.

It's safe to say Cerys Williams isn't like most mums. She had me when she was only seventeen – my age now. It freaks me out to think about that; I can't imagine how I'd handle having a baby at this point in my life.

Mum was at art college in Chelsea at the time and my father was, according to her telling of the story, a dusky, mysterious visiting lecturer with an unidentified 'foreign' accent who was completely besotted with her for all of five minutes. He disappeared before I was born and . . . Well, let's just say I haven't seen him since.

Sometimes I look in the mirror and try to work out how I could have ended up so different to Mum. In sharp contrast to me, she's delicately built, strawberry blonde and so pale she's almost transparent, and her eyes are a bewitching sort of blue-grey. I try to arrange the features of mine I know can't have come from Mum's side of the family into a person, so I can guess what my father would have looked like. Although I'm not entirely sure that's how genetics work.

Hugh's dad was a married man Mum had an affair with a few years later. I remember him, vaguely. He had the same pointy chin that Hugh has and he always wore gallons of aftershave. He stuck around sporadically for a whole year after Hugh was born, until it was obvious his promises of leaving his wife for us were entirely empty and Mum kicked him to the kerb in her typical, dramatic style (she loves to regale us with the story of how she cut up his shirts and flung the fragments out of the upstairs window).

Mum always wears a variation of the same outfit: a floaty kaftan, tied at her narrow waist, made of some kind of ridiculously expensive fabric ethically hand-woven by magical pixies or similar, a turban and a pair of huge dangly earrings from her vast collection. (Seriously, she has a bureau which spans the entire wall of her dressing room in which earrings sit displayed in neat little rows, like something out of *The Princess Diaries*). On another person, this look might be a bit much, but Mum is tallish and slender with a magnificent bone structure and, perhaps most crucially, the confidence to pull it off. She therefore looks like some kind of ethereal goddess from another realm. Or maybe Tilda Swinton. The only time I ever get any positive attention from the popular girls at school is when they are congratulating me on what a fabulous, stylish, laid-back, beautiful mother I have (and, I can tell, wondering why I haven't followed suit).

I'm nothing like my mum, but I do like her (most of the time). Sure, she's eccentric, prone to hysterical outbursts or randomly deciding we must all watch while she recites some Welsh poetry by candlelight or dances barefoot in the garden under the full moon, but she's also witty, kind and inspiring, in her own weird way. She left her home in Wales at sixteen to make it on her own in the radically different world of West London, then she raised Hugh and I by herself while simultaneously managing to climb the art-world ladder. She's wealthy now – not stupidly so, but we have a large, tastefully decorated house in a nice street in Surrey and Hugh and I both attend private schools, which is astounding when you consider my grandparents are sheep farmers from the Valleys.

Hugh isn't old enough to remember when we had no money, but I do – just about. I think that's why I'm generally less entitled than he is. On his last birthday, Hugh said he wanted a PS4 Pro, as well as about five games, plus a party at Byron Burger. All of which he got, of course. Mum spoils Hugh, in my opinion. On my last birthday, I asked for some herbs in terracotta pots to grow on the windowsill. Mum laughed for ages about that and told me I was severely abnormal. She still steals my rosemary when she's cooking, though.

Hugh has two main hobbies: PlayStation and winding people up. Apparently, that particular evening it was my turn. I decided I must halt the 'Loo has a girlfriend' conversation before it got completely out of hand. I turned my back on Hugh and looked my Mum directly in the eye so she knew I was VERY SERIOUS.

'Mum, I don't have a girlfriend. Hugh is lying.'

'She does!' Hugh retorted immediately. 'The new mixed-race girl at her sixth form. They've been all over each other all week, apparently, and Mia said she saw them kissing in a car park.'

Mia is in Year 9 at my school and absolutely idolises Hugh for reasons best kept to herself. For the past two years she's come to knock for him every morning so they can walk to their respective schools together, even though that involves her going about a mile out of her way. Hugh usually gives the impression that he tolerates her so as not to hurt her feelings, but I think he secretly loves it.

'That is so unbelievably stupid,' I declared.

'Don't call your brother stupid' Mum said, almost reflexively, because she always has to take his side.

'I didn't say *he* was stupid,' I replied, folding my arms and lifting my chin. 'I was referring to the notion of me kissing Aretha in a car park when I don't even have a car!'

'Oh, Aretha is it, now?' Mum twinkled. God, it was unbearable.

'Yeah, and . . . and Mum,' Hugh said, poking the sleeve of Mum's Liberty print kaftan while jiggling up and down in his seat. 'There's a picture of her on Loo's blog. Mia said,' he added hastily, no doubt keen not to give the impression that he had the slightest bit of interest in my blog.

Mum placed her finger tips under my chin and gently tilted my face towards her, a gesture she's perfected over the years and uses to announce that she is going to say something of the utmost importance to which we must all pay the closest of attention.

'Now, listen, my darling,' she said, earnestly, 'love is love and it's a beautiful thing, no matter who it happens between.'

'Apart from kids and paedos,' Hugh interjected.

Ignoring him, Mum continued, 'You must never be ashamed of who you are, carriad. And, to be honest, I always suspected, what with you having no interest in fashion or make-up . . .'

I could bear it no more. 'Mum! That's an outrageous stereotype!' I heard Hugh sing 'ooooooh!' but didn't let his crowing break my stride. 'I'm not gay and if I was I wouldn't be ashamed of it. I'd just tell you. Anyway, sorry to be a disappointment, but Aretha is just a friend. And I don't want to talk about it any more.'

Mum raised her eyebrows at Hugh, who giggled. I started determinedly chomping away on my lentil bake. They could both sod off.

Chapter 7

In the whole of my school career to date, I'd gone to a friend's house to socialise maybe ten times, max. And even then, it had mostly been in primary school, during a time when everyone invited everyone to their birthday parties, regardless of popularity. But now, here I was, on a Friday evening, standing next to Aretha as she let herself into her house.

It was a modest semi she shared with her mum Dawn, dad Delroy and brother Ezekiel (who was currently away studying Politics and International Relations at Bristol University).

The first thing Aretha did when Dawn came to the hallway to greet us was put her arm around her shoulder and say, 'This is my mum, who has been so supportive of my music and who I'm going to buy a mansion for to say thank you,' before pecking her on the cheek. It was like I was behind a camera and we were filming a documentary about her life. Dawn leaned into the embrace, smiling and closing her eyes, basking in the warmth her daughter was emitting, while I stood there grinning awkwardly.

We took off our shoes, leaving them in a heap by the front door and traipsed down a narrow corridor to the kitchen, which despite being small was bright and cheerfully decorated, giving the impression of tonnes of light and air. Dawn had laid out plates of crumpets oozing butter and what looked like home-made chocolate chip cookies.

'Help yourself, Loo darling,' she said, which immediately put me in a quandary. I didn't want to be rude, but I'd stuck to Aretha's diet plan for three weeks by now and my clothes were looser, my stomach flatter, my face thinner. I was hungry pretty much constantly and my throat felt sore and scratchy, although the intense sugar cravings which had made my head bang and my skin itch for the first ten days or so had died down.

I eyed the cookies, my mouth starting to water. Then I saw Aretha was looking at me, shaking her head. I made a conscious effort to snap back to the conversation with Dawn.

'Would you like a cup of tea?' she asked.

Compared with my home life, Aretha's seemed to be straight out of the Wholesome Family playbook. When I got home from school, often well past six because I had stayed late for piano, or drama, or some student council-related business, Hugh and I usually took it in turns barging each other out of the way of the fridge, swiping whatever dinner we could cobble together from leftovers and bits of cheese, before scurrying upstairs. I would study and Hugh would play PlayStation as Fiona trotted between each of our rooms demanding tummy tickles, until either Mum came home or we fell asleep – whichever came first.

Aretha's mum, by contrast, was making tea in an actual teapot, with a proper tea cosy, while asking us about our day.

I studied her as she bustled about the kitchen, placing a delicate china jug decorated with blue flowers on the table and filling it with milk. She was a couple of inches shorter than Aretha – not much taller than five foot, I'd guess – and much more dainty. She didn't seem like one of those people who deprived herself to stay slim, though. She never seemed to stay still for more than a millisecond, fussing over the snacks and repeatedly fluffing cushions, which I supposed must burn a lot of calories over time. I wondered if you could train yourself to be like that, or if it was just the way some people were designed.

Dawn had the same huge, almond-shaped eyes as Aretha and the same freckles across the bridge of her nose. She was naturally pretty and I couldn't imagine what she would look like if she wore make-up. Everything about her was soft and understated.

I told her about our production of *Merchant* and her eyes lit up.

'The quality of mercy is not strain'd.' She quoted the play's most famous line (which bloody Charlotte would get to perform as Portia). 'One of Shakespeare's finest, in my opinion,' she said, 'yet so often overlooked. I suppose it's because you have to be so careful the way Shylock is played. It can be anti-Semitic if you're not very careful with it'. What part are you playing, Llewella?'

When I told her I'd been given the role of the troubled merchant, she nodded and closed her eyes for a few seconds, as though trying to summon some appropriate wisdom.

'Of course, the most important thing to bear in mind with Antonio is that he is in love with Bassanio,' she told me.

'Really?' I replied, genuinely taken aback. 'I thought they were just really good friends?'

'How many people do you know who would actually die for their friends, however much they think they love them?' asked Dawn.

It was though I could actually feel some dusty cog in the recesses of my mind turning as I contemplated Dawn's question. When it came to close friendships, really the only frame of reference I had was my rapidly blossoming bond with Aretha. I stole a glance in her direction. She was scrolling on her phone using the thumb of one hand while disdainfully examining her chipped neon-yellow nail polish on the other. I felt a now-familiar rush of affection. I didn't think I was quite ready to die for her, but I also couldn't rule out the possibility of feeling that way at some point in the future. *Did this explain the dreams?* I wondered.

Over the past couple of nights I'd been having really vivid dreams of an . . . erm . . . adult nature (Certificate 18) involving Aretha. Usually, I wouldn't give this a second thought. I often had dreamland sexual encounters. The most bizarre one was with Foghorn Leghorn from Looney Tunes. I whispered details of the dream to Olivia in theatre studies the next day and she burst out laughing and told me she'd once had one about the meerkat from the insurance adverts. Then we'd spent the rest of the time we were meant to be working creating a flow chart to try and determine which fantasy was weirder.

But with Aretha it was different because she'd inspired the odd, fleeting doubt about my sexuality during conscious hours, too. I'd always assumed I was straight. Of course, I had crushes on women – the summer holiday where I became briefly obsessed with looking at vintage pictures of Gillian Anderson on Tumblr after seeing her play Dr Milburn in *Sex Education* being a classic example – but I could never distinguish whether it was because I wanted to be with them or wanted to *be* them.

You'd think going to an all-girls school would be an ideal environment to explore any curiosities about same-sex attraction, but in fact the opposite was true. There was always the suggestion that lesbians or bisexuals couldn't be 'trusted' in amongst so many girls. Grace and her gang of cronies actually started a petition to have Megan and James, who are gay and transgender respectively and both came out in Year 9, banned from swimming lessons. The student council told them to stuff their petition right up their bums, of course, but it still created a tense atmosphere. For all those reasons, it was actually far less embarrassing to talk about my Foghorn Leghorn fantasy than it would be to admit to the dreams about Aretha.

I remembered something my Mum had said during the phase where she became convinced she was psychic and would insist on reading our tarot cards and strategically placing crystals about the house (which only stopped after she trod on a jagged piece of rose quartz when she got up for a wee in the middle of the night) – if you dream about having sex with someone, it means they have something you want.

For wont of anything more insightful to contribute to the conversation, I said to Dawn, 'So, Antonio's gay, then?'

'Well, I don't think they defined themselves that way in those days,' she replied. 'Sexuality was seen as a much more fluid thing. Many academics believe Shakespeare's sonnets were written to his male lover, you know . . .'

'YEAH!' Aretha suddenly interjected, with a startling enthusiasm which made me spill a bit of the tea I was holding. 'It's only recently human beings have become so hung up on, like, defining sexuality and gender and all that stuff. I mean, look at Ancient Greece! All the emperors were shagging men for pleasure and women if they wanted to make babies.'

I waited for Dawn to correct Aretha – to tell her that it was

Ancient Rome, not Greece that had emperors – and was surprised when she didn't. If I'd made that sort of basic blunder at home, Mum and Hugh would have dedicated the remainder of the day solely to the pleasure of finding more and more elaborate ways to take the piss out of my ignorance. Dawn, however, smiled indulgently at her daughter, gave her a quick peck on the forehead and announced she had 'an enormous pile of marking that wouldn't do itself' before making for the door.

'Dad will be home in about an hour to make dinner,' she called over her shoulder, as she retreated to the sitting room.

Aretha grabbed a couple of cookies, announcing she was having a 'cheat day' as she did so, and beckoned me with a tilt of her head to follow her upstairs to her bedroom.

It looked like a music studio crossed with Santa's grotto. Every spare inch of surface and wall space was covered. Posters of Prince, Carole King and, of course, Aretha Franklin adorned the walls. Rows of fairy lights were strewn across the curtain rails and headboard. It was a fairly large room, but we had to gingerly pick our way across it to avoid colliding with a keyboard on a stand, two guitars and a large dressing table. On the dressing table sat a huge mirror with bulbs around the edge, like something from a film star's trailer.

A tall set of shelves towered over the scene at the opposite end of the room to the bed. Each layer was crammed with framed pictures of Aretha: Aretha on stage at a festival, taken from behind so you could only make out her silhouette against a vast backdrop of a cheering crowd which seemed to stretch out for miles; Aretha performing at what looked like some sort of recital, sitting at a piano in a shiny hall, her head thrown back and her eyes closed as she sang; Aretha outside Abbey Road studios, clad in a fur-lined puffa jacket, beaming at whoever was behind the camera.

'Who's that?' I asked, pointing to one of the rare photos which wasn't solely of Aretha, in which a distinguished looking man was clutching her around the shoulders and she was giggling into his armpit.

'That's my dad!' Aretha replied, like everyone should know that.

I looked again. Now I knew who he was, I could see the family resemblance. He was a lot taller than Aretha and had darker skin, but he had the same broad smile and dimples in his cheeks, as well as that intangible quality – which shone out, even through a photo – which makes you want to get to know someone.

We sat crossed-legged on Aretha's purple, paisley-patterned bedspread, her munching cookies while I tried not to dribble. We talked about our English homework, for which we had to analyse *Animal Farm* in the context of modern politics. We agreed that it wouldn't be that hard to draw parallels between current government policies and Orwell's dystopian fiction. Together, we looked at the last line of the novel: 'The creatures outside looked from pig to man, and from man to pig, and from pig to man again; but already it was impossible to tell which was which.'

I told Aretha it never failed to make me shiver.

The conversation soon turned to people we knew from school.

'Olivia's a bit of an odd one, isn't she?' Aretha observed.

I didn't know what to say. Olivia wasn't like the other girls at St Edith's, but that was why I liked her.

'I guess so . . .' I responded, careful to keep it noncommittal.

But then, I couldn't resist asking, 'Why do you say that?'

'Well, I mean, she's a textbook example of a person who lacks confidence so mimics everyone around them. Every time you said something at that rehearsal I came to she was like, "yeah, I thought that"!' Aretha adopted a high-pitched whine, which didn't actually sound much like Olivia at all, but I laughed anyway.

'Yeah, she's always been kind of shy in groups. But she loves acting and has done so well to get a lead role this year,' I said, conscious that I didn't want to be disloyal.

'Oh, wow. Sorry. I had no idea you guys were tight.' Aretha brought both of her palms forward in a gesture of surrender. 'I'll just shut up and stop slagging off your friend, shall I?'

Yet I found I didn't want her to, because discussing a mutual acquaintance was one of the things which made me feel like Aretha and I were in an exclusive club of two and I didn't want to sacrifice that, even if it meant poor Olivia had to take a verbal battering. She'd never have to know, I reasoned with myself.

'No, no! Not at all!' I backtracked, hastily. 'Olivia and I just do drama club and have theatre studies together, that's all. We aren't that close. And I think you're right . . . what you said about her copying me. She does it all the time.'

Aretha drew a large breath and opened her mouth to reply, just as there was a knock at the door and the man I now knew was her dad poked his head around it. I felt myself sit up a little straighter, wanting to make a good first impression.

'Hello, girls!' he said, smiling. 'I'm making ackee and saltfish for dinner. Want to help?'

Chapter 8

I sat at the kitchen table and watched Aretha and Delroy, side by side at the counter, preparing dinner in what was obviously a well-practised routine.

Delroy rinsed the fish and passed it to Aretha, who transferred it into a large glass bowl and used two forks to break it up into flaky chunks. Delroy playfully grabbed the fish's head and brought it towards Aretha's face, asking her if she wanted to eat the eye. 'It'll make you smarter,' he said, tapping his temple in the exact gesture Aretha had used when we'd discussed my mental health a few weeks back.

'Don't do that to Loo,' Aretha replied, barely glancing in my direction even though she was talking about me. 'She freaked out the other day when she was served a fish whole in a restaurant. I had to cut it up for her.'

'Is that right?' Delroy turned and narrowed his eyes at me, but there was a mischievous smile playing about his lips.

'I just don't like to think of anything I eat having once been alive.' I shrugged. 'I know it's silly.'

'Not silly,' Delroy reassured me, flicking a tea towel over his shoulder and turning his attention to a weird vegetable that looked a bit like a large lychee with black olives stuffed into it. 'There are lots of cultures that feel that way. What's your heritage? Is there any Indian in you?'

'Oh, uhm . . .' I hated this question. HATED IT. Not because

I wanted people to think I was white, but because it was kind of embarrassing to admit that I had no idea where half of me came from. 'I'm actually not sure . . . maybe?' I replied to a bemused-looking Delroy.

'Loo doesn't know her dad,' Aretha jumped in to fill the slightly awkward beat of silence that followed. 'It's such a shame for her.' She looked at Delroy. Her gaze could only be described as bordering on worshipful. She looked like that gif of Patrick from SpongeBob leaning on his elbows with hearts circling around his smitten face. It was fascinating.

I'd first seen the change in Aretha as Delroy's face peered around her bedroom door earlier. It was both stark and immediate. Gone was her usual confident persona, replaced instead by a person who was coy and adoring. Everything about Aretha – the set of her shoulders, the way she smiled and spoke – changed entirely when Delroy was nearby. It was like watching her in a theatre role, playing the part of 'Daddy's Girl'.

Of course, there was a part of me that wondered if this was just normal. I'd watched girls with their dads before, but only from afar and usually in sentimental settings, like the father-and-daughter dance at a relative's wedding. I knew the stereotype – mums spoiled their sons and dads their daughters, but I had no real experience to measure it against. Sometimes I felt like it might be nice to have an older, male version of me put his arm around me and tell me I was his Special Little Princess. But then I'd chide myself for betraying Mum and for buying into what was clearly a stupid fantasy I'd picked up from some Disney movie or similar.

I didn't tend to wonder what it might be like to have a dad often, because the concept was so far removed from everything I knew. You might as well ask me to think about what it would be like to be a Martian, or a hamster, or Ariana Grande. For lots of reasons, I'd got really good at just putting it to the back of my mind.

I watched as Aretha told Delroy an in-joke I didn't understand and he threw his head back to laugh heartily. It struck me that Aretha had two things I lacked: a loving, present father and a sense of who she was that stretched back generations . . .

I wondered what it would feel like if I could cook the food of my ancestors. (I knew of course how to make Welsh rarebit, but cheese on toast wasn't going to impress anyone.) Watching Delroy gaze fondly at his daughter as she twittered on about her day, I felt a lump form in my throat. I coughed to try and dislodge it and turned my head away.

'Loo, would you mind setting the table?' Delroy startled me out of my thoughts. 'Cutlery is in the top drawer in the dresser over there and place mats are in the one underneath. Oh and you need to set it for five. Steph is joining us in a bit.'

'Daaaaad! Whyyyyyyy? Ziek's not even here!' Aretha wailed, as I went over to the dresser to retrieve the necessaries.

'Aretha!' Delroy's tone was suddenly stern. 'Steph is Ezekiel's partner and she is therefore part of this family. She is welcome any time she wants. End of discussion.'

Aretha immediately piped down, which surprised me. At school she acted like she wouldn't be told what to do by anyone. I wanted to ask more about this Steph, but thought it best to drop it – the faint whiff of the altercation still hung in the air, like cigarette smoke. Instead, I asked if there was anything else I could do to help.

'Thanks, sweetheart,' Delroy replied, all crossness now gone from his voice. 'You can put some of the juice in the fridge in a jug and set out some glasses from that cupboard and then I think we're good.'

Aretha had her back to me, but I could tell by the way her shoulders had stiffened that she was annoyed. I wondered what Steph could possibly have done to provoke such ire.

The doorbell rang and we heard Dawn shout, 'I'll get it!' A few moments later, a person I could only assume to be Steph walked in. She was both imposing and incredibly beautiful and I wondered if the reason Aretha didn't like her was that she was a little intimidated. I knew I was. She was tall – perhaps even taller than me – with an enviable hourglass figure. She had velvety, almost inky-dark skin, a heart-shaped face and she wore her hair in long braids which reached down to her waist. She carried herself without a shred of self-consciousness – head held high and shoulders back, the way Dr Coleman told us to stand when we were trying to 'channel confidence'.

'Hiiiii!' Steph smiled, revealing perfectly straight teeth. She hugged Delroy, then Aretha, who grimaced.

'Hello, I'm Loo.' I offered Steph my hand nervously. I hated introductions and today had involved an awful lot of them. There was always a little voice in my head which said my posture, or my facial expression was all wrong and at any moment the person I was meeting would say 'everything about you is a fraud and you don't belong in this conversation!'.

Steph, however, shook my hand with both of hers and told

me it was a pleasure to meet me. Then she gave me a hug for good measure, just in case I was in any doubt that it was, indeed, a pleasure to meet me. I liked her immediately – she radiated friendliness – but I tried not to make that too obvious in front of Aretha.

Delroy was busying himself by flamboyantly chucking tomatoes and peppers into a pan, juices spattering across his chef's apron. 'Your timing's good,' he said to Steph, 'it'll be about ten minutes or so.'

Aretha grabbed my hand. 'Come on, Loo,' she commanded. 'We're going upstairs.' I waved vaguely in Steph's direction and followed Aretha meekly to her bedroom, curious to know what had caused this animosity.

Once we were safely in Aretha's bedroom with the door closed, I asked her about Steph. She and Ezekiel had met at college in East London two years before, it transpired, and hooked up a few months later. While Ziek had gone to university, Steph had opted to take a year out to decide on her next steps. In the meantime, she'd got a job working for some sort of techy start-up (she'd studied computer science at A Level) which happened to be not far from where Dawn, Delroy and Aretha now lived. Steph had taken to popping around for dinner about once a week, something Aretha was clearly raging about.

'Urgh! She's just so annoying!' she ranted in a furious half-whisper, as she paced the tiny square of available floor space in her room. 'She thinks she's so smart. And she is really hung up on race. Like, once she asked me if I considered myself to be black or white and when I said neither she gave me this big lecture about how it's not what your mix is, it's how the world perceives you or some bullshit. And Ziek's totally bought into it. Ever since he met her he keeps telling me to check my privilege and I'm like, oh my god you sound like you borrowed a personality from the internet, shut up.'

She exhaled, looking mutinous. I wasn't sure what to say, so she continued.

'I get this all the time from Black women! Every time I go to a club or post a picture of myself online, I get hatred for being light skinned. And half the time I swear it's only because men prefer light-skinned women and they're salty about it. But that's not exactly my fault. I didn't ask to look like this.'

Despite the awkward context, it was actually refreshing to hear someone speaking so openly about race. At home, I got the impression Mum didn't like drawing attention to the difference in my skin tone from hers and Hugh's, in case it made me feel like I didn't belong in the family. At school, the vast majority of pupils and staff were white and, although we occasionally spoke about racism in history or PSHE, it was always in a way that suggested it was an issue consigned to the past, no longer relevant to our liberal modern world.

One of our teachers even told us she didn't 'see colour' because she had 'friends of all different races'. I remember thinking, *if you don't see colour then how come you know they're different races?* But I didn't say that out loud. Unusually for me, I kept my thoughts to myself, because race was one of the few topics I didn't feel entitled to have an opinion on. I'd been raised by a white parent and lived in an overwhelmingly white community, after all. Plus, I wasn't what people thought of when they imagined a mixed person – half Black, half white. I didn't know where my place was in the conversation, or if I even had a place.

So, I didn't voice my frustration the last five times I had to buy panstick for our drama productions out of my own pocket, because the school only supplied stage make-up for white people. I guess that's what happens when the people in charge 'don't see colour'.

Having said that, I never really felt like anyone treated me any worse because of my race. I wasn't particularly popular at school, but I was fairly sure that was just because of my general personality, rather than the shade of my skin. It was also hard not to notice all the white girls in my school were using filters on Insta and TikTok which made them look like they were about the same colour as me – olive skin was apparently what everyone was aspiring to.

Once Aretha got her frustrations off her chest we went back down for dinner. I was sat with Steph on one side and Dawn on the other. I'd been worried I would have nothing to say, but was relieved to find conversation flowed naturally. Steph asked lots of questions and gave thoughtful responses to the questions I asked her in return. I wondered if I was doing the right thing, being nice to Steph, but she was so warm and interesting she made it difficult to be anything else. I kept one eye on Aretha, who was staring straight ahead like she'd gone somewhere else in her mind.

I can't say I really understood when Steph described what she did at the start-up (technology not really being my forte), but when we touched on politics everything she said landed with me.

'Systematic prejudice against Black people and other minorities is an indisputable fact,' Steph said. 'Even if discussions in media about racism are always centred around whether or not a person "feels" society is racist. They did an experiment at Oxford University where they sent out a bunch of CVs. They all had the exact same amount of qualifications and experience, but some of the names sounded African or Middle-Eastern. And, guess what? Those were the ones that didn't get a call back for an interview. Of course it's hard for an individual person to say the reason they didn't get a job is because of their heritage but when you zoom out, when you look at the patterns in the way people of different races are treated, you can see the discrimination so clearly.' As Steph spoke, it was as though I could feel my eyes being opened to issues I'd only been peripherally aware of in the past.

Delroy, who was attacking his ackee and saltfish like a man who'd been starved for a week, murmured the occasional 'mmm hmm' and nodded his head.

I asked Steph if there was anything I could do to help.

'Wow. How refreshing to hear that question!' Steph replied, with a brief, but pointed glance in Aretha's direction. 'You'd be surprised how little people ask it. Especially when they are of a minority background themselves, like you. They assume just because they aren't white they have no privilege, whereas the truth is that discrimination is complex. As a dark-skinned Black woman, I will statistically experience measurably more racism than those with lighter skin, for example.'

I felt, rather than saw, Aretha roll her eyes theatrically.

'But it's not just about skin colour,' Steph continued. 'Hair is a big factor, too. So, let's take you and Aretha as an example. Your skin tone isn't that different, but you have wavy hair and Aretha has curls, so the world will racialise her more than you. You are above her in the hierarchy of privilege.'

Aretha looked directly at us for the first time, her eyes wide. She seemed genuinely shocked. I was trying to absorb what Steph was saying at the same time as making sure Aretha was OK. Our eyes met and I did a very small smile which I hoped conveyed the twenty different things I was thinking in that moment. Steph seemed not to notice any of this.

'The most important thing is to challenge prejudice wherever you can and to listen and accept the experiences of others. Speaking of which, I have been talking at you for a very long time!' Steph laughed. 'Why don't you tell me more about you?'

For a dreaded moment, I thought Steph was going to follow in Delroy's footsteps and ask me questions about my heritage that I had no hope of answering. But instead, and to my immense relief, she said, 'Do you and Aretha have any classes together?'

'Only English,' I replied.

'Cool. What are you reading at the moment?'

'*Animal Farm.* I'm loving it, although I kind of wish we'd done *1984* instead.'

'Oh my god, *1984* is soooo good.' Steph almost knocked over her glass of juice in her enthusiasm.

'I wish it was on the syllabus,' Dawn interjected, reaching across to take mine and Steph's plates. 'Particularly when there are so many parallels to be drawn with governments around the world at the moment. I mean, look at what's happening to freedom of the press.'

'The party told you to reject the evidence of your eyes and ears . . .' I began.

' . . . It was their final, most essential command,' Dawn and Steph both finished with me and we grinned at each other, in that way only people who have just discovered a shared passion can.

There was a clatter of cutlery against plate and chair against floor, as Aretha suddenly got to her feet.

'Excuse me,' she said. 'I don't feel well all of a sudden. I'm going to my room.'

Then she practically ran up the stairs, slamming the kitchen door behind her in her wake.

Chapter 9

The next day, I was in the garden bouncing on my mini trampoline while going over my *Merchant* lines for the scene we were rehearsing the following week.

This was a technique I'd discovered during a visit to Nain and Taid's in Wales one summer a few years before. They have a massive trampoline in their back garden, which looks out over the gorgeous, lush green hills beyond. We were doing *Macbeth* (or 'the Scottish Play' as the Professor had insisted we call it, because saying 'Macbeth' out loud would apparently cause a curse to be placed upon the entire production) and, since I was only in Year 10 at the time, I'd been given the small-ish part of Macduff. I'd realised that the only way I could be guaranteed to remember my lines in spite of stage fright/distractions/my mum insisting on waving at me from the front row even though I'd told her in no uncertain terms this was forbidden etc, was if I knew them so well I could recite them automatically. So, I took to practising while bouncing furiously on the trampoline, attempting more and more elaborate routines which took greater and greater levels of concentration, until I could focus almost entirely on performing a side flip while saying my lines at the same time.

The mini trampoline wasn't quite the same, but I'd got into the habit of doing it now and it had become a superstitious thing. Plus, it counted towards the hour of exercise per day Aretha had said was necessary for me to 'continue my weight-loss journey'.

'If thou wilt lend this money, lend it not
As to thy friends; for when did friendship take
A breed for barren metal of his friend?
But lend it rather to thine enemy,
Who, if he break, thou mayst with better face
Exact the penalty.'

I recited.

The word 'enemy' took me back to the night before, at Aretha's house. After Aretha had stormed out of the kitchen, there was a moment where I wasn't sure what to do. My instinct was to follow her, but I didn't want to appear rude. Luckily, Delroy saved me from my internal dilemma by gesturing at the closed door and mouthing 'go on'.

As walked down the hallway I could hear Delroy ask, 'who is going to tell her she is grounded?' To which Dawn replied, 'she's too old for that now, Del. Anyway, maybe she really is feeling poorly.'

I don't know what I expected when Aretha opened the door – just a crack at first, then further when she saw it was me – but I was surprised when I saw she had tears streaming down her face.

'Come in,' she croaked, before turning and plonking herself on the bed, picking up a knitted blanket and hugging it to herself the way you see toddlers do in pushchairs. It was a side of Aretha I'd never encountered before and, wary of upsetting her further, I gingerly placed one half of my bum on the corner of her mattress and asked her if she was OK.

'Yeah. I'm fine,' Aretha replied, staring intently at a scratch in the purple paint right next to her head.

'Well, you're obviously not,' I ventured, with trepidation. 'Do you want to talk about it?'

I thought maybe she'd say no and then I'd have no choice but to concede defeat and go home. I hated unresolved conflict. The idea made my heart race a little faster.

'Argh, babes!' Aretha exclaimed, covering her eyes with the heels of her hands. 'Do you know what it was like for me, in there? Having to sit and listen to you sucking up to stupid Steph and then you and her and Mum bollocking on about a book I haven't even read? I might as well have not even been there!'

My stomach felt like it had dropped through the floor. I'd been so absorbed talking to Steph, at some point I stopped wondering how my behaviour might have been affecting Aretha.

'I'm sorry,' I said, 'I didn't think.'

'That's right, you didn't,' Aretha retorted. 'It's just so hurtful when you know I'm not as well-read, or posh as you to deliberately exclude me like that.'

'It wasn't deliberate—' I began.

'Or, maybe it's me,' Aretha interrupted, slumping defeatedly against her headboard. 'Maybe if I want to run with you and the Surrey crew I need to start reading more . . . up my game.'

'Don't be silly!' I exclaimed. I'd always thought of Aretha as intelligent, what with all the cultural knowledge she dropped into our conversations. It had genuinely never occurred to me to think otherwise.

'Oh, so now I'm silly?' Aretha sat up straight, looking me in the eye. 'You know, I'm just trying to explain to you how I feel and you're dismissing me.' She stood abruptly, beginning her now-familiar routine of pacing the few square centimetres of clear bedroom floor space. 'Oh my god, this always happens. I always think I've found a friend who understands me and I open up to them and they throw it back in my face.'

I thought of all the stories Aretha had told me about people who had judged her and mistreated her in the past because of jealousy. I imagined Aretha with a new friend in the future, describing our friendship in the same way, telling them how I humiliated her in front of her family after she'd trusted me enough to invite me round to eat with them.

I felt, with a solid, urgent certainty, that I could not allow that to happen. I would be different. I would be the friend who truly 'got' Aretha, with all her quirks and eccentricities and she'd reward me by letting me back into her sphere, the secret club of two I'd come to cherish since I'd known her.

'Tell me what I need to do to make it right,' I said.

She'd hugged me then, her soft curls pressing into the curve where my shoulder met my neck, and I exhaled, knowing I was forgiven.

'Just don't ever put me in that situation again,' she'd murmured.

I was jolted from the memory by the sound of my phone ringing in the pocket of my hoodie, which I'd chucked across a garden chair when all the trampolining began to make me sweat. I scrambled to answer it.

'Babe!' Aretha exclaimed. 'I've had a brilliant idea! Stop whatever you're doing and let's Skype!'

Aretha knew my phone was a hand-me-down from Hugh I'd acquired years before and found perfectly adequate for my needs. I could do all the blog stuff on my laptop and had an automatic filter which meant I could approve and/or reply to comments in bulk. I didn't tend to look at social media on the fly, saving it for specific times when I'd scroll through Instagram on my laptop, usually when I was bored, just to see what everyone was doing. Aretha, however, favoured communicating face-to-face, so we'd taken to chatting over Skype.

Obediently, I picked up my trampoline and put it in the garage, before bounding up to my bedroom. I took the stairs two at a time, intrigued by what Aretha's idea could be and also conscious of keeping her waiting. I noticed that the effort didn't leave me as out of breath as it would have done a couple of weeks before. I was getting fitter.

'So, I've been thinking,' Aretha leapt in immediately after a connection was established, as I attempted to get comfy on my bed. 'The whole toilet thing was a good gimmick to get you noticed, but I've been looking over your blogs and . . . aren't you starting to repeat yourself a bit?'

'Uhm . . . I suppose so,' I replied, trying to imitate the way Aretha was sat with her legs folded elegantly beneath her but quickly discovering I was nowhere near flexible enough.

'I mean, when you look at influencers who do really well,' Aretha continued, 'they're all about the personalities. They have really slick photos and talk about their lives so you feel like you know them. And then they can pretty much talk about any topic.'

'That's the thing, though,' I argued, slumping back against the wall 'I don't want to be an influencer. I want to be a writer. And the professional writer who came in to do a talk in Year 10 said—'

'If we get ourselves a massive following,' Aretha interrupted, 'you can get a book deal. I can get a record deal. We can do whatever we want. And we stand double the chance if there's two of us. The internet loves a double act.'

'Influencers usually do books about how to decorate your bedroom with paper chains, or stick plastic flowers in Play-Doh, though,' I reasoned.

'Look, babe, I get that. We all wish the world was different and that genuine talent was what got you noticed.' Aretha waved her hand in front of the screen in a dismissive gesture. 'It's like the music industry – artists are products now. Even the ones we're told started off posting videos of their songs on YouTube and just happened to be noticed by, like, Pharrell, or whoever, it's all bullshit. It's all been manufactured behind the scenes. And that frustrates me, too, so I hear you. But I love music and it's what I want to do with my life so I have to play the game. If you want to be a professional writer you need to have a plan, too.'

I hadn't thought of it this way. At school, we were taught that hard work and talent reaped reward. But the real world, a world of which Aretha had vastly more experience than me, was different. She was wearing me down and, as though sensing this, she steamed ahead. 'And I've been thinking, between the two of us we could massively expand the things we review. Like, I could talk about music. Or, if there's food, whether it's, you know, nutritious and good for you.'

'Do you . . . know enough about that stuff?' I asked, just as Fiona jumped up on to the bed and directed her backside at my computer, momentarily filling the screen with ginger bum hole.

'Nutrition, I mean,' I added hastily, picking Fiona up and manoeuvring her on to my lap – I didn't want Aretha to think I was questioning her musical knowledge.

'Oh, hey, Fi!' Aretha laughed, waving at the cat, who stared back at her with a vaguely murderous expression. 'Well, I've helped you lose weight, haven't I? You're looking great, by the way,' she added as an afterthought and I smiled bashfully, 'and I have all these allergies so I'm basically, like, fully vegan . . .' The shock must have shown on my face, as images of her chowing down on her king prawns and steak at Giuseppe's and the salt fish we'd eaten the night before flooded my mind. 'Not the whole time, obviously.' She giggled. 'I'm flexitarian. But I've had to do loads of research into what effect various foods have on the body. It's an area of my expertise, for sure.'

'Right, OK,' I said. If Aretha noticed that I was unconvinced by this, she pretended not to. Or maybe I did a good job of hiding it. After our mini fall-out the night before, I didn't want to risk rocking the boat. I also didn't want to disappoint or annoy her by telling her I was pretty sure there was more to being a nutritional expert than reading up on allergies on the web, or to appear ungrateful for the help she had given me. Anyway, Aretha was super smart. She'd probably absorbed more information than the average person.

'And it'll be so much fun!' The screen was momentarily a blur of Aretha's freckles and teeth as she pressed her face right up to the screen. 'Like, how many people in this world can say that their job involves being invited to hang out in cool places for free with their best mate?'

And it was that rhetorical question which decided it.

The way she called me her 'best mate', confirming that the affection I felt for her wasn't one-sided. The implication that phrase held of what our future could look like – a whirlwind of gigs, bars, restaurants, galleries, with Aretha getting us A-list treatment by bewitching everyone in her wake and me enjoying all the benefits of being her sidekick. The notion that I'd become more glamorous, more aspirational and more popular because the outside world would see us as a double act.

I beamed at the screen, all doubts suddenly forgotten, and nodded.

'How about we call the blog "Aretha and Loo"?' Aretha asked. 'I know it should really be Loo and Aretha, but that sounds too much like urethra, which is gross.'

I erupted into giggles, which Aretha took as my consent.

'The first thing we need to do is get some professional photos taken together,' she continued. 'One of my friends back in London is a photographer and stylist. I bet I could get her to do a shoot and hire her studio and she'd give you mates' rates.'

I didn't notice how, when the conversation turned to money, 'we' became 'you'.

Chapter 10

The following Saturday I found myself perched on a high steel stool (seemingly designed to inflict as much discomfort upon the user's bottom as humanly possible) in the middle of a stark white space somewhere in East London, while a woman called Crystal scrutinised my face with a gaze fixed somewhere between pity and disdain.

'What moisturiser do you use?' Crystal asked, gently stroking my temples in a way which might have been affectionate had she not been wearing the expression of a person being forced to clean up dog poo with their bare hands.

'Uhm . . . I don't?' I replied, sheepishly. Sometimes I slapped on a bit of the cocoa butter I used on my elbows if my face felt tight but, other than that, my pores were a product-free zone.

Crystal widened her eyes and gasped, as if I'd just confessed to enjoying spending my Saturdays sticking drawing pins into puppies.

'Your skin is very dehydrated,' she said. 'You really should invest in a good moisturiser with an SPF for the day, as well as a heavier night cream. And you want something specifically formulated for around the eyes, too, because the skin there is very delicate, as well as good quality lip balm. Lots of people your age don't think they need to moisturise but if you get into a good skincare routine now you'll save yourself wrinkles down the line.'

I nodded, hoping I was giving the impression that I was taking the slightest bit of notice. Mum was always buying extortionately priced pots of illuminating this and age-defying that and she never looked any different. Or at least not as far as I could see with my human eyes.

'I'll just do some basic skincare before we start on the make-up,' Crystal said, lining up an intimidating number of bottles, tubes and jars along what was once a mantlepiece but was currently being used as a makeover station. 'And then we'll have to get your hair into some sort of shape. We can do that while the moisturiser is sinking in. What time are you shooting?' she asked, looking over at Aretha, who was sitting in a battered armchair in the corner, scrolling on her phone.

'We have this place booked until four and Bea says we need about two hours to get the shots,' Aretha replied, without looking up. She had already been made up and looked almost other-worldly, even under the harsh strip lights. With her huge eyes and blemish-free skin, her make-up hadn't taken long at all. It seemed to mostly involve dabbing on about ten different kinds of highlighter, as well as applying drag queen-esque fake lashes and masses of her trademark glittery eyeliner. Plus, she'd squashed her own afro under a tight fitting cap and put another, even larger afro wig on top, which had taken all of about thirty seconds. I felt like quite the beauty burden, by comparison.

Bea was Aretha's 'official photographer'. She'd snapped and styled all Aretha's head shots and, Aretha told me, was a 'bit of a genius'. Said genius was shuffling around in the corner doing something with what looked like a large umbrella.

I didn't want to judge, but when we arrived at the studio and found it locked, Aretha had phoned Bea and I heard her muffled voice through the speaker say, 'Oh, is it today?' It hadn't exactly filled me with confidence. Bea had arrived about forty-five minutes later looking dishevelled, dressed in what I strongly suspected were the pyjamas she slept in. She practically fell out of her cab, laden with three suitcases full of 'looks' for Aretha and I, a camera on a strap around her neck, as well as several lights and the umbrella thing, which her cab driver kindly carted up the three flights of stairs to the studio. She didn't tip him.

Since then, Bea had been schlumping around the 'space' in an activity she called 'searching for angles'. She was one of those people who moved with infuriating slowness, as though through treacle. Even forming a sentence seemed to take her an eternity. Her eyes were perpetually half-closed and she was always forgetting what she was meant to be doing. But I trusted Aretha's judgment and, in fairness, the headshots she had shown me looked great.

Aretha had talked me through the plan for the shoot the previous evening, at her house. I'd invited her to mine but she didn't seem keen and said she needed to be home to accept an ASOS parcel with 'back-up accessories' she'd ordered for today's shoot.

In return for £1000 we would get a studio for four hours, hair and make-up, plus a set of high-quality pictures we could use to 'rebrand' as Aretha and Loo. This money would come out of the ad revenue from Loo Reviews but, Aretha explained, 'we will recoup it really quickly once we start getting brand collabs.' I found myself nodding, even though I barely understood.

In truth, I don't think my responses mattered that much one way or the other. Aretha had talked at a million miles an hour, barely pausing for breath as we sat on her bed pouring over her laptop. She'd created digital mood boards for each of us based on our personal styles. This was fascinating from my perspective as someone who had always believed I didn't have one. Turns out I'm best suited to 'conventional soft glam', which apparently means lots of smoky eyes and short skirts. She dropped names into the conversation I'd never heard before – Iskra Lawrence, Dina Torkia, Deji – and commanded me to research them for 'inspiration'.

'But ultimately,' Aretha declared, with the same unquestionable confidence with which she said everything, 'what we're going for is relatable. Not in a Zoe Sugg way,' she reassured me, as though that had been what I was thinking or I had half a clue what she meant, 'we need more of an edge.'

In the studio, Crystal was huffing with the effort of using two brushes to try and flatten my hair into submission. It remained resolute, sticking out in about twenty-five different directions.

'I'm going to need to wet it,' she sighed, eventually conceding defeat. 'Come with me to the toilet.'

'Bea,' she called over her shoulder, as we began traipsing down the staircase. 'can you put the looks out on the rails so I can see what they'll be wearing?'

'Oh, sure,' Bea replied, not moving.

By the time we had dampened the thick masses of my hair over a tiny, ancient sink in the toilet and got back up the stairs, the clothes were being assembled on two steel rails by Aretha. Bea continued to stare mysteriously at a corner.

'Here's yours, babe,' Aretha said, gesturing towards the left-hand rail with a flourish. 'There's some really nice pieces there.'

I gulped. Everything looked tiny.

'Uhm . . . I don't think these are going to fit,' I said, fingering a strappy crop top with broderie anglaise across the bust.

'You won't know until you try!' Aretha retorted, irritated, like I was a child refusing to eat broccoli.

'What size are they?' I asked Bea.

'They're, errr . . . twelves or mediums – Aretha told me that's what you were,' Bea replied solemnly, as though this had all happened due to a misfortunate accident and she genuinely couldn't work out how.

I held my breath, mind reeling. I'd been following Aretha's regime for almost six weeks and, while I had no idea how much weight I'd lost in pounds and ounces, I knew I was thinner. But I still wasn't thin. In fact, at six-foot-one with broad shoulders and hips, I didn't think even my skeleton would fit into the tiny slip of fabric I was holding gingerly between my fingers. That didn't stop Aretha contending that it would.

'Just put it over your head,' she insisted. 'There's some stretch in that top.' I looked around for somewhere I could change in privacy, but the studio was one large square with every corner exposed.

'Don't be silly, babes,' Aretha said, as though reading my thoughts. 'We've all seen a body before. Just whip off your top and try this one.'

Cringing, I did so. I felt goosebumps erupt across my skin as I lifted my oversized black T-shirt over my head. Bea and Crystal both looked away pointedly, which somehow made it worse.

I put both arms into the crop top, immediately feeling that the fabric wasn't stretchy enough to fit over my bust. Aretha, however, had moved around to the back of me and began determinedly yanking the top down. Ignoring my protestations, she eventually managed to squish me into the garment. I began to panic. The top was constricting my chest and I was struggling to breathe. The room suddenly felt too hot and too bright. I dropped to my knees, trying desperately to stave off the panic I could feel bubbling up inside me.

I went on to autopilot, my instinct telling me to employ the techniques I'd learned in therapy two years ago. I breathed in for five, out for seven, in through the nose, out through the mouth. After a few moments, I started to feel less faint. I began tugging at the top, impatient to feel my lungs expand to their full capacity.

'OK, OK!' Aretha said, rolling her eyes. 'If you're going to be like that about it, we'll find you a different top.' She giggled at Crystal, whose mouth was set in a grim line as she took in the scene.

'Are you OK?' Crystal asked gently, sinking down and stroking my arm. All the spikiness I'd sensed before, when she was despairing at the state of my hair and skin, had gone.

'Yes.' I managed a small smile.

'Good.' Crystal deliberately caught my eye and I noticed hers had a distinct twinkle. 'Because I have an idea . . .'

An hour later, I was standing in front of the full-length mirror we'd borrowed from the studio below, unable to comprehend that the reflection I was staring at was me.

As it turned out, Crystal was multi-talented. As well as being a make-up and hair artist, she also had a passion for clothes design and sewing. She'd sprinted to her car, which was parked a few streets away and returned red-faced and excited, brandishing what looked like a small metal toolbox. Inside were dressmaker's scissors, needles, thread and a small selection of fabric pieces.

Crystal had proceeded to slice and stitch my plain black T-shirt into something unrecognisably fabulous. She'd created what she told me was a 'boat neck', which flattered my broad shoulders and showed off my collar bone, now gleaming with the highlighter powder that had been dusted over it. She'd drawn the T-shirt in at the waist by adding stitches at the back. The fabric then fell loosely over my hips, giving me an hourglass silhouette. At the bottom, she'd added a thick band of orange silk which even I, with my zero knowledge of such things, could see complimented my skin tone perfectly. The makeshift dress sat a good four inches above my knee and my legs, which had also received the highlighter treatment and, lengthened by the three-inch open-toed sandals I had been coaxed into, looked endless.

Crystal had also insisted on trimming my hair, getting rid of several centimetres of uneven split ends I'd been cultivating over the years. She'd teased it into glossy waves, which were tumbling over one shoulder. She'd kept my make-up fairly simple, but my skin was glowing, my bushy brows were – according to Crystal – 'fleeky AF', and she'd painted my lips a deep scarlet, which made me look pouty in a way I'd never considered myself capable of up until that point.

I'm not going to lie, I was slightly in love with myself.

I spun on my heel, grinning, to face Aretha, who was stood behind me. She quickly plastered on a smile and her voice squeaked slightly as she exclaimed, 'you look great, babe!', clapping her hands together to emphasise her point.

But she obviously hadn't been expecting me to turn round quite so soon because there was a split second, right before she smiled, when she kind of looked like she wanted me to die.

Chapter 11

The photos looked good, in the end. They were mostly 'unposed' shots (i.e. actually very posed but meant to look as though we weren't aware of the camera) of Aretha and I laughing. We looked like the kind of young women other girls might aspire to be – glamorous, but not in a way that suggested we were trying too hard. Fun. Carefree. Confident. When I accepted Bea's invitation to look at the pictures through the viewfinder on her camera, I once again experienced the weird sensation of not being able to believe it was myself I was looking at.

Yet, there was something amiss, something known only to the people present that day, about the way those photos had been captured. Each time Bea lined up the shot, Aretha would start laughing spontaneously and I found her giggles contagious, so I'd chuckle too. But then, as soon as Bea confirmed she'd got the shot, Aretha's laughter would fade as abruptly as it began. The rest of the time, Aretha was sour and stony-faced. I suspected her mood had something to do with the vest top she'd tried to wrestle me into not fitting, but every time I tried to talk to her, she'd yell to Crystal that her eye make-up was dropping or her wig needed adjusting, derailing any conversation between us.

It was a relief when the shoot was over.

'What are we doing now?' I asked Aretha.

'No idea what you're doing, babe,' she replied, 'but I'm going on to a mate's house. My Uber's three minutes away.'

I'd ventured into Central London on a few occasions before, mainly for school theatre trips and Loo Reviews. It was less than an hour by train into the heart of the city, via Waterloo. Culture wise, however, it might as well have been Mars. Compared to Chiddy, London was so huge, sprawling and busy, I'd always been slightly terrified by it. I'd certainly never been this far out of Zone 1 alone. I hadn't been paying any particular attention on the way to the studio as Aretha had navigated us effortlessly from overground, to underground, to bus. I didn't want to admit that I didn't know where I was, but the thought of having to get back home unaided filled me with terror.

'Just look it up on your phone, babes,' Aretha said, when I voiced my concerns. I reminded her that I didn't have the sort of phone with access to live maps. Aretha smiled in a creepy way which didn't quite reach her eyes as she replied, 'that's really not my problem,' then she disappeared down the stairwell and out into the night.

I ended up helping Bea and Crystal pack up. I was too embarrassed to tell either of them I was sticking around because I was avoiding travelling back to Surrey alone.

'How long have you and Aretha known each other?' Crystal asked.

'Not that long. She joined my sixth form back in September. But it feels like we've known each other for ages,' I added, forcing myself to smile through my anxiety.

'That wasn't nice, what she did today. With the top.' Crystal was packing nail varnishes into a vast black plastic case and turned briefly when I hesitated to reply. I didn't know what to say. I suppose it wasn't a particularly nice thing to do, but I could also understand why Aretha had been annoyed. Bea had gone to the trouble of sourcing all those outfits for me and it must have been frustrating when it dawned on her that they weren't going to fit.

'Oh, you know. When you're tall, people always underestimate your size,' I eventually responded. 'It's a compliment, in a way. She obviously thinks I'm thinner than I am!' I forced myself to titter, like the whole thing hadn't bothered me at all, and the sound echoed around the cavernous studio space.

'Mmmmm,' was all I received in reply.

Finally, after handing them each a wodge of cash and waving them off in their respective taxis, I decided I couldn't put it off any longer.

I tried to look surreptitiously up and down the street, in order to get my bearings. The road the studio was on was stark and nondescript, lined either side with square, grey buildings, broken up by the odd patch of grass. A guy on a bike rode past me, close enough that my hair lifted in the breeze caused by the motion, and whistled. It was only then I realised I was still wearing the t-shirt dress and my lips were painted scarlet. The sun was rapidly setting. It would be dark soon. I suddenly felt extremely vulnerable.

I slipped out of my heels, which Bea and I had both forgotten didn't actually belong to me, and scrabbled around in my rucksack for the plimsoles I'd arrived in, taking care not to flash my knickers to the entire street as I did so. Once I was less wobbly on my feet, I decided the only thing for it was to go to the nearest bus stop and attempt to ascertain where I could get to from there. Hopefully, it would somehow relate to where I wanted to be.

The bus stop was cracked and covered in graffiti. It was difficult to make out the map which hung above the uncomfortable looking red plastic railing-style 'seats', presumably designed to discourage lingering. Finally, I was able to work out that the nearest major overground station was Liverpool Street. I decided I'd go there and ask someone official what to do next.

Not wanting to subject my bum to the tyranny of the red plastic railing, I entertained myself by standing near the pavement edge, nervously shifting my weight from foot to foot. The next bus was due in six minutes, the display informed me.

Two long minutes later, an ancient Mercedes with tinted windows pulled up next to me. The driver's window wound down to reveal a man of indeterminate age, dressed in a white tank top and a thick gold chain.

'Hey!' he said.

'Uhm, hey,' I replied nervously. I didn't want to appear rude. He could just be asking for directions (which would be unfortunate since I was entirely lost). Still, I felt my heart start to quicken.

'Where are you going?' he asked.

My mind spooled through possible responses. I didn't want to make him angry by telling him it was none of his business, but I also didn't want to be too specific and accidentally reveal too much of myself to a stranger. In the end I settled for 'home'.

The man grinned, revealing a gold tooth. 'You're cute, you know that?'

'Uhm, thank you,' I mumbled, looking at my shoes. I just wanted him to go away.

You always think you know what you'll do when you get unwanted attention from creepy strangers. If someone had explained the situation I was in at that moment to past me, I'd have said I'd tell the driver politely but firmly that I wasn't interested and to kindly move along. Yet, here I was showing gratitude for his attentions while trying to project fuck-off vibes using the power of telepathy. I wondered what Aretha would do. She'd probably charm this man into thinking fucking off was his idea, which was not something I considered to be within my skill range.

'Get in, I'll take you home,' the man demanded, leaning slightly out of the car to reveal a muscled forearm.

'No, thank you.' I cursed myself as my voice quavered a little.

'What, you want to take the bus?' the man said, managing to inject just a hint of a threat into the question.

'Yeah, I'll be fine. Thanks, though.' I somehow believed that if I kept thanking this man he would get the hint and go away.

'Come on, girl. It's getting dark and cold. I'll drive you wherever you want to go. No strings.' The man attempted to assure me, his grin becoming wider and somehow more sinister.

I was saved the trouble of thinking of a retort, since at that exact moment the sound of a loud horn interrupted us. Mercedes man had pulled into the bus lane and a red double-decker was impatiently trying to take its rightful place where his battered vehicle was currently parked. The man kissed his teeth and roared off angrily at high speed, skidding slightly as he did so.

I ran on to the bus, not even bothering to check whether it was the right one and sank, trembling into a seat. The other passengers eyed me curiously. I tried to be subtle as I focused on my breathing – in for five, out for seven. After a few minutes, I felt calm enough to stand, make my way to the front of the bus and ask the driver where we were going.

'Excuse me, do you stop at Liverpool Street?' I asked. The driver looked studiously ahead and ignored me. Thinking he hadn't heard, I drew breath to repeat my question, at which he silently pointed to a sign above his head reading PLEASE DO NOT TALK TO OR DISTRACT THE DRIVER.

It dawned on me that I had just outed myself as a tourist to a group of semi-curious strangers, any of whom could be rapists or murderers or a vast array of other criminal types you know London is full of if you have even a passing acquaintance with the six o' clock news. I felt my throat tighten. My mind began to spiral, imagining all the worst possible outcomes in this scenario. What if the bus crashed? What if someone followed me off it and dragged me into an alley and smothered me to death? What if I got really, really lost and had to spend the night wandering the dark streets of London alone, hungry and cold? What if I then got kidnapped and sold into slavery?

Just as I was imagining my Mum's tear-streaked face as she made a televised appeal for anyone who knew of my whereabouts, the bus came to a sudden, shuddering halt. I stumbled into the luggage rack as I tried to steady myself. The air was filled with the pungent scent of fried chicken as about twenty people lurched aboard, clearly drunk and very loud. They were cackling raucously, yelling drunken nonsense at one another, spilling stray chips and globules of ketchup on to the bus floor.

Everything was too much – too loud, too bright, too boisterous, too overwhelming. Every logical thought left my brain as somewhere inside me a voice began to chant, *you're going to die, you're going to die.* My breath started to come in painful, ragged gasps.

I hadn't had a full-on panic attack in over a year, but I remembered enough to know that one was now inevitable. There was nothing I could do to fight it. My head was swimming, my vision blurred. I was distantly aware that I was emitting a wheezing sound each time I exhaled. It felt like I was drowning. No one around me even glanced in my direction.

Every seat on the bus had now been filled, so I crouched on my heels, tucking my chin into my chest. I felt that we were coming to a stop again. Without pausing to consider what I was doing, I flung myself through the doors and on to the street, gulping in huge lungfuls of what passed for fresh air in this part of the city. The red plastic chair of the bus stop I found myself at now seemed like the most inviting place on earth. I lowered myself heavily on to it, shaking, with tears streaming down my face.

After what could have been seconds, minutes or hours, I finally felt strong enough to look up. I tested my balance, placing my weight on to one foot and then two. I still felt light headed, but my vision and hearing were returning back to normal. There was a dull pain in my chest, but it too was dwindling. It seemed the episode was passing.

I took in my surroundings. I was at a busy intersection, cars crawling along at a snail's pace in four distinct directions. Ahead of me, I could see rows of restaurants and bars, all heaving with Saturday night revellers. They spilled out on to the pavement to smoke cigarettes or move on to their next destination, letting out blasts of music with thumping basslines as they did. A pizza place was to my left, a Vietnamese restaurant to my right and, in the distance, I could just about make out the gleaming spire of the Gherkin.

A woman I'd guess was in her early twenties was striding down the road purposefully towards me. She wore a chunky scarf looped around her shoulders, skinny jeans and silver loafers. Her hair was shaved on one side and fell in short, post box-red waves on the other. She stopped when she saw me.

'Are you OK, lovely?' she asked in the kind of posh, nasal drawl I confess I had not previously associated with the East End. Something about the way she spoke reminded me of home.

'I'm lost,' I confessed. 'I'm trying to get home to Surrey.'

'Which station do you need?' she asked. 'Is it Waterloo?'

I nodded.

'Ah, brilliant!' she exclaimed, as though this were the best news ever. 'Then you're on the right road. Just look out for the 243 coming from that direction.' She pointed the opposite way to the Gherkin. 'It'll take you all the way there. Takes about half an hour, depending on traffic. You're in Dalston, by the way.'

I had never been more grateful to anyone in my whole

entire life. I exhaled properly for the first time in hours, feeling my shoulders sink. 'Thank you so, so much!' I said, feeling the urge to hug her, but some greater instinct telling me that would be disproportionate and strange.

'Hey.' She smiled. 'It's not a problem. You OK now?'

I nodded again, returning her grin.

'You take care of yourself.' She touched my arm briefly but kindly, before turning on her heel and continuing to take long strides towards whatever the night had in store for her. It was only after she'd become a tiny dot in the distance that I saw my reflection in the glass of the bus stop and realised what I looked like – my clothes inappropriate for the now-cold evening and what was once mascara in long black rivulets, snaking down my face.

What felt like eons later, I collapsed into my bed, hardly able to believe I'd made it. I was exhausted in that way you only know if you've had a panic attack and experienced the sensation of adrenaline coursing into and then leaking out of every cell in your body.

Blearily, I reached for my phone charger, ready to tuck my mobile away on the little stand on my bedside table where it lived overnight. I had a message from Aretha.

Hey babe u home ok ?? ☺ xx

I didn't know how to reply. I didn't want to be a drama queen, but I also thought she should know it hadn't been easy for me to find my way back after she'd dumped me unceremoniously.

Shakily, I typed:

Just got in. Bit of a mission getting home. Had huge panic attack on bus x

Seconds later, my phone beeped again.

O babes! U poor thing! At loud prty but will call tmrw so u can tell me wat happened or cry it out. Wateva u need ♥ Hope u ok. U know u can talk to me bout anything. Luv u xxxx

Chapter 12

I was in the wings, waiting for the house lights to dim so I could take my place for the opening scene of *Merchant*. I could hear the excited murmur of the crowd and smell the distinctive scent of dust and sweat, a residue left behind by hundreds of nervous teenagers like me who had waited in this exact spot to perform. I loved that smell, it brought to me in an instant a unique feeling of excitement, a sort of fizzing in my fingers and toes that I associated with theatre.

Suddenly, my heart began to race. I didn't know my lines. In fact, this whole thing was happening far too early. We hadn't even rehearsed most of the scenes. We were still weeks away from discarding our scripts. Why was this happening so soon?

'In sooth, I know not why I am so sad . . .' I whispered to myself, hoping that once I began reciting my very first line the rest would magically make themselves known to me. But I drew a blank. I panicked, frantically scanning the backstage area for a copy of the script. I'd just have to perform with the book in my hand. It wasn't ideal, but it was better than not knowing the words at all.

I spotted the familiar cover, a multi-coloured globe surrounded by vague, swirling shapes. I reached for the script, but when I opened it the writing was fuzzy and I couldn't make out the words. I tried to force myself to focus, but the black markings on the white page made no sense. We were seconds away from lights up. I tried to run, to find the Professor or Olivia, or even Charlotte to explain what was happening, to ask them to help, but it was as though my feet were nailed to the floor.

Just then, darkness descended, followed by the dazzling glare of the stage lights as the curtains began to draw back. I didn't know what to do. I wasn't ready. Why was this happening?

I hunched behind a prop table, hoping the audience wouldn't notice me standing there, helpless and confused. Then I heard a familiar voice, ringing out from the stage just in front of me.

'In sooth I know not why I am so sad . . .' it said. Someone else was playing Antonio. Why? Had I been replaced and not told? Was it because I wasn't good enough? I dared to glance upwards and could just about make out the masses of soft curls, their pale blonde ends almost silver under the spotlight.

Aretha had stolen my part.

I was shaken awake from my nightmare by the shrill, unwelcome sound of my phone ringing. My pyjamas were drenched in sweat and I'd become entangled in the sheets at some point during the night. I must have been thrashing about. This often happened the night after a panic attack, as though my brain and body were continuing to work through the residual anxiety left over from the events of the day as I slept. I reached across and pressed the 'answer' button, before I'd had time to register who was calling.

'Hey babe,' a subdued Aretha half-whispered in a soft, high tone as soon as the line connected. 'Just calling because I'm worried about you. Wanna Skype?'

'Uhm . . . Sure?' My groggy mind was still connecting dots, grasping to recall the events of yesterday, why I felt like I'd been run over by a truck and why the sound of Aretha's voice had caused me to shudder. 'I've just woken up, though. Can you give me ten?'

'Oh, OK.' Aretha sounded surprised.

I glanced at my little bedside alarm clock, a gaudy plastic monstrosity in the shape of the teapot from *Beauty and the Beast* given to me by my nain when I was a child and which I couldn't bear to part with. It was just after 1 p.m. I'd slept hard.

'Sorry, I'm just a bit drained,' I stuttered, as I attempted to unscramble my limbs from the damp sheets.

'No, no. It's fine. Speak to you in a bit. Just text when you're ready.' She hung up.

I dragged myself into the bathroom, splashing my face with cold water in an attempt to shake myself out of my stupor. I studied my reflection as I brushed my teeth. I looked tired. My face was puffy, there were dark, purpleish circles under my eyes and three spots had erupted on my chin during the night. As I squeezed them (I could never resist) I thought about what I was going to say to Aretha.

Yet, the more I went over the events of yesterday, the more I began to doubt myself. I wondered if I'd overreacted. I couldn't remember us making concrete plans to hang out after the shoot. Perhaps I had assumed. And at almost eighteen years old – a legal adult – was it acceptable that I couldn't navigate my way around London? Probably not, I concluded. In fact, I should have felt embarrassed for being so pathetic.

Aretha popped up on my laptop screen a few minutes later, complaining of being 'sooo hungover', although she didn't look anywhere near as frightful as me.

'How was the party?' I asked, because I was trying to avoid the awkwardness that would inevitably descend when we tackled what had happened the previous afternoon.

'It was amazing,' Aretha replied, pausing to swig water from a sports flask. 'It was at my friend from back home's house. She's working with a producer who also does Skepta's stuff and loads of other massive names. So there were, like, loads of important music people there. It was a really good opportunity for me to network. And there were people doing these really amazing impromptu acoustic performances until about 2 a.m. Argh, but I drank too much. I need all the water.' She waved the flask in front of the screen to demonstrate her point.

There was an excruciating silence before she added, 'how are you, though?'

'I'm OK,' I lied. 'A bit tired. It's been a while since I had a panic attack and I forgot how much they take it out of you.'

'Oh, poor you,' Aretha sympathised. 'Well, make sure you rest up today, babes. And eat all the good things. I can send you some recipe suggestions if you want – foods that help restore wellbeing. To stop you bingeing on sugar.'

'Thank you,' I managed to croak out. Seeing Aretha waving her water around had made me realise I was severely dehydrated, too.

Another awkward beat. I couldn't bear it. I had to know.

'So . . . I kind of got the impression you were annoyed with me yesterday?' I asked, my words tumbling out in a squeak as I confronted the elephant in the room.

'OK. We're going there. Cool,' Aretha replied, almost to herself. Then she returned her gaze to the screen. 'The truth is,

I was going to invite you to the party with me. But after the shoot . . . well. I'm sorry to say this, but I feel like I can be honest with you... I just couldn't be around you any more.'

I stared, astonished, at Aretha's image on the screen as my brain whirled. Images and snatches of conversation began to loop around my mind like clothes in a washing machine as I tried to work out what I had done wrong.

'It just seems like I'm more invested in our brand than you are, if I'm honest,' Aretha continued. 'I went to all the trouble of sorting the location, the stylist, the photographer for the shoot. All you had to do was show up. And then it just seemed like you were trying to make everything really difficult.'

I finally found some words. 'I'm so sorry. I didn't think about how it must have seemed . . . I . . . I am invested. I should have offered you more help. I didn't realise . . .'

'Hey, it's OK,' Aretha soothed. 'But, you know, I was researching panic attacks this morning and they reckon they happen because of the resistance we put up in the face of flow. Resistance is bad. You have to just go with where life is taking you and embrace it. That's probably why you freaked out on the way home.'

'Maybe it was,' I conceded, trying to fit this theory over my memories of yesterday, like a glass dome over a cake.

'So, anyway, what I think you need is some fun. Something to cheer you up. That's actually why I rang. Two weeks from now I've got a gig. Someone I was talking to at the party last night is doing an open mic in a pub in Hoxton and they've offered me a slot.'

'That's great!' I smiled.

'I know, I'm pleased!' Aretha grinned back. 'I mean, it's only ten minutes and it's quite near the beginning of the night, but the headline band are apparently really awesome and I thought we could stick around, make a night of it?'

'Great!' I replied. I recognised this as an olive branch and I felt myself start to relax a little. I'd screwed up what should have been a fun day at the shoot. Now here was a chance for me to make it better, to show Aretha I could be merry and carefree and that I didn't have a panic attack every five minutes. I needed to use this opportunity to paper over the crack in our friendship that I had caused.

'Count me in!' I said.

Chapter 13

The following Friday in theatre studies, I passed Olivia a note.

You know your really nice red top? Where's it from?

I saw her give a little start of surprise as she read it. I didn't think we'd ever talked about clothes before. She scribbled something and passed it back.

On ASOS I think, but it was ages ago. Why?

I'm going to a thing next weekend and I have ZERO clothes.

I did wonder why you were naked ;-)

Stop being funny and HELP ME.

You want to borrow the red top? You totally can.

Thank you, but I will stretch it with my giant bosoms and you will be annoyed. Just needed inspo.

Inspo? Who are you and what have you done with Loo, pls? :-)

'Olivia Turner!' our teacher, Ms Jameson bellowed, startling us both. 'What did I just say?'

'Errrr . . . listening?' Olivia replied, hesitantly.

'Before that?'

' . . . you're not?'

'That's right. So if you wouldn't mind putting that note away, turning your attention back to the board and behaving like the responsible young adult I know you to be, we can continue the lesson.'

Sorry, I gestured to Olivia under my desk as soon as Ms Jameson's back was turned, using the sign language we'd developed after years of sitting at adjacent desks.

No worries, Olivia signed back. Then, checking Ms Jameson's back was still turned, she mouthed, *Meet me in the common room at lunch.*

I knew if I said Olivia and I were hanging out, Aretha would want to join us. I also remembered what Aretha had said about Olivia being odd. So I told Aretha a small lie and said I had an essay deadline.

We used Olivia's phone to look at the website for the bar where the gig was happening, noting what people were wearing in the photos. We agreed I had absolutely nothing suitable. If I wasn't in my bootcut trousers and an oversized shirt for sixth form, it was jogging bottoms and a baggy jumper. It was clear something needed to be done.

I'd already checked my bank balance. While the photoshoot had dented my finances a little, they were still healthy. I could certainly afford to siphon off a little to make myself Hoxton-ready, but being a novice in this area meant I didn't know where to start.

Olivia filled her cheeks with air before blowing it out again. 'You know . . . I don't think I'm the best person to help you with this,' she conceded, reluctantly. 'I mean, I could tell you what I'd wear but that would be all wrong, probably. I've never been anywhere like this. It's hipster central. I don't want to be responsible for you looking like a tit.'

Her brows were knitted together in concern. I could tell she really wanted me to look good and was upset she couldn't assist. We sat in companionable silence for a while, the tops of our heads touching together as we stared at Olivia's phone and she scrolled slowly through the photo gallery.

'I know!' Olivia suddenly squealed, as she was struck by inspiration. 'Why don't you ask your mum?'

As soon as she said it, I knew Olivia was right. It could have been a reflection of my limited social circle, or it could be that she was objectively fabulous. Either way, other than Aretha, my mum was the coolest person I knew.

As was often the case, Mum was working on Saturday, so I didn't get a chance to ask her until Sunday morning. I found her in the kitchen, indulging in her usual routine – the radio was blaring some sort of obscure jazz which sounded as though all the notes were in the wrong order, the French windows leading out to the garden were flung open and Mum was sitting at the kitchen table, which was strewn with pages of the *Observer*, a half-empty mug of coffee and a plate covered in crumbs. She was wearing one of her trademark kaftans, but in a soft fabric which was probably cashmere. Even pottering around the house, Mum always looked fabulous. She was definitely the person to ask about this. I don't know why it hadn't occurred to me before.

She turned in a languid motion as she heard me approach. Her hair was backlit by the sun, making her look even more like some sort of alien-angel hybrid than usual.

'Morning, carriad. I bought some croissants, I did. There's still some left, if you fancy?'

'Thanks, Mum. Maybe a bit later.'

'Now, I know you think I haven't noticed all this weight you're losing but I have and if you're doing it for the right reasons and healthily, that's OK. But you are eating, aren't you?'

'Yes, Mum, I am eating. I've just cut out a few things temporarily.'

Mum narrowed her eyes and pursed her lips. I recognised this expression as the one she used when she was backing down for now, but was storing away the conversation to refer back to in case the issue ever arose again.

'Actually, I wanted to ask you something,' I began hesitantly. Mum raised her eyebrows and gestured at me to sit opposite her. I did so, picking up her coffee mug and fiddling with it nervously.

'Uhm. I need some advice. Fashion advice, actually. I've been invited to this bar in London next weekend and I don't know what to wear.'

Mum's grin spread wide, making her look like a beautiful Cheshire Cat. 'That,' she said, slowly and deliberately, 'is bloody marvellous.'

Five days later, I stood in Mum's walk-in wardrobe, twisting this way and that to get a better view of myself. I was wearing a jumpsuit, in a blue so dark it was almost black. It was made of a heavy, draped fabric with a slight sheen, two sizes smaller than I'd usually buy.

The trousers were wide and pooled at the bottom by my new, heeled shoe-boots, which made it seem as though I was literally made of legs. The top was sleeveless and the back was cut into a shallow V shape. My hair was up in a messy bun, with a few loose strands escaping here and there, revealing the nape of my neck.

'It's almost there,' Mum assessed, squinting as she appraised me, 'but you need an earring . . .'

I had discovered, during my incredibly brief time giving a crap about fashion, that those for whom it was practically a religion did this a lot – making plural things singular. Trousers, for example, were 'a trouser'. Shoes were 'a shoe'.

Mum carefully drew out one of her *Princess Diaries* drawers and selected a couple of pairs from her enormous collection for me to try. I picked the least elaborate, a delicate waterfall of intertwined silver and gold, which just brushed the tops of my shoulders. Mum was right, they 'set off' the rest of the outfit perfectly.

I didn't look as sexy or 'Insta-ready' as I had for the photoshoot but, I realised, that look hadn't really been me. I had felt like a child playing with her mum's dressing up box. There was irony to be found in the fact that I was now doing exactly that, yet I felt so much more comfortable. I looked sophisticated and interesting in a subtle way, but I hadn't deviated too far from the Llewella who chucked on whatever smelled the least for sixth form every day.

I picked up the boxy silver clutch bag I'd splurged on and

turned to face Mum, who was doing that thing the popular girls at school did when they got really excited – applauding rapidly but only using the very tops of her palms, so she wasn't actually making any noise. She walked towards me and placed her hands gently on my shoulders, my beheeled feet meaning she had to crane her neck to look me in the eye. She was about to have one of her wisdom-imparting moments, I could feel it.

'Now, listen, my lovely . . .'

I knew it.

'You're looking gorgeous at the moment and I think we've done a marvellous job with this outfit. But every time someone tells you you're beautiful tonight, I want you to remember that you always were.'

I rolled my eyes.

'Don't roll your eyes at me!' she admonished, pausing to regain the constant eye contact she kept when she was doing her wisdom thing. 'All this – the losing weight, the accessories, fashion, make-up – it's just icing on a cake. You're the sponge. And you've always been a beautiful sponge, you have. Don't forget that.'

I wanted to believe her, but something in my brain wouldn't let me accept it. Just as I was wondering why, Mum abruptly changed tone, snatched my clutch bag out of my hand, smacked me firmly on the bum with it and commanded, 'Now, go and have fun!'

Chapter 14

The bar was every bit as intimidating as I'd anticipated. Aretha had to be there early to sound check, so I had navigated my way using a combination of copious online research, pages of notes detailing bus routes and Tube lines and a hastily scrawled map of the walk from Old Street station.

The venue itself had that 'shabby chic' thing going on. The walls were papered with gig flyers, some yellowed with age, advertising everything from obscure bands I'd never heard of, to huge names like David Bowie and the Rolling Stones. Massive chandeliers of wrought iron hung from the ceiling, interspersed with the odd bare bulb on a freestanding light fitting. The furniture was mismatched – there were spiky-looking stools which reminded me slightly of the bum-numbing one I'd sat on to have my make-up done at the photoshoot, but there were also well-worn armchairs, the burgundy leather cracked after multiple backsides had collapsed into them, exhausted from partying. In their midst was the odd random decorative object. A wall-mounted stag's skull. A slightly ominous looking china doll with a pig's snout where her nose should have been. One solitary shelf of ornate, leather-bound, dusty books. It should have been incongruous, but somehow it all worked.

I found Aretha perched at the bar, her legs swinging from a high stool, chatting earnestly to a bald man with pointy teeth who looked a bit like a bird of prey. She was wearing leather hot pants, a faded T-shirt with her namesake on it, a velvet choker and chunky heels. I hovered awkwardly for a while, acutely aware I was interrupting what looked like a flirtation, until the bald guy finally noticed me, giving me a 'what do you want?' stare.

'Oh, hiiiiii!' Aretha leapt up and flung her arms around me. She seemed slightly manic, I noticed, although I put that down to pre-gig nerves.

'This is my best friend, Loo.' Aretha put one arm around my waist. 'And this is Stu. He's a producer. I was just telling him about my music.'

'I can't wait to see Aretha perform,' Stu said, with a lecherous wink. He looked me up and down in a way that made me feel like my carefully selected outfit had fallen away from my body and I was standing in front of him naked. I swallowed my discomfort. 'What are you drinking, Loo?'

What *was* I drinking? I'd spent so long preparing for this night and yet this, rather crucial, question was the one thing I hadn't considered.

Panicking, I said, 'Whatever Aretha is having.'

A few minutes later, I was clutching a huge, bulbous glass of something that looked like Lucozade, tasted like a cross between orangeade and the Tixilix cough medicine my Mum used to give me a as a child and, I had been informed, was called a 'spritz'. I didn't much care for the taste, but since Aretha and Stu were locked into an intense conversation I sipped it anyway for wont of anything else to do.

I surveyed the room. The women were all dressed the same,

in artfully ripped vintage band T-shirts worn with miniskirts, hot pants or sprayed-on jeans. There were lots of piercings and tattoos on show, as well as a vibrant array of rainbow-coloured hair. I was suddenly aware of the jumpsuit and how overdressed I was. It had seemed sophisticated back at home, but now it felt all wrong. I slipped Mum's glamorous earrings out of my ears and put them in my clutch bag.

When I looked up, a fourth person had joined our little crowd. She looked like she was of East Asian heritage and was about Aretha's height, but was rendered much taller by trainers with platforms so gigantic she might as well have been wearing stilts. She had on a barely-there skirt, with a corset top revealing two full sleeves of tattoos, as well as the head of a serpent at the base of her neck. Her hair was poker-straight, navy blue with a few violet streaks, and cut into a blunt bob. She wore rings of kohl pencil around her eyes in that way that is supposed to look slept in but, as I had discovered during my recent experiments with online make-up tutorials, actually takes ages to apply.

She had a high, saccharine voice and she didn't open her mouth very much when she used it, so it was quite difficult to work out exactly what she was saying.

'Aretha? Oh my actual god! How, like, mental that I'd see you here!' She practically jumped on Aretha, wrapping her in an enthusiastic hug.

'Babe! I know!' Aretha replied. 'I'm singing here tonight.'

'Shut up. Shut the actual fuck up. That's shamazing!' Despite an accent which had a distinct air of Kate Middleton, she spoke like she was in an American teen drama. Something about her made me wary, but I told myself to stop being judgmental and plastered on a smile.

Introductions were made and I learned her name was Medusa (which explained the back tattoo) but everyone called her Maddy. She and Aretha had been to music college together, although Maddy was a few years older. While they caught up on all the gossip involving their mutual acquaintances, Stu made half-hearted attempts to ask me questions.

After about twenty minutes of excruciating small-talk mainly involving Stu asking me if I was absolutely sure Aretha was single, Maddy put a hand on my arm and said, 'Charlie?'

I hadn't thought my name was that difficult to remember, especially as I'd shortened it for other people's ease. 'No, I'm . . . L—'

But before I could finish my sentence, she waved her hands in front of my face and said, 'oh, that's cool, that's totally cool,' before looking at me as though for the first time and murmuring, 'no, of course not.'

I was baffled.

'We're just going to the loo,' Aretha said, linking her arms through Maddy's and leaving me with Stu, staring into my fancy Lucozade.

'Oh my god, she's so amazing! Isn't she amazing? She's just so . . . so . . . amazing!' Maddy breathed, as she gazed up at Aretha with enraptured awe.

Aretha was on a small, makeshift stage performing to a backing track she'd been working on. The song was best described as an odd but not altogether unpleasant mixture of indie and nu-soul and Aretha's obvious enthusiasm for it was infectious – she was writhing around in her leather hot pants like Beyoncé at the Superbowl.

Maddy and Aretha had arrived back from the toilets vibrating with even more manic energy than when they went in. They talked at a million miles an hour, frequently interrupting each other or agreeing emphatically before the other one had reached the end of their sentence. This, along with the thumping base of the increasingly loud dance music the DJ was playing made it hard for me to follow the conversation.

Stu the Birdman had departed, perhaps sensing there might be a more compliant target for his affections elsewhere. He'd been replaced by a group of blokes whose names I couldn't remember, but who had been furnishing Aretha, Maddy and I with a steady stream of cocktails. At first, I wondered how accepting free drinks from strange men fit with my feminist credentials, but Aretha kept passing them to me and towards the end of my third delicious, sugary concoction it didn't seem to matter so much.

Just before Aretha went on stage, Maddy had told me they were having something called angel dust and that I should join them. I agreed, having long ago lost track of what was on the cocktail menu.

Almost as soon as I took my first sip of the angel dust cocktail, I was filled with an extraordinary sense of peace. My ever-present anxiety magically evaporated. I felt my chest and throat loosen. Contentment and joy trickled through every cell of my body, like warm honey. Maybe this was what other people felt when they drank. That being the case, I could definitely see the appeal.

Instead of finding Maddy's ceaseless twittering annoying, it was like someone had turned a dial in my head and I'd been tuned in to her frequency. She was right, Aretha *was* amazing. This place was amazing, too. And so was Maddy. And so were the random men bankrolling our bar tab. Everything here was love and nothing else mattered.

I felt safe too, like the bar was a cocoon, protecting me from the outside world. All around me was a spectrum of technicolour amazingness, set to the sound of Aretha's beautiful voice.

As I watched Aretha sing, I felt a swell of pride. That was my best friend up there, commanding our attention, doing what she loved. I felt myself swaying to the music and smiling so hard my cheeks ached.

All too soon, Aretha's performance was over and she leapt from the ramshackle stage and landed – superhero-like – on her chunky heels. She immediately snatched her half-drunk cocktail out of Maddy's outstretched hand. Then she grabbed me around my waist and put her head on my shoulder. I gave myself an internal high-five because it was me she chose to hug first.

'How was I?' she asked.

'SO good,' I replied, hugging her back with a ferocity that caused her to squeak slightly, then laugh.

'Aaaah,' Maddy cooed, as she watched us. 'How do you two know each other, by the way?'

I was about to reply 'from sixth form', when Aretha jumped in.

'Oh! I can't believe I didn't tell you this already! We have started an online brand together!'

'OMG, that's amazing!' Maddy grasped Aretha's hand. 'Do tell!'

So she did, and while I couldn't reconcile a lot of what she was saying with our little project – apparently we were 'hacks for young feminists, who don't see themselves represented anywhere else online' – I found myself nodding along every time Maddy glanced at me for confirmation.

'I'd love to be involved, somehow,' Maddy said, when Aretha had concluded her spiel.

'That would be increds!' Aretha replied, nodding frantically.

Somewhere in the recesses of my logical mind, the bit that had faded a little more into the background each time I raised my cocktail glass to my lips, a little bell rang. Aretha didn't wait for me to approve the idea of Maddy being involved. She also hadn't mentioned that the blog had started out as my project. She had boasted about our engagement and hit rate without acknowledging the years of work I'd put in to get us to that stage. But I quickly pushed the thought away. None of that mattered, I decided. All the mattered was what was happening right then – a moment in which I felt, for the first time in years, happy, well and like I belonged.

'And now we dance,' declared Maddy, sashaying towards the stage and beckoning for us to follow. We found a spot right between the speakers. The next act appeared, an indie-rock three-piece who barely fitted on the tiny platform.

At first, I was self-conscious that we were the only people dancing. I looked at Aretha, who had her hands flung above her head and her eyes closed. She looked so relaxed and joyful. I decided to copy whatever she was doing until I felt as carefree as she appeared to be. My 'fake it 'til you make it' technique worked. I could feel the bass pulsing through the soles of my feet. Even though I had never heard the song before I was singing along, using lyrics I made up on the spot. The three of us laughed and danced until every last drop of our cocktails had been slurped and our faces were shiny with perspiration. Then, it was time for a loo break.

These toilets would have been absolutely slated on Loo Reviews, I thought, as we squished ourselves into the dim, damp, reeking space. I felt a fleeting moment of sadness as it occurred to me the only Loo Reviews I'd be doing from now on would take place in my own head. Maddy and Aretha went into the cubicle together and I could hear much rustling and giggling. Through my cocktail fug, I dimly registered that this was weird. I tried to stow the memory away somewhere safe in my brain, knowing I'd want to revisit it later.

I ran my wrists under the cold tap and tried to repair any sweat-damage to my make-up and hair. Everything was blurry and unfocused, like someone had put a filter on reality, and there was ringing in my ears. Yet, I still felt serene. I smiled at the cracked mirror and an understanding seemed to pass between myself and my reflection.

When they emerged, Aretha once again put her arm around my waist.

'Thank you so much for being here tonight, babe,' she said.

'Of course! My pleasure. I'm having a great time.' I grinned.

'It means a lot that you get to see what I do,' Aretha continued. 'You know, I've spent a lot of time watching you being brilliant – getting straight As in English, or in rehearsals for that play – and it makes me feel like . . . what am I bringing to the table?'

The Aretha I'd seen the day she cried after dinner at her house was back. Although I'd seen her this way before, it still took me by surprise. The rest of the time she was so sure of herself, to the extent I'd had to defend her when comments were made about her being 'up herself' by other sixth formers. I opened my mouth to reassure her, but she was off again.

'You're so pretty and clever and talented, babes.' She was watching me in the mirror above her basin and I noticed that her pupils were enormous. I felt like I could dive into her eyes. 'Why would you even want to be friends with me? I'm only at your school because they offered a subsidy on fees for "BAME"' – she made air quotes with her fingers as she said this – 'students.'

This was news to me. I turned and looked at Aretha, whose presence in my life had changed it so quickly and completely, and I felt an overwhelming surge of love. I put my arm around her shoulder.

'I'm friends with you because you are brilliant,' I declared. 'And it doesn't matter to me how you got in to St Edith's, I'm just so glad you did.'

'I love you,' said Aretha.

She was so vulnerable and beautiful in the subdued light of the bathroom. I thought about Antonio the Merchant and how he'd willingly risked death for his BFF Bassanio. I thought about Dawn's question, 'how many people do you know who would actually die for their friend?' and I felt a new certainty blooming somewhere in my belly. It was telling me the bond I had with Aretha was the type you'd sacrifice everything for.

'I love you too,' I replied. And I meant it.

It felt like we floated back to the dance floor. There were more people on it by that stage, and a guy, who might have been one of the ones who bought us cocktails earlier – everything was too fuzzy to tell – grabbed my hand and pulled me too him. I giggled. It was an unfamiliar sound – I'd never heard myself laugh that way, before.

He leaned into me and I felt hot breath as his lips brush my ear. 'You're stunning,' he said. 'Are you single?' Giddily, I nodded. He grinned. He had dimples in his cheeks and green eyes. He dipped his head towards me again. I lost all ability to think about anything other than if he was going to kiss me. My first kiss.

But before I could find out, I felt a sharp tap on my shoulder. I turned round. Aretha looked furious. I saw her mouth *what the fuck?* I couldn't work out what was going on. A few minutes ago we'd said we loved each other and meant it. Or I had, at least. I just stood there, confused.

After a few seconds of us being locked in this stand-off, Aretha marched out into the smoking area, a small patio surrounded by trees strung with fairy lights. I followed her.

'What's wr—' I began.

'You knew I liked him!' Aretha shouted.

'I didn't! I promise I didn't!'

'Oh, whatever,' she retorted. 'You know, at some point you're going to have to grow the fuck up.'

I couldn't work out how to make it stop. I needed to make her see this had all been a genuine mistake, but my mind was completely blank.

Aretha took a step towards me, looked me in the eye. Then she laughed.

'Oh my god. Babes. You actually had no idea, did you?'

I shook my head. She put her arms around my waist.

'Sometimes I forget you don't know how to interact with men. I forgive you. It's not your fault your dad didn't care enough to stick around.'

It was like I'd suddenly been plunged under water. I could hear my heart beat in my ears as I struggled to take a breath. Aretha, oblivious, took my hand and led me back inside the club.

I faked a smile and tried to dance, but my body felt weak and empty. I told myself again and again that Aretha couldn't have known how much her words would hurt me. But somewhere else, somewhere really deep down in the pit of my stomach, I knew that the bag of poison had burst.

Christmas

'How all the other passions fleet to air,
As doubtful thoughts and rash-embraced despair,
And shuddering fear, and green-eyed jealousy!'

The Merchant of Venice
Act 3, Scene 2

Chapter 15

'Why did you drop out of the play, Llewella?'

I closed my eyes as multiple internal voices competed to answer what should have been a simple question.

'Because I am weak.'

'Because I was confused.'

'Because . . . I don't know.'

And then, a voice louder and more resonant than the rest.

'Because Aretha made me.'

Finally, I settled for trotting out the line I'd rehearsed so many times before, when my Mum, Olivia and even Hugh had asked me the same thing.

'The first couple of months of a blog are really crucial to its success. The Aretha and Loo brand needed more of my attention to ensure it got off the ground. I was spreading myself too thin and something had to give,' I replied, robotically.

Linda pursed her lips slightly, nodded and wrote something down in her notepad.

Linda was my therapist. She had a kind, round face, masses of messy dark hair streaked with grey and she wore at least two rings on each finger, in variations of silver and turquoise. Her office was always warm and full of bean bags, scatter cushions and fragrant candles which made the air smell like a sweet shop. I felt safe there.

Despite this, I was annoyed with myself letting things

get to a stage where I needed to be back here. Linda and I had done so much work together after what happened in Year 10. We'd plotted the arc of my panic attacks so I could identify and halt them in their embryonic stages and I'd learned techniques to control my breathing and separate my paranoid anxious thoughts from my 'rational self'. I really thought I was cured.

I couldn't pinpoint exactly when anxiety once again became a permanent fixture in my life. It had hooked its long, spindly fingers around my insides slowly and gently at first, squeezing a little more with each passing day until, quite suddenly, I couldn't breathe.

It was Mum who had found me in the upstairs bathroom before the last day of term, slumped over the toilet seat covered in sweat and taking raggedy, painful breaths. I'd only gone in there to brush my teeth. With nothing to focus on but the tickling sensation of my electric toothbrush as I moved it slowly from tooth to tooth, my thoughts began to spiral. The next thing I knew, I couldn't stand up.

'What's caused this?' Mum had wanted to know. People always ask that when you have a panic attack and it's usually the most difficult question to answer. Often, you don't know. And when you do know, it's usually something stupid like 'I started thinking about how many obstacles there are between here and the front door and what would happen if there was a fire and I needed to get out'. That's just your brain inventing a scenario to make sense of the panic. Often, the real reason is much more elusive. That's why I needed therapy – to try and work out what was really going on.

'The last time we spoke,' Linda said in her careful, soothing way, 'you talked about how important drama club is to you. How it's one of the only spaces where you can completely forget about anything troubling you. Knowing what you know now, do you think it was the right decision to give it up?'

NO.

'Well . . . I can't exactly give up my A Levels. And if it's a choice between drama and student council, then being a prefect looks better on my UCAS form,' I replied. 'The only other thing is music. But Aretha and I have been putting videos of us performing together on YouTube and it's good for the brand, so . . . That only left *Merchant*.' My voice cracked a little as I said the name of the play and I swallowed rapidly, fighting the tears I could feel prickling at the backs of my eyes.

'This brand you keep referring to.' Linda's bright blue eyes looked at me intensely over the silver rims of her glasses. 'Is that the same blog you were writing before? The one about toilets? Last time you said that was just a passion project for you. It seems to be taking up a lot of your time now. What's changed?'

EVERYTHING.

'It's kind of the toilet blog, but it's completely different now. Me and my best friend Aretha have turned it into a lifestyle blog and YouTube channel. If it gets enough advertising revenue it will be a massive help to me at university. Plus, if it really takes off it can be a potential career.'

There were a few moments of silence as Linda licked the tips of her fingers and flicked back through the notebook resting on her knee. It was covered in a green velvety fabric and for a while I just let myself be mesmerised by the patterns in its texture. The combination of the warmness of the room, the vanilla scent from the candles and the gentle 'swooshing' sound as Linda turned pages was hypnotic.

'I can't see any mention of this Aretha in my notes from our sessions before,' Linda said, at last. 'Is she a new friend?'

'Yeah . . . She only joined our sixth form in September. Although, we have become close really quickly. I can't imagine life without her now!' I tried to chuckle, but it sounded weird, like a sort of strangled cough.

'Why don't you tell me about her?'

I took a deep breath, unsure where to begin describing the phenomenon that was Aretha Jones.

'She's amazing!' I enthused, after a brief pause. 'She's a brilliant singer and she used to live in London. She's really pretty and wise and talented. I feel lucky to be her friend most of the time. Lots of people have treated her badly in the past because they have been jealous, so she sometimes has problems trusting people . . . So, I try and show her, you know, that it's not like that with us . . .' I trailed off. There was a pause.

'Hmmm,' Linda said, eventually. 'How does she treat you, though?'

'She's been really good about my anxiety,' I replied, the pace of my speech quickening. I was obviously failing to convey to Linda how brilliant Aretha was and I felt frustrated, like I was doing her a disservice. 'It's really got in the way recently, when I've needed to have a day off from the blog because I'm not feeling well. And even though Aretha's put so much into the project and I'm slowing down our progress, she doesn't say anything.'

Linda said nothing, just leaned back in her battered old armchair and gave me a meaningful look. We stayed like that for a moment or two, me trying to resist the urge to fill the silence. Eventually Linda took off her glasses, which were attached to a pretty gemstone chain around her neck and rested them on her rather spectacular bosom.

I knew this signal well by now. We had run out of time. The session was over.

After my meetings with Linda I always went for a long walk. I understood, of course, that therapy sessions had to be finite, but the way they ended always jarred a bit. We'd be wading through some deep well in my psyche and suddenly Linda would put her glasses on her boobs. Walking helped me to shake off the residue of the conversations we'd had and all the feelings they'd stirred up.

I crunched through the light frost that had settled on the leaves scattered along the pavement, imagining my anxious energy dissipating each time I swung my arms and propelled myself into the next step. Fleeting vignettes from the past three months passed through my mind, but I knew by now not to attempt to analyse them. Going to therapy was like shaking a jar of glitter – it jumbled your subconscious into a swirling mess and it always took a while for it to settle down again.

It started to rain. I pulled the hood of my coat up around my ears and tucked my chin into its collar, trying to stave off the worst of the fat, freezing droplets which sailed towards me on the bitter wind. I was so angry with myself.

If you'd have asked me my wishes and ambitions for the new year, being back in therapy would definitely not have been amongst them. I had thought I was being so vigilant, zealously applying all the tips and techniques from my first set of sessions with Linda. I couldn't believe I'd allowed myself to get back to square one.

The only thing I could think of that I'd let slip was my anxiety journal. Linda had encouraged me to rate my anxiety from one to seven every day (she subscribed to the theory that when asked to rate something from one to ten, everyone just picked seven without really thinking about it). Then I had to make a note of what I'd eaten, how much exercise I'd done, how long I'd spent studying, how much sleep I'd had the night before and anything unusual which had occurred. At first, I completed it religiously, but after a while and as I'd fallen into a familiar routine, I got bored of putting the same thing. Over and over I'd written:

ANXIETY LEVEL: 3
Food: Breakfast - toast, lunch - jacket potato with cheese and coleslaw, dinner - leftovers with cheese, snacks - Pringles, Maltesers and an apple
Exercise: Walked quite a lot
Study: Four hours after school
Sleep: Six-ish hours (tried for eight but ended up reading)
Unusual circumstances: Nothing exciting happened

I tried to map out in my mind how my anxiety journal might look today:

ANXIETY LEVEL: 6
Food: Nothing until after therapy, then 'overnight oats'.
(Aretha's recipe - not that appetising.)
Exercise: Walked to and from Linda's office, two miles away

Study: None yet
Sleep: Four-ish hours (couldn't get to sleep for ages so ended up taking laptop to bed and working on the blog)
Unusual circumstances: Aretha is away - feel very lonely

Aretha had gone to London to stay with Delroy's sister Gladys for the Christmas holidays. For the first couple of days I'd received regular text updates – usually pictures of Aretha next to festive decorations, head thrown back in laughter. Lately, though, my texts asking how she was doing or what she was up to had gone unanswered.

I pulled my iPhone out of the pocket of my coat. The screen taunted me with its blankness.

Aretha had convinced me to get one of the latest models of smartphone, arguing that being able to upload and edit posts and respond to comments at any time was important if we wanted our blog and channel to reach their potential. I'd drawn money from my rapidly dwindling Loo Reviews fund, telling myself once again that you had to 'speculate to accumulate'.

I had only a few hundred pounds left of my original nest egg. Aretha had wanted us to put it all in a joint account, but the bank told us we couldn't do this until we turned eighteen, which wasn't until March for me and June for her. Aretha therefore had to come to me every time she needed something – a new outfit, or a prop, or a train ticket. I could tell she resented this and, to be honest, it didn't make me feel great, either.

Sometimes I thought we were being too frivolous with our spending, but I never vocalised this worry. Aretha had such a clear idea of what the brand was and where it was headed and her knowledge of the cultural landscape was much greater than mine.

I trusted her when she told me what was needed and how much was a reasonable amount of money to acquire it. In order to 'compete' with the biggest names on YouTube, she said, we had to have new clothes and accessories in virtually every video we made, mountains of make-up, as well as various props and backgrounds.

She, through no fault of her own, was relatively poor and I, through no merit of my own, was not, so it was only fair I stumped up the cash.

Aretha styled us and created themed 'sets' for us in her bedroom. The blog had become more about visual content – photos or videos of Aretha and I with brief captions. I missed writing for fun. Sometimes, I found my mind drifting back to the conversation Aretha and I had right at the beginning of this project, when she assured me the brand would help me become a professional writer. I wondered if she had forgotten about my ambitions. I lacked the confidence to bring it up, though, in case Aretha thought I was questioning her competence.

I was responsible for posting the content after Aretha had edited it, as well as monitoring and responding to the comments, which were diminishing with each passing week. At first, our audience had been confused about the abrupt change of style and content from Loo's Reviews.

Where's the toilet review?

We miss your toilet humour, Loo!

Preferred Loo's old look.

Who's the new girl?

That girl with the afro can fuck off, tbf.

I always tried to get to the negative comments and delete them in the draft folder before Aretha could see them. On the rare occasions one slipped under my radar, she took it in good humour (well, better than I would have done, anyway), sighing and saying, 'so many jealous people.' She assured me we just hadn't clicked into our audience, yet. I had to be patient. We would get there.

I believed her. I had to. I'd spent so much time and money on this project that to give up now, when we could be on the precipice of everything Aretha had promised, seemed foolish. Plus, I couldn't bear the idea that I'd sacrificed my part in *Merchant* for no reason.

Even thinking about it weeks after the performance had taken place, the fact that I'd abandoned the play made my heart ache. Although it was Aretha who suggested I quit, it was only after I'd complained to her about how tired I was trying to juggle everything. At first, she had thought I was trying to imply we should stop doing the brand. She asked if I'd mind if she carried on doing it with someone else, since she'd put so much time into it which she could have spent on her music. I was mortified. I told her how important Aretha and Loo was to me.

'Nothing is more important,' Aretha had replied, solemnly, putting her hand over mine.

I remembered vividly the look of shock and disapproval on the Professor's face when I'd told him I was quitting. He didn't get angry or try to dissuade me. He simply said, 'Well, that is your decision,' took the pencil which had been tucked behind his ear and tapped it against his teeth, then turned on his heel and slowly walked away. Which was, of course, much worse.

That evening I'd had fourteen missed calls from Olivia, along with text messages which read:

what happened?!! xxx

and

R U OK? xxx

and

here if you want to talk xxx

I'd hidden beneath my duvet, hugging Fiona close to me and letting the soft fur on her back absorb my tears.

I really wanted to be mature enough to go and see one of the performances of *Merchant,* which happened just before we broke for Christmas, but in the end I just couldn't bring myself to. I couldn't bear the idea of hearing someone else say the lines I'd rehearsed and memorised, of watching another person act out the character of Antonio, who I'd earmarked as mine.

I'd asked Aretha if I could go to hers the night of the play to take my mind off it, but she said she was going clubbing with Maddy. I thought she might invite me, but she didn't. I still cringe when I remember how I'd tried to wangle an invitation. I'd told Aretha I felt 'kind of down' about the play being that evening. Aretha thought I was trying to blame her and reminded me it had been my decision to quit *Merchant,* that she'd given me the opportunity to get out of the brand. I'd spent the rest of the call apologising.

Dejectedly, I trampled back home, forced down the unctuous gloop that was Aretha's overnight oats and plonked myself at my desk. I had work to do, but I couldn't seem to stop staring into space. It could have been seconds I sat there in a daze, or it might have been hours. I genuinely couldn't tell. I looked at the detritus of my failed study session – text books opened at random pages, scattered around where I sat on my bed, my laptop's screen blank and accusing, having been left untouched.

I reached for my phone. It was just past 4 p.m., which meant I'd achieved precisely nothing in the three hours since I'd been back from my session with Linda. Instead, my brain had the same questions and memories on spin cycle – why wasn't Aretha returning my calls? What had I done? How could I make it better? And then there was that insistent inner voice, repeating like a mantra, *Something is wrong. Something is wrong. Something is wrong.*

I noticed I had two missed calls and a voicemail from a withheld number. Thinking it might be Aretha calling from another line, I dialled in.

'Hello, this is a message for Llewella Williams. My name is Jess and I'm a researcher for *English Breakfast!*. We'd like to chat to you about your blog. Please call me back on 0207 . . .' Hastily, I tapped the number into my phone.

I hesitated before I hit 'dial'. If it was about the blog, shouldn't I wait until Aretha was back so we could call together?

I saved Jess's number and called Aretha. It rang twice before going to voicemail.

I took a deep breath, feeling it catch painfully on the now eternally-present lump in my throat. Anything, I eventually decided – I'd do literally anything to distract me from how I was feeling, right now. So, I called Jess.

'Llewella!' Jess exclaimed before I'd had a chance to speak. 'Thanks so much for calling back! Do you have a minute to chat?'

'Uhm, hi . . . Sure,' I stuttered.

'Great!' Jess spoke with what I can only describe as intense cheerfulness. I wondered if it was just her personality or whether TV people had training to make them sound perpetually wired. 'So, basically, one of the exec producers here has been looking at your blog and he, like, LOVES it. He thinks it'd potentially make a really good regular feature for our show. Do you know *English Breakfast!*?'

'Of course.'

Everyone knew *English Breakfast!*. You couldn't avoid it. Aside from hundreds of thousands of viewers who watched it on their TVs each morning, you couldn't go on social media without seeing a clip of its forthright male host expressing 'controversial' opinions while his glamorous female co-host sat next to him looking uncomfortable (whether due to the voracity of her colleague's views or the fact she was always wearing a skin-tight bandage dress was unclear).

'Wonderful! And would doing a segment for us be something you're open to?'

'Maybe,' I replied, carefully. 'I mean, obviously I'd have to check with Aretha first, since we share the blog.'

'Oh.' Jess sounded confused. 'Sorry, I've looked at the posts the producer sent over and I could only see your name. I didn't realise there were two of you. But anyway, that's something we can look into. Basically, we *love* the toilet thing and the way that you talk about it. It's such an important, issue, you know?'

The realisation hit me like a sucker-punch. They didn't mean Aretha and Loo. They were interested in Loo Reviews.

'Anyway, think about it,' Jess said, sensing my hesitation. 'If you did want to come in we'd do a screen test and take it from there. Obviously we'll pay all your expenses. And if it does go ahead you'll be paid for your time. You have my number, maybe give me a call tomorrow when you've had a chance to think it through?'

'I will. Thanks, Jess.' I sounded robotic, even to my own ears, but I was finding it impossible to pretend to be normal.

I stared out of the window. Fiona was prowling about in the back garden in that proud, defiant way she has, sniffing things intermittently.

This could be a really important opportunity. I mean, obviously it would be another thing to balance with my A Levels and I'd have to get a better understanding of how much of my time it would involve. But it would direct more traffic to my blog and, since Aretha and Loo was connected to it, could potentially be a way of us finally finding the 'audience' Aretha kept talking about. It was also a chance to top up my bank account, during a time when the Aretha and Loo project was haemorrhaging money. I knew it would be difficult to sell this to Aretha, but I also felt determined to try.

Because more than anything, I gradually realised, I wanted

this. The performer in me wanted the chance to shine. The writer in me wanted more eyes on my work.

My brain was back to front – normal things other people did every day with ease, like texting a friend or getting on a London bus, were the proverbial mountains I had to climb when I was feeling anxious. Yet activities most people found terrifying, like performing and public speaking, I relished. The thought of landing the gig eased my anxiety and made my chest swell with excitement. I knew I would never forgive myself if I didn't at least give the audition my best shot.

I tapped out a text to Aretha, writing and re-writing it until I eventually settled on:

Just had a call from some tv people re my blog. Can you give me a call? Xx

As I knew she would, she called me back immediately.

As soon as Aretha's smiling face popped up on the screen, I felt a profound sense of relief. I had convinced myself I must have accidentally done something terrible and her lack of contact was punishment. Yet, she didn't appear pissed off at all. I recognized her auntie's sitting room from the pictures she'd sent and I could see two of her cousins playing a video game in the background.

'Hey!' Aretha said. 'Got your text. What's up?'

So, no small talk, then. No asking how my Christmas had been or how I was feeling. Straight to business. Maybe I *was* being punished, after all.

I tried to relax. It was important I phrased this right. 'Hey. So, this woman just called me from *English Breakfast!* and she said they've been reading Loo Reviews. They apparently, uhm, like it. A lot.' I squinted apologetically, hyper-aware of the treacherous conversational tightrope I was currently walking. 'They want me to go in and do an audition and maybe turn it into a regular slot on the show . . . and I really want to do it. I think it could be good for us. For the brand.'

'How so?' Aretha asked, coldly. Her smile was still plastered in place, but it no longer reached her eyes.

I explained my theory of how increased traffic to the blog could connect us with an audience for Aretha and Loo, as well as my thoughts on our financial situation. I held my breath through the pause that followed.

'I don't want to tell you not to go for an opportunity,' Aretha replied, almost as though she were talking to herself. 'No . . . I definitely don't want to say that to you. It's your decision.'

I knew then that my sales pitch hadn't landed. She didn't want me to do it. I was of course wary of upsetting Aretha and conscious of the tension it might cause in our friendship, but the sense of wanting, or rather needing to do the audition was stronger.

'OK, well, I'll just go along and see. It probably won't come to anything. But I'll let you know.' I was trying to be as diplomatic as possible, trying not to show how excited I felt, or to blurt out all the thrilling thoughts I was having about what the audition might entail and what I would wear for it. 'How is everything with you, anyway?' I asked, attempting to deflect the awkwardness radiating from my phone.

'Yeah, it's cool. Listen, babes, I have to go. I just rang to check in. Speak soon, yeah?'

And with a click, she was gone.

Spring Term

'The devil can cite Scripture for his purpose.'

The Merchant of Venice
Act 1, Scene 3

Chapter 16

By the time the start of term rolled around, Aretha had clearly had a chance to get used to the idea and was being much more positive about my audition.

'Thing is, babe,' she said, over lunch, 'you can tell them how to describe you on that text thing at the bottom of the screen. So you can be, like, "Llewella, co-founder of Aretha and Loo". And then everyone who watches will see that, every time you're on.'

'Good idea,' I replied, glad she was on board.

'I was even thinking we could print a T-shirt with the two of us on it for you to wear. It's all about brand recognition. I was watching this video by this branding expert who said the average person needs to see you seven times before they even remember your face. More, if you want them to remember your name as well. So, the more we can get images of the two of us out there, the better.' She barely paused for breath before adding, 'And if it all goes well, or even if they really love you at the audition, maybe you could talk to them about doing it with the two of us. I mean, I didn't love the toilet thing, but if toilets are what they want, I can do that.'

My chest tightened. Toilet reviews were my thing. My original idea. I didn't want to share. Was I being childish? I couldn't tell. With my anxiety disorder resurfacing, it was becoming harder to separate my gut instinct from the irrational, paranoid stuff which was part and parcel of mental illness. Was it anxiety's voice telling me Aretha was trying to muscle in on an opportunity I'd earned, or was it me? I honestly didn't know.

I recalibrated the fantasies I'd had about *English Breakfast!* coming to fruition, putting Aretha into the picture instead, and came to the conclusion that it wouldn't be so bad. In fact, having her there to bounce off and share the experience with would be really fun. As Aretha herself had said, what could be better than being paid to hang out with your bestie? And it would increase the chances of Aretha and Loo taking off if we were seen as a double act. I decided to go with what Aretha was saying and write off my concerns as anxious nonsense.

Before I could do that, though, I needed Aretha to acknowledge that this opportunity had come up, for both of us, because of the groundwork I'd laid down. It didn't bother me whether the outside world thought Aretha had been part of Loo Reviews the whole time. This was about the shared understanding we had, between the two of us. I couldn't have explained why that seemed so important. Yet, there was no dismissing the certainty I had about it.

Clumsily, I tried to articulate what I was feeling. 'I agree it's a good idea to try and do this together,' I began, 'and I'll definitely talk to them about that at the audition. But, you know, just to say at this point . . . not that it matters loads, but just to, you know, acknowledge . . . I was doing Loo Reviews for two years before I even met you.' I rushed to finish the sentence and held my breath as I awaited Aretha's reaction.

Nothing could have prepared me for what she said next.

'The thing is, babes, that really isn't my fault'

***

The morning of the audition, I turned this way and that, examining various angles in the mirrors scattered about my mum's walk-in with a critical eye. I got a distinct sense of déjà-vu. I was wearing the dark blue jumpsuit again, but this time I'd paired it with trainers with a slight platform and some gold hoop earrings. I'd lost more weight since I bought it, partly through sticking to Aretha's regime and partly because the constant anxious knot in my stomach didn't leave much room for food. The fabric sagged loosely around my chest, stomach and hips, mourning the ghosts of my dissipated flesh. I could see my collar bone protruding above the boat neck. For the first time in my life, I was beginning to look small. The logical, feminist part of me knew it was wrong, but I couldn't deny that I liked it.

I'd spent most of the previous week watching tutorials on YouTube, working out how to achieve that elusive 'no make-up' look (which ironically involved using more products and more complex techniques than the more traditional 'just make-up' look). My hair was freshly washed and loose, apart from a few strands at the front which I'd pinned on top of my head. Did I look like a young woman who was about to land herself a job in TV? I had absolutely no relevant knowledge I could use to answer this.

My phone chimed, alerting me that the car *English Breakfast!* had sent to bring me to the studio was waiting outside. It was ten minutes early but that was OK – so was I. Pausing on the stairs to give Fiona a quick rub behind each ear for luck, I stepped out of the front door and potentially into a new future.

I knocked next door. There were still a few months to go before I turned eighteen, so I needed a chaperone for the audition. Mum was working as usual, so our neighbour Wendy had agreed to step in. Wendy used to babysit Hugh and me before we got old enough to look after ourselves. We used to love going to hers because she always had those really thick yogurts which were like eating a pot of cream.

She came to the door in a yellow-and-white striped jumper and jeans. It made a change from her usual uniform of a burgundy quilted dressing gown (which she called her 'house coat') and slippers. She had a slender build, a neat little silver-grey bob and was always grinning in a way that suggested she was on the verge of mischief. She reminded me of an elf.

'Ready?' Wendy asked, clapping her hands together while hopping from foot-to-foot in an excited little jig.

'It'll probably come to nothing. You know ...'

'It will with that attitude!' Wendy admonished. 'I've known you since you were this high' – she pointed at the air around her waist – 'and if anyone should be on telly, it's you. Now let's go and . . . SMASH IT!' She punched the air as we made our way towards the car.

I was nervous, but in a good way. It's difficult to explain, but there's a massive difference between the kind of thrilling anticipation I get before a performance or big event and the crushing, painful panic attacks I experience for no apparent reason. It's the difference between butterflies in your tummy and the biliousness you feel before you're about to vomit. Or the difference between the pleasant exhilaration of a rollercoaster and the genuine terror of a car crash.

But I couldn't think about car crashes, just then. Instead, I reread the email Jess had sent me for the hundredth time. This was just a screen test, it explained, to see what I was like on camera. There was nothing for me to specifically prepare, but they would ask me some questions about Loo Reviews – what inspired me to start it and what were the best and worst toilets I'd ever reviewed, that sort of thing – and record my responses. I wouldn't get any immediate feedback, but they'd watch the tape at their next production meeting and if the execs liked me, they'd be in touch to discuss next steps.

I tried to think of the presenters I liked and what made them compelling or special. I didn't watch TV often, but when I did it was usually a political show of some description which Mum would have on in the kitchen during breakfast.

I liked the people who gave intelligent, thoughtful answers and challenged the status-quo the best. Afua Hirsch was a favourite of mine, as well as Akala and Deborah Francis-White. I always cheered when any of them appeared on screen. But could I replicate their cleverness, bravery and spirit? And more importantly, could I do it while discussing toilets on *English Breakfast!*?

As though she knew what I was thinking, a text from Mum popped up at that precise moment.

Just b urself, carriad. Love u. Call me after

It was exactly what I needed to hear. I smiled, as my phone pinged again with another text, this time from Aretha.

Good luck Remember to ask about us doing it together. Txt me str8 after to let me no wot they say.

The car pulled up to what looked like a warehouse. The bleak grey exterior clashed with the cheerful *English Breakfast!* logos emblazoned across it – white text on a brash orange background with a fried egg instead of a dot above the 'i'. A security guard asked for my name, checking his clipboard before opening the car door for me.

'Welcome, Ms Williams,' he said. 'If you go through to reception I'll let them know you've arrived.'

The combined effect of being chauffeured here, having doors opened for me and being addressed in such a manner made me feel like the Queen. Or at least *a* queen. I committed the feeling to memory, knowing that if I screwed up the screen test today I might never experience it again.

The next hour was a blur of corridors and clipboards. Wendy and I were introduced to what seemed like a gazillion producers, runners and assistants, all of whom looked like a slight variation on the same person – thin, white women with bouncy ponytails, on-trend yet understated attire and wide, permanent smiles. In the dressing room, a make-up artist removed my carefully applied efforts and restarted from scratch using a thick foundation too light for my skin. I almost spoke up but then looked at her kit and noticed that, amidst the oceans of brushes and palettes, there was only one generic mid-brown foundation for Black people, one which could only be described as 'orange' and then about five shades of light beige. If it was a choice between looking like a vampire or Donald Trump, I supposed the former was preferable.

The make-up artist applied layer after layer of eyeshadow until the skin around my eyes started to sting. She told me she was 'emphasising my crease'. I thought this was a particularly horrible way of saying 'I'm making your eyes look bigger'. She added a tonne of blusher and fake lashes, so that by the end

I looked like a budget Kardashian, as well as about ten years older. As I looked uncertainly at my reflection, I was assured by the make-up artist that the camera 'washes you out', which was why she'd trowled it on so thick.

I snapped a photo of myself grimacing and sent it to Aretha. She replied with a photo of herself wearing a terrible synthetic long brown wig and witch-like make-up, at what looked like a Halloween party.

Reminds me of this ☺!

After make-up, we were taken to a small room with squishy sofas lined against two of the walls and a coffee table with a platter of exotic fruit, a bowl of Quality Street and a pile of newspapers. The runner who'd led me through the maze of corridors and past closed doors with names I vaguely recognised on stars on the front, instructed me to help myself and told me Jess would be with me in a minute. Wendy, perhaps sensing that I was trying to focus on what was ahead and wasn't in the mood to make conversation, just smiled and gave my hand a little squeeze.

I picked up and put down the same green triangle from the bowl of chocolates about five times, debating whether quickly soothing my grumbling tummy with a sugar hit or not smudging my lipstick should be my priority. This had become a ritual for me, recently. Foods which were theoretically 'banned' called to me like sirens. I'd have lengthy internal debates with myself, reasoning that just one bar of chocolate, or slice of cake, or bagel, couldn't possibly undo the months of hard work I'd put in while the other half of me retorted that I hadn't come this far only to fall back into bad habits.

Once, I spent twenty minutes staring at a bag of tortillas, rendered statue-like in my furious contemplation. I only snapped out of it when Hugh came into the kitchen and asked me whether I was trying to stare out the Doritos.

I'd just decided to go for it, lipstick be damned, when the room was filled with noise and movement. The atmosphere shifted, as though the air itself was trying to announce that a famous person had entered.

'Good show, Cyrus,' said a petite woman wearing a head-mic, as she removed a small clip from the tie of the barrel-chested man before her.

'As usual,' boomed a familiar voice with an Antipodean twang. 'People can say what they want about me but I always deliver a fucking good show.'

The assembled staff tittered sycophantically.

I tried not to stare at Cyrus Peyton, but it was difficult. When you're so used to gawping at a person in disbelief as they spout 'look at me!' opinions with only a thin screen and the internet between you it's hard to curb that impulse once the screen is removed.

In real life, Cyrus, *English Breakfast!*'s co-host and self-appointed 'voice of common sense' was much shorter than he looked on TV. He couldn't have been more than five foot eight and yet he still cut an imposing figure, with broad shoulders and dyed jet-black hair styled up into an unnatural looking peak. A huge beer belly hung over the belt of his trousers. He had smoker's lines around his mouth and a deep, natural-looking tan. His body had clearly enjoyed some indulgent times and he didn't care who knew it. His only concession to vanity, aside from the ludicrous hair, was a mouth full of blindingly white veneers.

I wondered why it was that when women had money they spent vast quantities of it on looking like they had miraculously stopped ageing on their twenty-first birthdays, whereas powerful men could just let nature take its course. I didn't think about this for too long because the answer was very obviously 'sexism'.

Cyrus had a disproportionately large head, making his close-set hazel eyes seem even nearer to one another. His face was set into a permanent sneer, which reminded me immediately of something Nain always said: 'If you look at an old person, you can always tell whether they've spent most of their life smiling or frowning. After forty, people start to get the face they deserve.'

As though he could feel me staring at him, Cyrus glanced towards me, but without turning his head, or breaking stride from the bollocking he was giving one of the team for not 'cutting to a VT' fast enough. When his minion was sufficiently cowed, apologising profusely and promising it would never happen again, he turned to face me.

'Well, who do we have here, then?' He smiled, but not in a friendly way. One of his eyebrows was raised and his eyes swept my body, taking me in from head to toe. It reminded me of the look Stu the Birdman had given me on the open mic night in Hoxton. Once again, it had the effect of making me feel vulnerable.

A woman with a head of mid-length, pale-pink waves put her hand on Cyrus's shoulder and manoeuvred herself so she was standing between us.

'This is Llewella!' she declared, and I recognised the same

high, cheerful voice Jess had used on the phone. 'She's doing a screen test with us today!'

'Excellent!' boomed Cyrus. 'Good luck. I'm sure you'll be fabulous. Although you might want to rethink the chocolate,' he added, gesturing to the green triangle, which was still in my hand, poised somewhere between the table top and my mouth. 'The camera adds ten pounds, you know!'

And, having dispensed his wisdom, he was gone. I could hear him chortling to himself all the way down the corridor and into his dressing room.

'What a thoroughly unpleasant chap. I shan't be watching him again,' Wendy observed in the slightly stunned silence that followed.

I hadn't particularly liked Cyrus before I met him. He was always belittling people my age, calling us 'virtue signallers' and 'snowflakes', yet I had always assumed it was an act – something he was doing for attention and viewing figures rather than because he genuinely believed what he was saying. Plus, *English Breakfast!* was just bit of fun, something you rolled your eyes at, before tutting and getting on with your day.

But, seeing him in the flesh had ignited an altogether different response. In fact, it had only taken two minutes of being in his company for me to know with absolute clarity that I hated Cyrus Peyton.

Chapter 17

When Jess told me how well the screen test had gone and that she was sure she'd be in touch very soon, I'd tried to shoehorn Aretha into the conversation as casually, yet as forcefully as possible. But I could tell Jess's mind was elsewhere, probably already thinking about the next thing she had to do that day, and she brushed my comments away with a 'yes, of course, we can talk about that later down the line'. I knew, somewhere deep down, that it wasn't going to happen.

'You just coming off shift, then?' the driver asked – a different one than had brought us in – as we sat in static traffic.

'Oh, no. I was just there for an audition,' I replied, grateful for the distraction from thinking about how I was going to broach today's events with Aretha.

'Is that right?' I could see him raising his eyebrows in the rear-view mirror. 'You know, I had that Kiara Patel in the back of my cab, once. Such a laugh, she was. We were best friends by the time I dropped her home!'

'Ooh, I like her!' said Wendy.

'Yeah, she's great,' I replied, meaning it.

Kiara Patel was *English Breakfast!*'s resident chef. You didn't see many brown or plus size women on breakfast TV and Kiara defiantly bucked that trend by being both. She'd made a name for herself after winning a TV cooking competition about ten years ago. I remembered watching it with Nain when I visited in the summer holidays. Kiara was our favourite and we would cheer her on. We weren't the only ones – the viewing public had instantly fallen in love with her bubbly charm. Since then, clips of her giggling (and accidentally setting fire to stuff) while knocking-up culinary delights in the corner of the *English Breakfast!* studio had gone viral and she'd firmly cemented her status as a national treasure.

Kiara had been walking by while Jess and a cameraman were setting up for my screen test in the recently vacated studio. She'd smiled warmly at me as she'd walked up behind Jess and looked through the viewfinder of the camera.

'Oh yes, bab,' she'd declared in her thick Brummie accent. 'You've got it. Look at those cheekbones! You're stunning!'

'Thank you!' I'd replied shakily. Perhaps sensing my nerves, Kiara had spent the next few minutes giving me some advice on how to project my voice, perching one cheek of her vast bottom on the edge of the famous desk usually occupied by Cyrus and his co-presenter Jemima. Then she wished me luck and gave me a hug. The combination of her abundant curves and the fact she smelled like coconuts made the hug a comforting experience, like being enveloped in a warm marshmallow – exactly what I needed in that moment. As she sashayed away, pausing to throw a wink over her shoulder, I found myself thinking everyone should have a Kiara in their life. The woman was pure sunshine.

Perhaps it was Kiara's intervention which had made the audition go so well. As soon as the camera began rolling, any hint of my nerves disappeared. Jess asked me questions and instructed me to include an element of what she had asked in my answer, since she'd be editing her voice out to create the showreel.

I'd talked about why I thought toilets were important, how they were missing from most reviews of public spaces. I described the worst toilet I'd ever reviewed and what my perfect loo would look and smell like. About halfway through it occurred to me how much I was enjoying myself. The time flew by and, before I knew it, I was being escorted out of the building and sent on my way.

The cab finally left the bumper-to-bumper congestion of central London behind and I couldn't put it off any longer. I'd already fired off a brief text to Mum to say it had gone well and I'd fill her in later. I had nothing left to do but text Aretha.

Hey! The audition went really well. I spoke to them about us doing it together but they weren't keen.

No. Too harsh. I deleted it.

Hey! Just out of the screen test. I spoke to them about you and me doing it together and they said they'd think about it.

That wasn't right either. I didn't want to give her false hope.

Finally, I settled on:

Hey! Just out of audition and on my way back to SE. Will fill you in later.

Perhaps it was cowardly, but at least I had bought myself some time.

No one apart from Mum, Wendy and Aretha knew what I had been doing that morning. Yet, as I made my way to my afternoon history class in my jumpsuit and troweled-on make-up, I could feel the stares of curious eyes on me.

'Nice new look, Loo,' said Grace, as she passed me on her way into the common room. It wasn't said kindly and I heard her cronies erupt into laughter. As the door swung closed I just caught a glimpse of Olivia, who gave me a sad, sympathetic smile.

I reminded myself that sarcasm was the lowest form of wit, put my shoulders back and carried on walking, silently rehearsing the comebacks I wish I'd been quick enough for. Sod them, I decided. None of them had just come back from a TV studio.

I could barely concentrate as Mr Copeland took us painstakingly though the demise of Cardinal Wolsey that afternoon. Instead, my mind kept coming up with increasingly disastrous potential outcomes of my looming conversation with Aretha. In one, she said I was a traitor and she was going to tell the whole school what a terrible person I was. In another, she laughed in my face, declaring that *English Breakfast!* were never going to call back and that I was an idiot to ever take the whole thing seriously. But the scenario my brain kept coming back to was one where Aretha made me choose – pursuing this opportunity or being her friend. And if it came to that, I genuinely didn't know what I would do.

My anxiety was back, having been briefly swept to one side by the excitement of the audition. I felt sweat prickling as it fought to make its way through the thick foundation on my face and my breathing was shallow.

After what felt like an eternity and also not enough time, the bell rang. Steeling myself for a 'rip the plaster' moment, I headed towards the door.

'Miss Williams,' Mr Copeland interrupted. He had always

insisted on calling us by our surnames, ever since Year 7. I supposed it stood to reason that a history teacher would be enamoured with archaic practices. 'May I have a quick word before you go?'

Was there a more terrifying sentence in the English language than 'may I have a quick word'? It never, ever led to anything good. Reluctantly, I sat opposite Mr Copeland's desk at the front of the classroom, feeling self-conscious in my very-much-not-usual garb.

'How are you, Miss Williams?' Mr Copeland entwined his fingers and put them on the desk in front of him, leaning forward expectantly. I couldn't recall him ever asking me that, before. Mr Copeland wasn't generally known for his people skills and I had no idea how I was expected to reply.

In the end, I settled for a noncommittal, 'Errrr. Good. Thanks,' resisting the urge to add an instinctual 'How are you?'.

'It's just, I've noticed you seem distracted in class lately. And your last couple of essays haven't been up to the usual standard I would expect from you.'

At this, he pulled two of my most recent essays out of the drawer in his desk, fanned out slightly so I could see the grades on both. There, in damning red pen, were two Bs. I couldn't let this happen again. I swallowed hard, trying not to cry.

'Are you aware of this dip in your performance yourself?' Mr Copeland asked.

I was and I wasn't. Of course, I knew I'd had less time than usual to complete my essays lately, because so much had been taken up with Aretha and Loo stuff. Plus, even when I did have time, I often found it difficult to concentrate. But I was still

153

shocked to learn this had impacted my grades. I got straight A*s. This wasn't just what I did, it was who I *was*.

'I'm sorry,' I replied. 'I've had a lot on recently. I will try harder.'

'That's a good start,' said Mr Copeland, carefully, 'but that's not really why I'm asking. I know you've . . . um' – he groped for the right words – 'errr . . . struggled with your mental health in the past and I just wanted you to know, if there's anything I can do to support you, I'm here.'

I stared determinedly at my lap, humiliated. I knew what Mr Copeland was really implying – I was failing and I needed to 'buck my ideas up', as Ms Trebor was fond of saying when she was telling us off.

'It's not that,' I lied. 'I've just had a lot going on lately. But I'll make sure to prioritise better. Sorry, again.' I snatched up the essays and jammed them in my bag while praying Mr Copeland would take the hint and end the conversation.

'If you're sure,' he replied, watching me levelly. I felt like a fish, floundering out of water, being eyed calmly by a cat waiting to pounce. 'But my door is always open if you need to chat.'

'Thanks. Great!' My voice sounded high-pitched and slightly hysterical as I scuttled out of the room. Out of the frying pan and into the fire.

Aretha was waiting for me as I picked my way towards my locker, carefully avoiding the shoes, rucksacks and other detritus flung there by the sports lot as they eagerly made the transition from classroom to their natural habitat on the playing field. I found I couldn't look directly at her, so instead fixated on the contents of my locker: three text books; a review of *Merchant* at the National Theatre I'd torn out of a newspaper and forgotten to throw away; a mini Troll doll Olivia had given me as a good luck charm before *Macbeth* ('It has red hair! It's Scottish!' she'd insisted) and a sorry-looking, rapidly decaying banana.

I felt Aretha's hand on my arm as she muscled into the space beside me, no doubt wondering what was so very fascinating. 'So, what did they say?' she asked, with absolutely no preamble.

'So . . . I told them about how you and I are doing a blog together now and how we make a good double-act,' I answered, truthfully.

I risked a glance in Aretha's direction, focusing my gaze on her left ear because I knew if I caught her eye I'd fall to pieces. I could see, even in my peripheral vision, that she had a 'get on with it' look on her face.

'Yeah. Anyway. They said that's something we could discuss later down the line.' I felt a shift in the air around us and it made me gabble. My mouth ran away with me, spilling out sentences I hadn't intended to speak. 'To be honest, I have no idea how my screen test even went. They probably won't even ask me back. The whole thing is such a long shot. So we should probably just focus on Aretha and Loo and forget about it. Sorry. I'm sorry not to have better news.'

In the moment of silence which followed, I was scared. Which was ridiculous. It wasn't as though Aretha did or said anything terrible when she was upset. If anything, she was the victim in this scenario. There was absolutely no logical reason for the fear I felt in the pit of my stomach.

'It's cool,' Aretha eventually replied, taking a step away from me. I knew by now this was code for 'things are very far from cool'. I found myself frantically planning ways to make her like me again, anything I could do which might prevent the week of surly silence or cutting remarks which usually followed an 'it's cool' moment. Then, it hit me.

'Hey, I've just realised!' I exclaimed, louder than I had intended. 'We never exchanged Christmas gifts! I still have yours wrapped in my wardrobe! Shall I bring it over to yours this evening?'

'Sure. If you like,' said Aretha. And then she spun on her high-tops and marched away, yelling 'see you later' as she went.

She didn't even bother to turn her head.

Chapter 18

Linda told me I should write my worries down when I felt overwhelmed.

'Then you can take three highlighter pens and use different colours for things you can control, things which have a solution but you need someone else's help to solve and things you have no power over at all,' she'd advised.

I hadn't really understood the point of the exercise at the time. But as the same anxious thoughts looped frenetically in my increasingly tired brain, I was scared that if I didn't get them out somehow, my head would explode.

'Really tune into what your mind is telling you,' Linda had instructed, 'and write everything down, no matter how silly.'

Sitting at the desk in my bedroom with a notebook folded at a blank page in front of me, I closed my eyes and stopped trying to fight my anxiety. Instead, I tried to lean into it so I could hear what it was telling me. Without warning, an image of the inside of my skull came to me, with thoughts swirling wildly in ugly acid greens, urgent reds and ominous dark greys. I imagined myself jumping into the vortex they created, immersing myself in the chaos so I could see it clearly. I watched as the worries darted and weaved in and out of my vision, spelling brief words or making familiar sounds before popping like bubbles.

When I flicked my eyes open, I was surprised to notice

a number of words written on the page in front of me in my own looping handwriting. I had not remembered picking up my pen and yet, I must have done.

Grades slipping. The first item read.

This had been playing on my mind a lot. The situation which had eventually led to me having disappointing GCSE results had begun in much the same way, with Bs and then Cs circled in harsh, red pen at the top of my increasingly shoddy work and teachers gently probing as to the cause in hushed conversations at the ends of classes. After a while, I'd started deliberately sabotaging myself, leaving essays until the very last minute because, I'd reasoned, it was better to fail knowing you had never really tried in the first place.

I resolved not to let that happen again. I would make sure I carved out time to do my work properly and promised myself I would double my efforts to make sure I got my A*s. This was a problem I alone had the power to control. I highlighted it in the yellow I'd selected for this category.

Weight - scared I will put it all back on.

Another yellow. Aretha's diet and exercise regime was working, so all I had to do was stick to it. It was a question of willpower. No one could help me with that.

Audition - really want EB gig. I'd scrawled next.

I had the presence of mind to realise this should be highlighted in pink, the colour I'd chosen for worries I had no control over. The audition was done. I'd tried my best. There was nothing for it but to await the outcome.

Aretha.

That was all I had written for the next and final entry,

but it was much larger than the rest and underlined twice. I sighed, wishing my subconscious had been a bit more forthcoming. Using another of Linda's techniques, I asked myself what I wanted to happen.

The answer was came to me in a nanosecond. I wanted things to go back to how they were before we began the Aretha and Loo project. Those first few blissful weeks of our friendship had been long talks in which we shared our secrets, observations about sixth form – as I'd been encouraged to see it through Aretha's newcomer eyes – and a huge amount of laughter. Other than the intimacy we'd once shared, that was what I missed most – the in-jokes which made us giggle until our faces and stomachs ached.

How had we lost those things? Why did the prospect of seeing Aretha now make me anxious rather than excited? Was it my fault?

I'd taken hold of the thought thread and it was dragging me down a rabbit-hole of self-doubt. *You are selfish,* the thoughts whispered, *you choose the chance to be on TV over your friend. You betrayed her. No wonder she resents you.*

And yet, another thought interrupted, *you still want it. You're desperate to get that slot on* English Breakfast!*.*

So you're going to have to work harder with Aretha. Let her know how much she means to you. You can have both. You'll only be happy if you can have both.

With a new-found determination, I highlighted Aretha's name in yellow. Then, I picked up my bag containing her Christmas gift, slung it over my shoulder and marched resolutely out of my own home and towards hers.

***

The door was answered by a boy my taid would have described as 'a lanky streak of dribble piss' on account of his tall, slender frame. He had the same skin tone as Aretha, but other than that looked exactly like a skinnier version of Delroy – same broad, warm smile, same twinkle in his eye. I knew immediately he must be Ziek.

'Hiya, I'm Loo. I'm here to see Aretha,' I said, reverting to my most awkward self and holding out my hand for him to shake.

Ziek took my hand and shook it solemnly, the faintest hint of a smile playing around the corners of his mouth.

'Loo. Of course. I've heard all about you from Steph. I'm Ziek. Come in.' He beckoned me with a tilt of his head down the now-familiar long corridor to the kitchen, which was empty.

'Would you like a drink? We've got cola, water, juice. Aretha's upstairs, by the way,' Ziek said, opening the fridge door and gesturing at its contents.

'Great! I'll just have a water, thank you,' I replied, hovering uneasily as he poured in silence. 'I'll, er . . . just go up and see Aretha, then. Nice to meet you!' I blithered, tripping slightly on a chair leg as I made my way to the door.

'Nice to meet you too, Loo. See you again soon, I hope,' Ziek shouted to my rapidly retreating back. I'd only known him about three seconds but I could already tell Ziek was impeccably mannered. This surprised me a little and I realised it was because I tended to measure all brothers against Hugh, who, if he could be bothered to open the door at all, would merely have grunted and gestured vaguely upstairs before running back to his PlayStation.

Before knocking on Aretha's bedroom door, I set my glass

of water on a nearby chest of drawers, reached into my bag and pulled out the small, meticulously wrapped package I'd been saving for her since early December. I'd first seen the necklace in the window of a jewellers on the high street, when I'd been shopping for some make-up in town. I'd always thought those split-hearts in silver and gold with 'best friends' written on them were a bit tacky, but this was gorgeous. Instead of being heart-shaped, it was a chunky circle of mother of pearl. It looked a bit like a shiny soft-mint. It was cut diagonally and each half-circle dangled from a long silver chain. In tiny writing, which looked like it had been typed on to the surface, one half-circle bore the word 'friends' and the other 'forever'.

The necklace was quirky and unusual, but understated enough that we could wear it with practically any outfit. I'd decided to give Aretha both halves so she could choose which she wanted and I'd take the other.

As I approached her bedroom door, I heard Aretha's voice, loud and indignant.

'She can absolutely fuck off, with that,' she was saying. 'I'm not going to sit here and take it.'

I hesitated, wondering whether this was the kind of conversation I should interrupt and, more crucially, who she was talking about.

'Every moment I spend with her I'm not . . .' she continued, followed by some muffled words I couldn't make out. It was then I knocked, lifting the gift to eye level.

'Ta daaaa!' I sang, with a slightly desperate enthusiasm, when the door opened. 'Happy belated Christmas!'

Aretha was scowling and I saw she had earbuds in and her

phone in one hand. 'Hang on a second, I'm on a call,' she said, turning back towards her bed and leaving me standing on the threshold, feeling like an idiot.

'Yeah, I can't talk now, babe. She's just turned up,' Aretha said, holding her phone out in front of her. I could just make out a swish of navy hair and realised she must be FaceTiming Maddy. 'Chat later, OK. Bye! Love you!'

She couldn't have made it any more evident that she had just been talking about me.

Aretha was sitting cross-legged on her bed, so I made my way over to her and dropped the package carefully into her lap.

'I bought this for you,' I said, sitting next to her. Aretha shifted slightly so our arms were no longer touching.

'Thanks,' she replied, ripping off the paper. She took in the two necklaces without emotion.

'I thought we could have one each,' I explained, unnecessarily. Anything to cut the atmosphere in the room. 'But I wasn't sure if you wanted "friends" or "forever"?'

'Oh. Uhm . . . friends, I guess?' Aretha was unenthusiastic and I found myself wondering if she would have preferred the vintage Prince LP I'd found in an independent record shop, or the earrings shaped like musical notes I'd seen in the same jewellers where I'd bought the necklace.

'Great!' I grabbed the 'forever' half and fastened it around my neck. By the time I'd done so, Aretha had chucked the box containing her half on to a pile of miscellaneous junk spilling out of the bottom of her wardrobe.

I decided that, unless I wanted to leave right then and proceed to spend a sleepless night wondering what I could have done to deserve such a reaction, I'd have to address the tension.

'Do you not like it?' I asked.

'No, it's cool,' Aretha replied.'I just can't pretend I'm not annoyed with you, right now.'

I took a deep breath, steeling myself. 'What did I do?'

'If you really don't know, I'll tell you.' Aretha sighed. 'You give off this impression you're, like, all about equality but when it comes down to it you'll just do whatever benefits you.' I couldn't put my finger on exactly why, but it felt as though she'd practised saying these words before.

I was too taken aback to reply.

'Steph already explained it to you, but it's like you've deliberately forgotten.' Aretha continued.

'When it comes to how Black you're perceived to be, it's more about the texture of your hair and how curly it is.'

'I thought . . . you didn't believe what Steph says?' I squeaked.

'When did I ever say that? Steph's all right, you know. You need to calm down about her and listen to what she has to say because you might learn something. As much as you're mixed race too and we're almost the same colour, people don't look at us the same. No one stares at you when you get on a train. No one follows you around a shop thinking you're going to steal something.'

I knew this was true. I'd seen it with my own eyes. I mumbled something about my privilege.

'That's right! You are privileged,' Aretha almost spat. 'You have straight hair; someone could put a light foundation on you and you'd just look like a white woman with 'exotic' features.

And that's what the media wants. Of course *English Breakfast!* only want to take you and not me.'

I thought Aretha was going to accuse me of not trying hard enough to ensure she was included. It had never occurred to me that Jess's reluctance to entertain us doing the segment as a double act was to do with Aretha's race.

The impact of that realisation knocked the air out of my lungs and the words out of my mouth. I'd had moments in my life where relentless anxiety had managed to convince me I was all but worthless, but I'd never once doubted I was a good person, before. I always thought I was the type to do the right thing. And yet here I was, so intent on pursuing an opportunity for myself I hadn't been able to see I never deserved it in the first place. I hadn't earned it, any more than Aretha had asked for her tight curls.

'I'm so sorry,' was all I could manage when I eventually found my voice. 'What can I do to make it right?'

'I was talking to Maddy about it just now,' Aretha said, confirming my earlier fears, 'and she said if she was in your position, she would refuse to take the job unless they agreed we could do it together.'

Chapter 19

'Well, obviously we're incredibly disappointed. Is there anything we can do to change your mind? Budgets are tight, but I'm sure we could add another couple of hundred to the fee, if that would make a difference?'

Jess had rung to say the producers loved my reel and were willing to offer me a regular weekly slot for a trial period of three months, pre-recorded to fit in with my studies. I turned eighteen in a few weeks and we'd be filming after that, so I didn't technically need my mum's permission, but they'd prefer to have it nonetheless.

They proposed to send me with a hidden camera to investigate the toilets of some of London's most prestigious and expensive venues. It would help if there was something major (and preferably gross) I could find wrong with them.

When the time came for me to tell her I couldn't take the job, I struggled to get the words out. They wrestled with the lump in my throat and clawed their way on to my tongue, which felt weighed down with disappointment and regret.

'It's not the money,' I explained. 'I talked it over with Aretha, you know – who I do my blog with – and we agreed that we need to focus on opportunities which are for both of us, right now. Is there any chance she could be involved with this?' I'd already asked twice, but I wanted to ensure I'd done everything I could.

'As I explained before' – there was a hint of irritation in Jess's voice – 'because of the format of the segment, it would really only work with one person. And the producers thought you were so funny, likeable and articulate on screen; they were really keen on you.'

Because I have straight hair and could pass for Caucasian in the right light, I added, silently.

'Why don't I give you some more time to think about it?' Jess asked. 'Ideally, they'd want to start filming as soon as possible, but I'm sure they'd wait a few weeks for you to discuss it with, maybe your mum? What does she think?'

'Oh. I haven't talked to her about it, really,' I admitted. I could try and fool myself that this was because we were both so busy, but in reality it was because I knew exactly how she'd react. She'd be so proud I aced the screen test, but would be baffled and disappointed by my decision not to pursue a creative opportunity. I wasn't sure I could bear the look on her face.

'Well, then maybe you're being a bit too hasty?' Jess ventured, gently. 'Let me come back to you in two weeks. Give you some time to percolate. OK?'

And without waiting for an answer she said a swift farewell.

As resignations went, it wasn't what you might call successful. Although, was it even a resignation if I hadn't taken the job in the first place?

I laid back on my bed, letting out a huge sigh as I did so. The past few days had really taken it out of me and I physically ached. Hunger had become a constant companion and impossible to separate from the gnaw of anxiety in my stomach. Sometimes, I felt light-headed and I knew it was because I hadn't eaten enough. But I was terrified of regaining the weight I'd lost, which was also one of the few things I actually felt proud of myself for, right now. Plus, I was worried what Aretha would think if I abandoned the plan she'd made for me, on top of everything else causing a rift between us.

Every cell of my body was willing me to rest, but I couldn't. According to my all-new study regime, I had another three hours to complete before I could sleep. Determined to fend off yet another dreaded B, I'd created a rigid and relentless timetable, shoe-horning extra study into every previously unaccounted-for moment. I took a deep breath and prepared myself to knuckle down, just as the doorbell rang.

I padded downstairs and was surprised to see Olivia standing on my doorstep, holding two paper cups. It was so weird to see her out of context. I saw the briefest flicker of something cross over her face when I opened the door – it could have been disapproval, or maybe concern, but she covered it up quickly with a wide smile.

'Hellooooooooooooooo!' she sang. 'We haven't caught up in about three thousand years, so I am here bringing thee gifts of hot chocolate!' She pushed one of the cups towards me with a flourish. I hesitated for a moment, hearing Aretha's voice saying *empty calories*, before taking it. An awkward silence followed.

'So, errrr . . . Can I come in?'

I felt conflicted. On the one hand, I could recognise that Olivia was trying to be kind. On the other, I had so much study to do. Panic began to flood my body. My mind was leapfrogging between two images: Mr Copeland's face when he took the B-graded essays out his drawer and my promise to myself I wouldn't let it happen again, written and highlighted in yellow. Suddenly, anxiety was replaced by annoyance.

Who did Olivia think she was, showing up out of the blue and disrupting my plans?

'Oh, uhm. Thing is, I really have a lot of study to do. So it's not really a good time.'

'Everyone can spare ten minutes for sweet, sweet friendship and hot chocolate! It's good for our mental health!' Olivia declared, refusing to take the hint.

I bristled. 'Actually, mental health is a lot more complicated than so-called self-care bollocks on TikTok. I've been really poorly recently and a cup of refined sugar isn't going to help with that. In fact, if you knew anything you'd know it's likely to make me worse.'

Olivia looked like I'd slapped her. 'I'm really sorry. I didn't know how bad things have been for you, but I was worried about you. That's kind of why I'm here.'

'Well, thanks, but like I say I really don't have time, right now.'

I went to close the door, but Olivia stopped it with her foot.

'Let me just say one thing and then I'll go,' she promised, taking a step back and putting her cup of hot chocolate carefully on the ground. I felt my jaw tighten. 'I'm not going to pretend I understand exactly what's going on with you right now, but I was so shocked when you dropped out of *Merchant*. And then every time I see you it looks like you've lost more weight. And then . . . the other day I looked at your YouTube channel and . . . Those videos aren't you, Loo. It's like you're pretending to be someone else. And you don't need to, because you're brilliant as you—'

'Yes, well,' I interrupted, because I felt like I was going to start crying and I didn't have time for that either, right now. I wanted to get her off my doorstep as quickly as possible.

'You're the only person who seems to think so and since you have no understanding of how media or blogging works you'll forgive me for not taking your opinions on board.'

'This isn't you speaking, now. This is . . . This is her, isn't it? That Aretha girl?'

'That Aretha Girl' is my best friend!' I yelled, startling us both.

'She's manipulating you. That's not what a true friend does.'

'How would you know? It's not like you have any.'

Olivia gasped and stumbled slightly, knocking her hot chocolate over with the heel of her boot.

'Oh, god, I'm sorry.' She dropped down on to her haunches, trying fruitlessly to clear up the spillage with the end of her rainbow scarf. As I watched her, scrabbling around on the ground, flustered and red in the face, my heart ached. Being mean to Olivia was like kicking a puppy. I shouldn't have done it. I wanted to tell her I was sorry but sensed it was somehow too late. She stood and I could see her eyes were shining with tears.

'I'll leave you alone now,' she said and practically sprinted down the street. I closed the door and sank down on to the soft carpet as my own tears began to trickle.

I'd let my anxiety take over and my mouth run away from me and I was too tired and hungry and confused to work out how to make it better. Without thinking, I took a sip from the cup still in my hand. It had gone cold.

***

I was jolted awake when a sliver of sunlight made its way through my hastily drawn blinds. My lower back throbbed painfully, my mouth was dry and I had made a wet patch on my exercise book where I'd drooled on it in my sleep. At some point I must have crashed out at my desk. I had assumed that was the sort of thing that only ever happened in films.

According to Mrs Potts, it was 5 a.m. I had exactly two and a half hours before I needed to be up for sixth form. I peeled myself out of my chair and crawled into bed, not even bothering to get undressed. Keeping my eyes half-closed, I reached for my phone to set an alarm. Without thinking, I pressed 'yes' when a notification asked me if I wanted to deactivate airplane mode.

Two messages beeped their way into my consciousness and despite my tiredness, I couldn't resist taking a peek. One, weirdly, was from Mum.

Hi Carriad. Didn't want to wake you when I got in last night. Let me know when you're up. I'd like to have a cwtch and a chat.

Odd.

The second was from Aretha.

Tried facetiming u but ur phone's off. CALL ME I WANT TO ASK YOU SOMETHING

I could feel my heart hammering in my chest as I spooled through options – some plausible, others which even I, in my panicked state, could see were highly unlikely – for what Aretha might want to ask. Had I done something else wrong? Did she want more time commitment to Aretha and Loo? I was barely managing to juggle my workload as it was. I suddenly felt too hot and threw my duvet off and on to the floor. I swung my legs over the side of the bed and dashed over to the window, spots appearing in the corners of my vision where I'd stood up too fast.

I opened the window wide, sticking my head out and gulping down the fresh early-morning air. I stayed like this for a few minutes, before reluctantly picking up my phone once more.

Sorry, was studying and had phone on airplane mode. Awake now so call me when you're up. I sent to Aretha.

There was no possibility of going back to sleep. I crept to the bathroom and showered, thinking I could perhaps squeeze in an hour of study before breakfast. As I tiptoed back down the hall in my towel, Mum's head appeared from behind her bedroom door.

'Morning, lovely!' she exclaimed, far more cheerfully than the early hour warranted. 'I'm glad you're up. It's a beautiful morning, it is. I was going to do some yoga in the garden. Want to join me? It's good for your brain, they say.'

Ten minutes later, Mum and I were downward-dogging on parallel yoga mats under the cherry tree in our back garden. Mum was, of course, dressed in a way which was both appropriate and stylish – her mint-green, three-quarter-length linen trousers and matching embellished top fluttering gently in the breeze. I, by contrast, was in a thick pair of joggers and baggy T-shirt, sweating despite the coolness of the morning.

Mum flipped effortlessly into a forward lunge, raising her slender arms elegantly above her head and looking up at her thumbs. I attempted to copy, wobbling precariously and feeling like a buffoon.

'They say when you do yoga it connects you to your real inner self,' Mum intoned in her special 'spiritual' voice, which kind of reminded me of ASMR and therefore always made me want to laugh.

'When your mind, body and soul are in unity, you can access the power of who you really are,' she continued.

'You do realise these are just words you're saying, Mum? You're not actually forming coherent sentences?' I replied, blowing my hair out of my eye ruefully as I wobbled over and landed on my bum. My cheeky retort earned me one of Mum's 'looks'.

'Let's get into lotus position,' Mum commanded, folding herself into a perfect cross-legged triangle. I put one leg out to the side and folded the other inwards, because I am not as flexible as my mother, which is not a thing anyone should be able to say. Mum closed her eyes and made sort-of 'hmmmm' sounds with her lips closed every time she exhaled. I joined in half-heartedly, unable to decide whether doing or not doing the noisy breathing thing made me look more silly.

After a few minutes of this, something miraculous happened. I was overcome by a sense of peace for the first time in as long as I could remember. It was like a snow plough had arrived and driven through all my anxious thoughts, clearing a path where I could stand and just be, without the burden of anxiety. I made a mental note – crisp morning air + smell of damp grass + loads of stretching/falling over = magic.

I let myself revel in it. Mum and I sat serenely side-by-side on our mats for some time before she pierced the bubble.

'I wanted to talk to you about something, carriad,' she said.

'Oh, yeah?' I kept my eyes closed, sensing that the impending conversation would be easier that way.

'I know you've been going to see Linda and it's not my place to interfere in that process . . . but I think we should talk about what happened before. Last time, I mean. Because that conversation never got resolved, did it? And if we don't resolve it, this thing with the panic attacks. Well, it might keep happening.'

I forced myself to keep breathing. Of all the things my Mum could have wanted to talk to me about, this was the topic I was least prepared for. I was powerfully conflicted. On the one hand, I knew she was probably right. I'd been avoiding talking about the thing that originally triggered my panic in Year 10, even with Linda. But on the other hand I just didn't feel ready. Not yet.

'Mum, you don't have to do this,' I replied, eventually. 'It isn't fair on you. And I can talk to Linda about it . . . I will talk to her. I promise.'

'You never let me finish the story, though. You don't know the full thing. Isn't it better to know?' Mum pleaded.

Oh no. Oh no no no no.

'Hello, you two yogi bears!' Wendy's head appeared over the bricks of the wall which separated our gardens. 'Isn't it a lovely morning?'

Taking advantage of the interruption, I stood abruptly, giving myself another whopper of a headrush as I did so.

'Hi, Wendy. I have to run. I'm going to be late for sixth form. Thanks, Mum. For yoga. It was . . . fun,' I gabbled, grabbing my mat and running into the safety of the house.

Easter

'You do me now more wrong
In making question of my uttermost
Than if you had made waste of all I have.'

The Merchant of Venice
Act 1, Scene 1

Chapter 20

The ancient, two-carriage train thundered squeakily through endless lush green hills as we made our way to West Wales.

Aretha had, randomly, scored a gig at Aberystwyth University's arts centre. The plan was to go from there to my grandparents' in Carmarthenshire, which was sort-of on the way to where we would be finishing our Easter holiday – a big night out in Bristol with Ziek and his friends from university. That, it turned out, was what Aretha had wanted to ask me – could we turn her latest gig offer into an extended adventure/road-trip? I'd been practically giddy with relief when she'd told me she wanted to spend time together over the holidays, taking it as a sign that my former friendship crimes had been absolved.

It would be strange, I reflected, as we sped past perhaps the thousandth flock of sheep we'd seen so far, to see streetwise, glamorous Aretha in my nain and taid's sleepy little Welsh village. Like watching a horse walk on its hind legs. Nonetheless, I was happy to spend a solid week in her company, away from potential interference from Maddy or Jess. (I was yet to break the realities of non-existent phone signal in rural Wales to Aretha.)

But first we were headed to Aberystwyth, a seaside town on Cardigan Bay, which bordered the Irish sea. My grandparents had taken me to Aber a couple of times when I was little. I had memories of eating fish and chips straight out of the paper on one of the many iron benches shaped like dragons which lined the seafront, a male voice choir belting out tunes with gusto on the pier and, most exciting of all to my then child-self, the funicular which took you up and down the giant hill on one side of the bay. I was looking forward to going there again.

Aretha had been asleep since Shrewsbury, her head resting on the train window and her feet propped up on the seat opposite her and next to mine. Technically, the two legs of the journey – London to Birmingham and then Birmingham to Aber – were about the same distance, but the second part took much longer owing to the lack of a high-speed rail line. We'd left Surrey at 7 a.m., so while it was only just past midday, it felt much later.

I let out a humongous yawn and wondered why it was that travelling made you so tired when you were mostly just sitting. As the train slowed to pull into the next station, the change in speed shook Aretha from her nap.

'Are we there yet?' she croaked, weakly.

'Almost. About half an hour away, I reckon. We've just stopped at Machynlleth,' I soothed, patting her foot reassuringly.

'Excuse me?' Aretha laughed. 'Is that actually the name of the place we're in or did you just sneeze?'

I forced a laugh. I'd had variations of this conversation with English people on so many occasions and every time the other person was convinced they were being original and hilarious when they mocked the Welsh language. Right on cue, Aretha said, 'tell me the name of that place, again.'

'Llanfairpwllgwyngyllgogerychwyrndrobwllllantysiliogogogoch,' I obliged, reciting the town with the longest name in the UK (which was pretty much every Welsh person's party trick).

'That is so fucking weird,' Aretha said dismissively, curling back into her sleeping position as though I was the one who had insisted on saying it for no reason. 'Hey, babes.' She suddenly leaned forward, putting her hand on my knee. 'You won't leave me on my own tonight, will you?'

'Of course not. Why would I?' I replied.

'Well, you know, you'll be among your people and I'll probably be the only Black person there and . . . I might need someone to have my back, is all.'

I had to stifle a laugh. The people of Aberystwyth were so friendly you would discover practically the entire life story of everyone you happened to bump into while walking along the beach.

Aretha had never been to Wales before and was applying the English blueprint to her expectations. In England, it seemed as though all the racists lived by the sea (which is strange, as you'd think they'd want to be further inland, away from foreigners). But Celts were different. They'd been invaded and pillaged and generally fucked over by the English many times throughout history and therefore the Scottish, Irish and Welsh identity was forged in struggle. I was sure Wales had its share of racists, but the overriding sense was that outsiders were welcome, for they were unified with the Welsh in their otherness. At least, that's the impression I'd always got as a visiting brown person.

'I have your back. Always' I promised Aretha. She took my hand, squeezed it, smiled and then leaned back into her slumber.

When we arrived in Aberystwyth, it looked totally different from how I remembered it. The whole place seemed to fizz with excitement and purpose. My memories were mostly full of families and old people on their holidays. But we were visiting in April and everywhere we looked there were students. I could see students through the window of The Cambrian pub opposite the train station, already lining up pints. Students on their way home from lectures, clutching books to their chest, heads down in concentration. Students queuing for lunch in Spartacus, the sandwich shop. Students talking and laughing on street corners.

In summer, Aber enjoyed a few weeks of glorious sunshine. The rest of the year, I later found out from the amused woman behind the reception desk in our B&B, was pretty much constant gale-force winds and torrential rain. As Aretha and I made our way from the train station to the seafront, we were hit by diagonal winds so strong we struggled to stay upright.

We dragged our tiny wheelie cases along the pavement which ran parallel with the beach, where high waves were crashing noisily, creating spectacular foamy splashes as they did so. We paused briefly to take a picture of Aretha for our shared Instagram, the grey skies behind her, seagulls circling overhead, her curls pushed flat at the crown and blown out to one side by the wind. I chose a flattering filter and uploaded it quickly with the caption WE'RE HEEEEEERE!

Our B&B was a slender, tall building painted blue and white. It smelled of fry-ups. It wasn't unpleasant; I'd always loved the smell of bacon, although I'd never tasted it. We were sharing a twin room on the top floor, with a small bay window overlooking the sea. When you weren't being battered by the howling winds, the view was actually breathtaking.

We took it in turns to shower and change, washing off the hours of tedious train ride that had brought us here. Aretha had a sound check at four, which gave us a few hours to explore.

'It's so random to be here,' I mused. 'How did you even get this gig, by the way?'

'Stu got it for me,' Aretha replied distractedly as she tied her hair into a tight top knot.

'Stu the Birdman?' I exclaimed, incredulous, before remembering that was my private nickname for him.

'Ha! Yeah, I guess he does kind of look like a bird,' Aretha acknowledged.

'You stayed in contact with him?' I still couldn't quite wrap my head around it.

'Of course! He's really well connected and very into my music. In fact, he's driving up here, now.'

'He's coming all this way to see you?' The words were out of my mouth before I could assess how they might sound.

Aretha just gave me a look which somehow managed to convey incredulity that I would even question why someone would drive eight hours to watch her perform, and impatience at my slowness to get on her page. We fell into an uncomfortable silence.

My mind whirred. I didn't know why it bothered me so much that Stu was going to be joining us. Perhaps it was because I'd got the distinct impression of 'creep' the one and only time I'd met him. Maybe it was because Aretha hadn't told me she'd been in contact with him since. We were meant to be best friends and that's the sort of information I assumed a best friend would share. Maybe it was because they'd seemed really flirty and there'd been no mention of where he was going to stay tonight. Visions of those two sharing the twin bed just a few feet away from mine filled me with horror.

I had a sudden and vivid memory of Olivia describing Aretha as manipulative during our argument. Aretha certainly did have a talent for persuading everyone around her to behave in a way that bestowed maximum benefit and minimum inconvenience upon her. Was that what Olivia had meant?

I tried to push that last thought away, to dismiss it as bitchy, unfair or perhaps as a paranoid symptom of my heightened anxiety. Yet, another part of me knew I'd hit on a profound truth – one which, as if I'd superglued a pair of sunglasses to my face – I'd be forced to view everything through from that moment on.

I'd always wanted so badly to find someone who truly got what it was like not to belong in Chiddy, so I'd dived head-first into my friendship with Aretha, seeing only what we had in common. Yet, there were so many more things I couldn't understand or, if I was being honest, didn't really like about her. Then again, isn't that what friendship is – seeing the truth of a person beyond the shiny facade they present to the world on first acquaintance, or on social media, and loving them in spite of their flaws? And it wasn't like I was perfect, either.

I thought again of all the people who'd betrayed Aretha in the past and how I'd vowed never to be one of those people. I'd committed to her, and now our friendship was inextricably tied up with the blog – into which I'd invested money, as well as time.

I looked out again at the wild, Aberystwythian sea. Maybe I was in over my head with Aretha, but I was so far out in the metaphorical sea of our friendship that the shore was just a distant speck – too far to even contemplate swimming back to. And even if I could, what did the safety of the shore have to offer me, really? Did I want to go back to being the frumpy, lonely girl I was before Aretha came into my life?

I had to keep going and see where the waves would take me.

Chapter 21

After we left the B&B, Aretha and I headed into town in search of food. What with Aretha's sound check, we weren't sure when we'd next have the time to eat and wanted to line our stomachs. We found a pub advertising two meals for £7.99. I stared hungrily at Aretha's huge plate of fish and chips while picking at the only vaguely 'healthy' thing on the menu – yet another salad.

The pub was a strange hybrid – dank and dingy inside, but two of its walls were made of glass, which made it the ideal vantage point for watching the general hustle and bustle of the town.

We'd only been there for about ten minutes before we were descended upon by a group of three guys. There was something about the way they plonked themselves down next to us without asking which made me tense. Aretha, however, never missed an opportunity to show off. Within minutes, she'd pushed her food to one side and was deep in conversation with these lads, regularly throwing her head back in coquettish laughter.

Aretha turned her chair towards the best looking of the three, at which point he immediately stretched out one leg in a fairly obvious demonstration of ownership. This left me in an awkward thruple with the other two, who were trying to come up with a topic of conversation but obviously resenting it.

I decided the best course of action was to tune out, concentrate on trying to be enthusiastic about my salad and only speak if addressed directly. I was just contemplating trying to find an excuse to get up – maybe if I could find some black pepper it would make my meal more appetising - when Aretha's voice cut through my thoughts.

'Oh my god, I *absolutely* agree,' she was saying. 'I've had male friends be falsely accused of that kind of thing and it was so awful for them. Their only crime was dating a girl who clearly had mental health problems.'

I could hear a high-pitched noise in my ears as all the blood rushed to my head. She couldn't be talking about what I thought she was, could she?

'Correct,' the guy responded, pointing his pint at Aretha and smiling. 'And feminism doesn't help. You're told to "always believe the woman" and of course that makes it really easy for a girl to make a false accusation. Men are powerless, these days.'

The words were out of my mouth before I'd even had a chance to consider whether or not they were a good idea.

'How do you explain rape convictions being at an all-time low of less than five per cent then?'

Aretha actually laughed. She placed her hand on the forearm of the alpha guy. It was meant, I supposed, to be a placating gesture, but it also informed me in no uncertain terms whose side she was on.

'Where did you hear that statistic, babe?' Aretha asked. Her tone was breezy, yet I could tell she was moving in for a slam-dunk.

'In that assembly we had.' I saw alpha guy raise his eyebrows. Aretha obviously hadn't told him we were still at school. 'You know, the woman who came in from the rape crisis charity. You were there!' I cursed myself for the tremor in my voice.

'Babe, you can't trust statistics from charities. Of course they're going to say that. They have to keep themselves in business. You need to do your own research. Go on YouTube.'

'Yes! Precisely!' her new best mate chimed in, practically patting Aretha on the head for her willingness to uphold the patriarchy. I glared at him. He had a smug smile on his face.

'Llewella doesn't have a dad and she's gone to an all-girls school since she was eleven.' Aretha told him, as though I wasn't there. 'She doesn't get how hard it is to be a man, these days. It's not her fault. Be gentle with her! Whereas *I* have an older brother and an amazing dad I just adore. I know most men aren't bad!'

And then Aretha partially stood up, swivelled her bottom around in a neat gesture and sat on this guy's lap. I watched in disbelief as his hands immediately made their way to her thighs. He whispered something in her ear. Aretha laughed and nodded.

It was as though I was watching the scene on TV, or through an observation panel. I examined what was before me – three middle-class white men, statistically more likely to win the lottery than be falsely convicted of rape, using a fake victimhood narrative in an attempt to pull my friend. In fact, I thought to myself incredulously, they were actually bonding over a mutual scepticism about sexual assault, as though that was an appropriate subject matter for flirtatious banter. And my supposed best friend, who knew I struggled with mental health issues, had all-but-declared that women like me were the problem. It was, as the internet would say, 'unbelievable scenes'.

'I don't think all men are bad,' I said, standing up. 'But I do think you're pretty heinous.' Then I marched over to the bar.

I don't know what Aretha said to those boys after that, but I do know she was at my side within minutes, telling me she didn't think having a 'hissy fit' like that had been 'the right thing to do'.

I was angry, but I also hated that there was unresolved tension in the air. Instinctually, I started composing apologies in my head, trying to see the situation from Aretha's perspective. But I knew that I was right to challenge that awful boy, so maybe it was Aretha who needed to apologise, for once? But every time I tried to bring it up, Aretha said we should park it for now because she wanted to concentrate on her gig.

I went to the toilet and just stood in a cubicle, breathing heavily, wanting to claw my own skin off. I was on the verge of a panic attack and felt like having one would actually be a relief, like when you need to sneeze and just want to get it over with. But I couldn't make it happen. I wanted to run up to the shore and scream out to sea. I felt trapped, like a bumble bee buzzing around a glass jar.

In the end, I decided my only real option was to get myself thoroughly pissed.

'Seriously, I think I'm going to vom,' I whined, as we made our way back along the seafront the following morning.

The crashing waves, which had seemed so dramatic and captivating the day before, were now pounding the beach to the rhythm of my rapidly blossoming hangover. The very last thing I needed in that moment was to be getting on a coach (widely acknowledged to be the most chunderous of all transport), but that was the quickest way to get to my grandparents'. Crucially, since I had paid for this trip and justified it as content for Aretha and Loo, it was also the cheapest. I made a faint groaning noise, which was swallowed up and carried away on the winds.

Aretha, conversely, had never looked perkier. She had a stronger constitution than I did, perhaps because she was more used to drinking. She'd taken off her shoes and jumped down on to the beach, where she was currently cartwheeling alongside my slow, reluctant footsteps. I watched her for a moment, trying to pierce through the fug of sickness and headache and work out how I was actually feeling about the previous' nights' events. My memory would only permit me access to them in non-chronological, blurry chunks.

Aretha had performed a short, intimate gig in one of the studio-style rooms in the Arts Centre and afterwards everyone in the audience wanted a piece of her. We were invited to the Student Union. They were having a 90s themed night. We danced to the Spice Girls, the Red Hot Chili Peppers and other bands I vaguely recognised in the sweaty central hall with students dressed in infinite combinations of neon accessories and combat trousers.

We'd found ourselves at a house party. Aretha and Stu the Birdman disappeared for a long time. I sat on a musty-smelling sofa next to a gay guy called Gavin who kept telling me I was fabulous and ruffling my hair. He gave me some poppers. I took them, having lost the sense to refuse. I felt briefly dizzy and then the feeling faded as quickly as it had arrived.

I wondered aloud what the point of poppers were. Gavin told me they relaxed your arsehole so you could have anal sex. I think I was too drunk to be embarrassed.

I'd met the president of the Feminist Society. I'd slurred my way through the tale of Aretha and the rape defenders from the pub. We'd talked for a long time after that. I don't remember exactly what she said. I do remember emphatically agreeing with all of it.

Aretha had wanted to go swimming in the sea. I'd tried to dissuade her by pointing to all the signs along the pier which read DON'T DRINK AND DIVE. I remember thinking they were hilarious, those signs. I laughed at them for ages.

The last thing I recall was watching Aretha's silhouette as we lay side by side in our beds. She'd been so many people in the time I'd known her. The defiant performer who stood up to the school bully in assembly. The observant newcomer who'd made me see my town and school with fresh eyes. The confident woman who could banter with waiters and tell what was good prosecco. The free spirit who promised the possibility of adventure wherever she went.

But she'd also been the insecure child, hugging her blanket and crying because she felt left out of a conversation. A person who blew hot and cold. Someone with the power to make you doubt yourself, delivering character assassinations with a smile on her face. And, as I had seen that night, she was someone who bought into conspiracy theories on the internet and would turn on the sisterhood in a heartbeat if it meant the chance to flirt with a good-looking boy.

Which one was the real her? Was I the only person who

saw behind the various facades? Or was I just another in a long line of admirers, shaping Aretha into the person they most wanted her to be? And if that was true, what did that mean for us, and everything we'd invested into Aretha and Loo?

It felt like I was on the cusp of an epiphany before everything faded to black.

Chapter 22

I insisted on sitting at the front of the coach, knowing this would reduce my chances of being sick. Luckily, it was full of old people who set about reading, knitting or sipping from Thermoses of tea, meaning a minimum of noise and disruption. I managed to fall asleep almost immediately.

I startled awake, as though by instinct, just as we were pulling into Llangunnor, the village where my grandparents have lived their entire lives. What had once been their working farm was now disused, but they still kept the land and lived in the old farmhouse. It took a huge amount of upkeep and sometimes I worried it was too much for them. On the other hand, that house and my nain and taid were impossible to separate; I just couldn't imagine them living anywhere else.

Wiping dribble from my mouth with one hand, I nudged Aretha with the other, beseeching her to look at the lush green hills and valleys undulating into the distance which never failed to fill me with warmth and wonder.

'Yes, I know,' she replied. She seemed annoyed, but I was too hungover to be bothered to work out why.

As I knew he would be, Taid was already at the bus stop waiting for us. He was standing poker-straight as always, wearing a smart pair of grey slacks (no doubt ironed to within an inch of their life by Nain). Ifan, their ancient Border Collie, was sitting obediently next to him, the dog's posture just as rigid and expectant. I hadn't told my grandparents exactly what time we'd be arriving and wondered guiltily if he'd been standing there all morning.

'Sut mae, annwyl!' Taid exclaimed as I jumped off the coach, giving me a brief peck on the cheek before setting about getting our bags from the driver. He was visibly older and weaker than the last time I'd seen him and my instinct was to help him, but I stopped myself. It was a pride thing – he came from a generation where men carried the bags and women let them.

'And this must be Aretha!' Taid smiled as the coach drove away, belching its puke-making fumes in its wake.

'I am!' Aretha wore her most charming smile, all irritation now gone. 'It's a pleasure to meet you, Mr Williams.'

'Oh, please, call me Dai,' Taid replied and gestured towards his ancient van, a relic from his farming days, which would take us to their cottage on the outskirts of the village.

As we navigated the twists and turns of country roads, I glanced over at Aretha, looking for signs that she regretted coming here. When we'd arranged this trip, the extent of her knowledge was that I had 'family, somewhere in Wales' and she'd concocted our holiday plans on that basis. I don't know what she was imagining, but it probably wasn't a rickety old cottage nestled on the site of what was once a farm, with no phone signal and only two old people, a deaf collie and half an accidental flock of sheep for company.

She seemed perfectly content, though, chatting to Taid about her gig in Aberystwyth and how she was finding her first visit to Wales.

'It's beautiful here!' Aretha exclaimed, gesturing out of the grubby window.

I'd never noticed how Taid's van smelled of wet dog before. Or if I had, I'd associated it with the pleasant anticipation of spending some time in my grandparents' gentle, slow, cosy world. Now, I was a little embarrassed.

'It is lush, indeed,' Taid agreed. 'Every day when I wake up, I thank the Lord I'm Welsh!'

Aretha laughed, but it was lacklustre and confused.

'It's a lyric,' I explained. 'A Welsh band called Catatonia sang it in the 90s and Taid's been saying it ever since.'

'"International Velvet", that song was called,' Taid confirmed. 'Whatever happened to that Cerys Matthews? She was lovely, she was.'

We had this conversation every time I came to visit, which was less than I would have liked since sixth form began.

'You need to update your crushes, Taid,' I said, gently teasing him in that way only family can. 'What about Katherine Jenkins?'

I heard my vowels elongate as I said Katherine's name. I was slipping into a Welsh accent, like I always did within minutes of seeing my grandparents. I saw Aretha notice it too and roll her eyes. I made a mental note to try and rein it in.

'Where to you from, then, Aretha?' Taid asked, as the long dirt track leading to the farmhouse came into view.

'Where . . . to . . . sorry, uhm . . .' Aretha jostled with the unfamiliar phrasing.

'He means where are you from,' I explained, suddenly feeling like an interpreter. Which I suppose, in a way, I was. 'Not your heritage,' I added hastily. 'Just, like, where did you live before you came to Surrey.'

'Oh.' Aretha looked at her lap.

I replayed and analysed the last few minutes, looking for any evidence of Taid or me being offensive or insensitive. I knew Aretha would be filing away her observations, ready to pronounce judgment on Taid, this village, Wales generally.

'London,' she eventually replied, vaguely.

I could see the net curtains in the windows of the cottage twitching as we approached. Nain always came to the front door to greet visitors, but made sure she appeared just as they reached the front stoop in the hopes of giving the impression she had better things to do than linger at the door. In reality it did exactly the opposite, of course – she could never wait for people to ring the heavy iron cowbell which hung outside. When she materialised she looked just the same – short and round (Mum had inherited Taid's slender stature, whereas Nain's boobs and hips had skipped a generation to me). As she stood on tiptoe to envelop me in a hug I inhaled her comforting scent – she always smelled of lemon soap, talcum powder and baking.

'Come in, come in!' she instructed us with a wave of her arm, not bothering with formalities. 'Who wants a cuppa, then?'

'I'd love one, thanks Grandma,' I replied.

Nain stopped abruptly and turned on her slippered feet to look me in the eye.

'What's this "Grandma" all about, then? Is that what they call us in that London?' Nain had never understood the distinction between Surrey, where I actually lived and London proper, which she would always refer to as 'that London' if she was about to slag it off. 'Well, you'll be calling me by my proper name of Nain if you expect an answer, around here.'

She chortled before continuing her (surprisingly speedy for an old person) walk to the kitchen.

That was me told, then.

Everything was the same and yet different. As I took in the shelves rammed with miniature cottage ornaments (why? They could literally just go outside if they wanted to look at a cottage), the low beams, real fireplace and endless doilies and cushions it was as though I was seeing it all through two sets of eyes – my own and Aretha's. I was gripped by a sudden fear as I remembered Aretha's stricken face the day me, Steph and Dawn had made her cry because she felt alien and excluded. How was she going to cope when Nain, Taid and I inevitably fell into our old habits, rituals and in-jokes, honed over lifetimes?

It had been a mistake to bring Aretha here, I realised. But it was too late to do anything about it now.

As it happened, the next two days in Llangunnor passed without incident. Aretha was happy to tag along on the long walks Taid and I took each morning with Ifan, to help Nain bake Welsh cakes and listen to their stories about what this place was like back when it was a working farm. These wholesome activities were photographed and videos made, ready to be posted to the blog when we had wifi.

There was endless footage of Aretha larking about with Ifan.

'Animals love me,' she declared, as Ifan was reprimanded for trying to hump her leg for the millionth time.

When it came to interacting with Nain and Taid, Aretha nodded politely, laughed in all the right places, ate everything that was put in front of her but there was something missing.

Her sparkle, that innate Aretha-ness which warmed the air around her as though she was a human radiator, was gone.

I wanted Nain and Taid to see the Aretha I'd fallen for – the one who could walk into any public place and emerge with five new friends, who laughed and sang for no discernible reason and was using all her passion and energy to propel us both into a more successful future with the Aretha and Loo brand. I wanted them to understand why she was the only friend I'd ever brought to meet them. Yet instead, they got to meet a version of her who was bland and, if not exactly surly, certainly subdued.

'Are you OK?' I asked her on the second night, as we lay side-by-side in the converted attic containing parallel twin beds for when Hugh and I visited.

'Sure,' Aretha replied. I couldn't see her, but I imagined her lying ramrod straight, staring at the ceiling, the crocheted blanket pulled under her chin.

'It's just ... you're very quiet,' I observed.

'Yeah,' Aretha agreed and then, with a hint of a giggle, 'but I would be, wouldn't I?'

'Is something wrong?' I turned on to my side so I was facing her, even though we were enveloped in the total, pitch-black darkness of the countryside and I couldn't see her. Aretha, who was used to the omnipresent noise and lights of the city, had said it was 'creepy'. I found it soothing.

'No, babe. No, nothing's wrong. It's just ... your grandparents. They're a lot.'

'They are?' I thought about Nain, who could be stern and no-nonsense but worked hard to ensure everyone's needs were taken care of, cooking and baking and washing and scrubbing all day with her muscled forearms. And Taid, with his eccentric sense of humour and penchant for telling long, meandering stories which went nowhere, but were entertaining nonetheless. Maybe they were 'a lot' to an outsider.

'I always think,' Aretha continued, a yawn in her voice, 'meeting a new friend is like listening to one track from an album. You might love it and want to play it all the time, but it's only when you hear it in context of the rest of the album that it actually makes sense. Whenever I meet my friends' families, it's like hearing all the other tracks.'

I was stung by the casual reference to meeting other friends' families. As though this trip, which we'd planned and enthused over and which felt to me like an exclusive shared experience, was something Aretha did all the time.

'You make total sense now I've met your grandma,' Aretha concluded, her words garbled with approaching sleep. I waited for her to elaborate, but her breathing gradually slowed until it became deep and rhythmic and I knew I'd lost her to dreamland.

I tried to match my breathing to Aretha's, hoping that would usher in a blissful slide into unconsciousness and respite from the anxious thoughts which were now swirling around my brain. Was this trip a test? Had I failed? Was I like Nain? And if I was, was that a good thing? Had Aretha seen something about me she hadn't liked? Should it even matter?

Round and round the worries went like a malevolent whirlwind until, exhausted and irritable, I eventually drifted into fitful slumber.

Chapter 23

I was startled from dreamless sleep as the sun was rising. I watched the shapes in the attic illuminate and reveal themselves to be pieces of furniture or discarded clothes, as though they too were waking up. I felt as though I was on hyper-alert, my breathing a little too heavy, my focus a little too sharp. Hunger was gnawing at my gut.

It was impossible not to eat 'bad' foods at Nain and Taid's, but I'd only nibble the corners of Welsh cakes, leaving other white carbs untouched on the mountainous plates of dinner we were presented with each evening. Knowing I wouldn't be able to drift off again, I swung my legs out of bed as quietly as I could and tiptoed downstairs in my pyjamas, thinking a cup of tea might quieten my grumbling tummy.

Nain was already awake, dressed in an immaculately pressed skirt and cardigan and bustling about in that busy way she has – I don't think I'd ever seen her relax in my entire life.

'Bore da, carriad!' she said, cheerfully.

'Bore da, Nain,' I replied, slumping into one of the heavy wooden chairs around the rough-hewn table at the opposite end of the kitchen and rubbing my sore eyes.

'Don't rub, Llewella,' she scolded, 'you'll give yourself wrinkles. And what is it you're after? Tea, is it?' Nain was already putting tea in the pot, not waiting for my reply.

She put a half-full glass bottle of milk, two mugs, some sugar cubes and a heatproof mat for the teapot in front of me.

To my surprise, when the teapot was ready she brought it over and sat down opposite me. Usually, in the mornings, Taid and us visitors ate and drank and Nain was a constant blur of activity around us, wiping and refilling and trying to persuade me to eat a sausage because the pig it was made out of had a 'very lovely life'.

'Now, my love, I'm glad you're up, because I've been wanting to have a chat with you.' While on the surface they couldn't have been more different, in that moment she was so much like Mum. I recognized all the signs of a Williams matriarch getting ready to impart some important advice. I was starting to see what Aretha meant when she talked about families and albums.

'You've not been yourself these past few days and I'm wondering if it has anything to do with . . .' She raised her eyes upwards to indicate the place where Aretha was still asleep, two floors above us.

'Don't you like her?' I blurted out, anticipating a negative answer and wondering how I would feel if it came.

'Whether or not I like your friend is not the point,' Nain stated, which startled me. She was usually quick to pronounce judgment on people she didn't 'take to', declaring them ill-mannered, self-absorbed or, the worst insult she could ever bestow upon a human, 'lazy'.

'This is the first time you've bought a friend to meet us, so she must be important to you,' she continued, making me wonder if she'd gone down the same assuming-Aretha-and-I-were dating route Mum and Hugh had. 'I said to Taid before you came, I'm so glad you're making good friends, at last.'

Ooof. That smarted.

'And I said to him, "you know what, Taid?", I said, 'I don't care what this friend is like. I don't care if she has three heads!"'

Please, please don't say 'I wouldn't care if she was black, white or purple', I prayed, silently. This was not a good time to discover Nain was a racist who'd made an exception for my brown self because we're related. Thankfully, she did not.

'I told Taid I wouldn't be watching her, whoever she was. I'd be watching you. I wanted you to be yourself, I did. Because that's the sign of a good relationship – whether you're friends or whatever else it is. You know it's right if you can be yourself. And right now, Llewella, you're not yourself. You turned up here looking so small. All thin and quiet and nervous, you were. So what's wrong? And tell me honest because I'll know if you're lying.'

It was such a kind, insightful thing to say and it was so overwhelming to think of my nain – my strong, capable nain – taking the time to think about and notice all of this that I immediately burst into tears. I tried to put my head inside my pyjama top, embarrassed at my sudden show of emotion, but Nain gently pulled my hand away.

'There, there, my lovely,' she soothed. 'It'll be all right.' Then, reaching for one of her favourite phrases, she added, 'Nothing's insurmountable apart from death. Tell me what's wrong.'

It all came tumbling out, then. I told Nain about giving up Loo Reviews and my part in *Merchant* and how whenever I thought about someone else playing Antonio it made my heart ache. I told her about all the money and time and energy I'd put into Aretha and Loo and how I couldn't turn my back on it now, even though it wasn't working. I told her about the audition for *English Breakfast!* and how I wanted it so badly, but felt like I couldn't pursue it because I'd only got the opportunity through unearned privilege.

I didn't stop to think about whether my elderly grandmother, who lived out in the sticks and thought Instagram was a brand of kitchen scales, really understood the dilemmas I was wrangling with. Whether or not Nain had any advice of value to offer, it felt good just to get it all out.

When I'd finished, Nain went to get me a hanky so I could blow my nose. Then we sat and drank our tea while I calmed down a bit. Eventually, she spoke.

'Do they teach you, at school, about when the gay people supported the miners?'

'Uhm, no. I don't think so.'

'Well, it was brilliant, it was. It was back in 1984, before you were born, little one. And Margaret Thatcher had closed all the mines. It devastated us in Wales. All those men, who thought they had a job for life, no longer able to support their families. Whole communities destroyed. A right bitch, that Thatcher was.'

I gasped. Nain ever, ever swore.

'She took away the power of the unions, so we couldn't even ask them to try and help those families. Then, one day, this camper van turned up in the Dulais valley. It was full of gays and lesbians from London, it was, and they had eleven thousand pounds with them. That was an unimaginably large amount of money, in those days. They'd raised it by collecting for the miners and come to drop it off directly. It was the biggest donation they'd had from anyone.'

I was not at all sure how this story was relevant to my life, but was fascinated nonetheless.

'That was the beginning of an alliance. Welsh miners from the Swansea valleys travelled to London to do the Pride parade the following year. It was quite something, these traditional men who'd never knowingly met a gay person in their life, going to protest for their rights. You wouldn't look at those two groups of people and think they had anything in common. But they were both fighting against the government and they knew they'd be stronger together.'

'That's amazing,' I said, wondering why Mr Copeland spent weeks on end teaching us about Henry VIII's marauding penis when there was history like this to be learned.

'The point is,' Nain continued, 'we all have our struggles. We could spend a long time sitting here at this table debating who had it worse – the miners who lost their livelihoods and didn't know how to do anything else, or those people being beaten and spat at in the streets just for being who they were, but what mattered in the end was that they supported each other.'

'So, are you saying I should have tried harder to get Aretha on TV with me?' I asked, trying to process what this meant for my situation.

'No. That's not what I'm saying. You've always been the same.' Nain smiled at me fondly. 'Ever so opinionated and ready for a fight, but only because you couldn't bear for anything to be unfair. That's what we love about you. But you can't change everything all at once.'

'But if I take this slot on TV . . . I'm stealing it from

202

another person, who is darker skinned or poorer than me. I'm maintaining the status quo!' I argued.

'What nonsense!' Nain was cross, now. 'If anything, they're more likely to hire someone whiter and richer than you!' She sighed, clearly exasperated but making an effort to remain calm. 'Look here. Yes, your mother has done well for herself and you've got a bit of money, now. And yes, I suppose Aretha looks more mixed race than you do, what with her hair, and that might mean some people are nicer to you. And I'm proud of you, I really am, for recognising that. But ask yourself this – if you want to be able to change things, are you in a better position to do that now, sitting crying at this table, or if people were seeing you on the telly all the time?'

'I guess . . . if I had a platform and a bit of influence, that would be better,' I conceded, sniffing away the last of my tears.

'Well, exactly. You have to think of it as an opportunity to get in the tent. And you know what they say – it's better to be in the tent, pissing out.'

I couldn't believe it – two swears in one conversation. I stared at Nain in astonishment. She smiled, then sighed.

'Who knows where this could lead? One day you could be in a position to hire all the Black and brown people and gay people and Welsh people!' Nain raised her mug of tea at this, in a 'cheers'. 'And Llewella' – she dipped her head to catch my eye – 'they wouldn't have offered you this chance if they didn't think you deserved it. You're an excellent writer and speaker. And before you think it, I'm not just saying that because I'm your nain.'

I opened my mouth to protest then closed it again, letting Nain's words sink in for a moment.

'Now, what would you like for breakfast?' she said.

I blinked, looking around the kitchen and noticing that everything seemed brighter. I was breathing normally for the first time in ages and the lump in my throat had diminished to the size of a pea. That feeling of relief, I realised, was because I had allowed myself to entertain the idea that Nain might be right. What if I did deserve this chance? What if the best thing I could do was grasp it with both hands, see where it took me and remember to give a leg up to people less lucky when I got there?

The more I thought about it, the more the hope Nain had planted grew until it had bloomed within me, filling me with optimism and certainty. I had to do this. I'd hate myself if I didn't.

I decided I'd phone Jess on Nain and Taid's landline later that morning. The grace period she'd given me to think her offer over had only just expired, so I hoped she'd be pleased to hear from me.

Now, the only obstacle was breaking the news to Aretha.

Chapter 24

In theory, I knew it would be best to put off talking to Aretha about my U-turn over *English Breakfast!* until after our night out in Bristol. I knew her reaction wasn't likely to be positive and I didn't want to sully what should be a fun occasion. Not to mention that this was our last chance to let off steam before the summer term, which was famous for shit-getting-real on the exams front.

Unfortunately, my anxiety wasn't amenable to logic. I felt like if I didn't tell Aretha straight away (and then find a way to make her OK with it) my internal organs would burst out and explode all over the floor. As we sat on the coach which took us to Cardiff train station, where we would change for Bristol, I did my best to give the impression of cheerfulness. I was nodding, smiling, approving captions to go with the pictures we'd taken at Nain and Taid's, but my mind was coming up with potential ways of broaching the subject.

In the end, the words jumped out of my throat of their own accord.

'Aretha,' I began, once we were settled on the train. Unsurprisingly, she snapped to attention. (When do you ever say your friends' names out loud, really?) 'I need to talk to you about something.'

She just looked at me, eerily still. I took a deep breath.

'I've been thinking about *English Breakfast!* and whether, actually, it might be a really good thing for me to do. I know what you said about opportunities being given to people who look like me, but if I keep turning them down I won't be able to influence anything and make sure in the future they're given to people who look . . . you know . . . like you.'

I'd said it wrong. I wanted to take my words back, pluck them out of the air, put them in my mouth and swallow them back down. But I couldn't. They were out there now.

'Well, now I know,' Aretha replied, after an excruciating silence.

'What does that mean?' I asked, only half-wanting to know the answer.

'You've made it very clear where your priorities are. And that's cool. Good to know.' She crossed her arms, sat back in her seat and looked pointedly out of the train window. An awkward silence followed.

'It's not that I don't value our friendship, or I'm not committed to our brand,' I replied, eventually.

'No, no!' Aretha interrupted, faux-breezy. 'It's just you value this TV thing more. I get it, like I said. And I'll know what to do from now on.'

I had no idea what that meant, but I didn't like the sound of it.

This part of our journey was less than an hour, but it felt like an eternity. Aretha was staring at her phone, her thumb a blur as she typed who knows what to god knows who and refused to meet my eye. After asking her if she wanted anything from the snack trolley and receiving a curt 'no thanks' in response, I gave up and tried to do the same, flicking aimlessly between Instagram, emails and our blog.

I looked at a picture of Aretha and me out walking in the valleys with Ifan. Taid had taken it after getting to grips with the rudiments of camera-phone technology, courtesy of the crash course I'd given him.

I still can't believe you can record a video using your telephone. Marvellous, he'd breathed, reverentially.

Lately, when I'd looked at pictures of myself, my eyes were drawn straight to my stomach, searching for evidence that I hadn't dreamed the past six months and the fat which used to sit around my middle was, in fact, gone. I'd lie in bed at night, unable to sleep, scrutinising pic after pic, scouring for any sign that the old Llewella, fleshy and lumbering, was re-emerging. I'd even edited one shot to smooth out a fold in my top which made it look as though I had a roll of fat just above my belly button. I still felt ashamed whenever I thought about that. Once, we'd been asked to pick a topic to do a speech in English and I'd chosen the way Photoshopped images on social media affect our self-esteem. I'd become part of the problem.

This time, I dragged my eyes away from my stomach and forced myself to look at my face. I saw what Nain had been talking about at the kitchen table. My teeth looked too big for my mouth. I was smiling, but somehow also looked sad. Sad, tired and, as Nain had said, 'small'.

I could cover myself in layers of foundation and concealer, contour and highlight. I could plump my hair and apply false eyelashes. I could force myself to laugh and to give the impression I was living my best, most glamorous and fun-filled life. But unless something changed, this girl, the one staring back at me from the screen, would always be underneath.

'Exit! There!' I shouted, pleased at having spotted the sign pointing to the way out, after Aretha and I got off the train at Bristol.

'Listen, babes,' Aretha began, grabbing my arm and leading me to an empty bench at the side of the platform. 'I've been thinking and I've decided it's best if you don't come tonight. I've checked the timetable' – she gestured towards her phone – 'and there's a train back to London in twenty minutes you can catch if you hurry.'

'Oh. Uhm. OK,' I said. I was too blindsided to argue. Besides, what choice did I have, really? It was her brother, her night, so – her decision.

'It's just, I have to have a difficult conversation with Ziek. And, I guess, Steph,' she went on, 'and it might be awkward if you're there.'

'OK.' I was completely lost for words and we sat in silence for a moment, both staring at a trail of pigeon poo on the ground in front of us.

'Don't you want to know what I need to talk to them about?' Aretha prompted, after a while.

'I wasn't sure if you wanted to tell me.'

'Well, actually' – Aretha's tone was sharp – 'there's a lot going on for me right now.'

She was implying that I should have noticed something was wrong and asked her about it. But wasn't that exactly what I'd tried to do at Nain and Taid's? And I'd been told Aretha's strange mood was because my grandparents were 'too much' ...

'I'm bipolar,' Aretha blurted out.

I tried to hide my shock, thinking about how unhelpful other people's shock had been when I'd opened up to them about my own mental illness. Part of me was relieved. At least mental health issues were something I had experience of – another thing Aretha and I now had in common. As awful as they could be, this might cement our friendship. I scrabbled for something positive or hopeful to say.

'I met some people with bipolar disorder when I was getting therapy. You know, first time. And there were loads of ways they had found to manage it. There's really good meds now—'

'Oh, I'm not going to take pills,' Aretha interrupted. 'I was reading up about meds for psychosis on this forum and it said they stop you being creative. And, as you know, music is the most important thing to me in the world. I'm not going to sacrifice that. I'm going to have to find a way to deal with it without help.'

'Well, you don't have to take meds, I guess. I mean, I don't know, obviously because I'm not a professional, but I think you can do other stuff as long as you have medical supervision. Who did you talk to at the surgery? My GP – that's Dr Abraham – is really good on mental health stuff. You could talk to him—'

'You didn't listen,' Aretha interjected, calmly. 'I am not going to let my personality be squashed by men in white coats. My doctor doesn't know. No one does. Apart from Maddy.'

'Then . . . how do you know you're bipolar?' I asked, confusedly.

'I have all the symptoms. Like, one day I feel like the most confident person in the world. Then, the next day I feel really depressed. That's manic depression,' she enunciated each syllable, like I was too much of an idiot to understand.

I curbed the impulse to correct her, to remind her that people didn't use the term 'manic depression' any more, and instead tried to focus on being helpful.

'You need to be diagnosed to get support,' I countered. 'And … if you haven't been seen by a doctor it could be something else. My therapist says—'

'Why would you think I care what your therapist says?' she snapped. 'I didn't tell you because I want you to fix me. I told you because I thought you might be a bit more understanding and give me a break, for once.'

'I'm … I'm sorry. I do understand—'

'Well, actually, you don't!' Aretha screeched, causing several heads along the platform to turn as I shrank into my hoodie. 'You think because you have "anxiety"' – she actually made air quotes with her fingers – 'you understand everything. Bipolar is a serious condition. A real mental illness. Something people really suffer with. And you would THINK, after how understanding I've been of your ISSUES you would show me the same respect!'

I didn't trust myself to speak. Everything I said was coming out wrong and seemed only to make Aretha angrier. So instead I just stared at her shoes, trying to focus on breathing normally.

After a while, I found a tiny sliver of my voice. 'OK, well, tell me what you need,' I tried.

'I need you to stop questioning me!' Aretha retorted. 'I need you to support me LIKE FRIENDS DO.'

The problem was, that was what I thought I had been doing.

I'd responded the way I wished other people had when I was sick – telling her it was going to be OK, letting her know she wasn't alone, making practical suggestions instead of just wringing my hands together and telling her how terrible it must be for her. But this clearly wasn't the type of support Aretha wanted. I was messing it up. I wracked my brains, trying to work out how I could do a better job. Aretha sighed.

'Look, you're obviously in shock. This is big news. Why don't we talk about it properly back in Surrey, yeah? You've got to get a ticket and you'll miss your train if you don't hurry. And I have to go meet my brother. He's just text to say he's in the car park.'

And with that she stood abruptly and stalked away, leaving me with a sixty-pound train ticket to buy and a whole lot of thoughts to unravel.

Summer Term

'Thou art too wild, too rude and bold of voice;
Parts that become thee happily enough
And in such eyes as ours appear not faults;
But where thou art not known, why, there they show
Something too liberal.'

The Merchant of Venice
Act 2, Scene 2

Chapter 25

On the first day of term, Isobel and Kara practically skidded up to me in the common room with massive (and, I won't lie, fairly rare) grins on their faces.

'We've got it!' Isobel declared, bouncing on the balls of her feet.

'Great!' I replied. 'What, though?'

'The school motto, of course!' Kara laughed.

'Oh, right!' I smacked myself on the forehead in what I hoped was a sufficiently self-deprecating gesture. In an effort to catch up on my studies, I'd been MIA for the last few student council meetings and with everything else that had been going on, the campaign to change the crest had slipped my mind. I was actually quite angry with myself for letting it slide – it was a chance to leave a legacy and make a difference.

'Go on . . .' I encouraged, knowing they were deliberately holding back in order to be as dramatic as possible.

'Facta non verba,' they said in unison.

Isobel turned her notebook round, where the words were sketched out as a crest and I traced them with my finger.

'So that's . . . behaviour . . . not . . .' I wondered aloud, trying to translate on the hoof.

'Words!' Kara finished for me. 'Or – actions speak louder than words'. It was my idea, actually. What do you think?'

'I like it,' I replied, honestly. 'Have you put it to the whole council?'

'Yup, we've voted on it already. It was unanimous. But since it was your idea to change the crest, we wanted to check you were happy before we took it to Ms Tidwell.'

Isobel was practically vibrating now, her eyes sparkling. I'd forgotten how that felt – to be so excited about a project it energises you as though you are a solar-powered battery soaking up the sun. When was the last time I'd felt that way about something? Maybe *English Breakfast!*, but not much else lately.

'I'll email you and let you know what Ms Tidwell says,' Kara said, walking away from me backwards as the bell rang shrilly, announcing first period.

Facta non verba.

I stood hugging my folder to my chest for a few minutes after that, turning the new motto over in my mind. I couldn't put my finger on why I felt so freaked out. I felt as though my brain was trying to tell me something, to mark the moment as significant. But the harder I grasped for it, the more evasive it became.

It was Aretha who pulled me out of my reverie.

'Babes! Woo!' She waved in front of my face, smiling indulgently, as though I was an extremely elderly person she had the burden of looking after. 'We're late for English.'

The last time I'd seen her, she'd been screaming at me at Bristol train station. This had, apparently, been forgotten. She looped her arm through mine and marched me out into the throngs of students scurrying along the corridors, chatting loudly and cheerfully about the 'amazing' night she'd had with Ziek and Steph on Friday and how she was 'sorry I'd missed it' along the way.

'But, GOOD NEWS!' she exclaimed, stopping abruptly outside the wood and glass-panelled door of our English classroom and putting both hands on my upper arms. 'It's my birthday in four weeks and it's going to be HUGE!'

'Yay!' I did a thumbs up, forcing myself to smile. Aretha giggled.

'And as my best mate, it's your job to help me plan it.'

Double yay, I thought, ever-so-sarcastically, then caught myself. I was making an effort to smooth things over, so it was important I didn't let my distaste for the idea show.

I'd spent all weekend turning over what Aretha had said on the station platform, having imaginary conversations with her in the mirror above the bathroom sink every time I went for a wee (which, with the anxiety, was often). I had reached the point where I genuinely felt like I might go mad, having those same, endless, washing-machine style thoughts and never reaching a satisfactory conclusion.

Linda had taught me I should 'channel my anxious energy into something productive' when I felt like this. So I began looking up symptoms of bipolar disorder on charity websites, which led me to their 'advice for friends and family' pages and forums.

I'd been struck by a phrase which kept coming up – knight's-move thinking. So-called because it mimics the way a knight's chess piece moves diagonally across a board. Knight's-move thinking is when someone doesn't reach the conclusions of a person thinking in the usual, linear way, but instead goes to places which could, from the outside, seem confusing or irrational. In one of the chatrooms I visited, the mum of a teenage boy with bipolar disorder described sending him out to buy a bag of potatoes for dinner and him returning two hours later brandishing an empty china jug. They were going to eat roast potatoes with gravy and gravy belongs in a jug – somewhere along the line, the jug turned into the item she had originally requested, in his head.

I thought back to all the times Aretha's responses had shocked or baffled me. With the benefit of my new knowledge, they made more sense. All the advice said you should never challenge a bipolar person's delusions, but instead show genuine curiosity and empathy. It wasn't my job to try and find a shared reality Aretha and I could agree on – a 'right and wrong'; a mutual understanding of the world around us. If I did so, I'd push her away. It *was* my job to hold Aretha's hand through whatever upside down, *Alice in Wonderland* territory her mind was taking her into. It meant letting go of my understanding of reality and fitting myself into hers.

Her occasional cruel or thoughtless acts weren't deliberate. None of this was her fault. I kept thinking about what Aretha had yelled at me during our last, fraught exchange in Bristol. *I need you to stop questioning me!*

So, I had decided, I would do exactly that. I'd fight my anxious nature and allow myself to go whichever way the winds of Aretha's mind blew us. I knew how lonely mental illness could be, so however hurtful Aretha's behaviour, I wanted to support her.

Still, the prospect of planning a birthday celebration filled me with cold dread. I've never really seen the point of making a huge deal out of birthdays. I mean, why do we even celebrate something so utterly mundane as being born? Literally every human alive has done it, so it's not like it's a major achievement.

'Big' birthdays are a particular nightmare. When my eighteenth rolled around in late March, Mum had bought me a beautiful Tag Heuer watch. I'd put it in a drawer, not trusting myself to wear it without smashing it or leaving it on a train. Occasionally I would take it out and stroke its beautiful white-and-chrome face, before nestling it back carefully in its velvet presentation box, to wait until I was sophisticated and graceful enough to wear it. Mum, Hugh and I had rainbow cake and a glass of prosecco after dinner and that was the extent of it. I'm not sure anyone else even knew. It was perfect.

I'm aware, of course, that I'm in a minority of people who feel this way. Most people want to do something significant on their eighteenth, in particular. My year group mostly opted to hire out Oceana, the local nightclub. I sometimes watched the videos of these events on socials. They showed my classmates silly-drunk on Archers and lemonade and dancing fanny-first in front of their horrified parents, before throwing up in an alley.

Aretha clearly had bigger plans.

Grace and Sam appeared from around a corner, strolling along in a nonchalant fashion in spite of also being late.

'Oh, hi, Aretha,' said Grace, as though I wasn't there. 'Can't wait for your birthday!' Then she blew a kiss before skipping away, whispering something to Sam, who laughed.

'OMG could she be any more fake?' Aretha said, as soon as she was out of earshot. 'Promise me, babe, that whatever we end up planning for my birthday, it'll be way better than hers.'

'Absolutely.' I mustered a smile which belied the complete lack of confidence I felt in my ability to keep my promise.

Chapter 26

Mercifully, my involvement in Aretha's birthday planning was minimal, in the end. A friend of Maddy's (ridiculously posh) boyfriend Seb gave her cut-price access to a stately home, about forty-five minutes' drive away in rural Surrey. Aretha had asked us to contribute £100 each, which would pay for a room for the night and dinner. We'd been instructed to wear 1920s *Peaky Blinder*-style clothes, in keeping with the grandeur of our surroundings.

As my taxi trawled down the long driveway, a Gothic-looking building encircled by immaculate lawns came into view. I tried to swallow my nerves. I didn't know exactly who else was invited and wasn't sure if I'd know anyone other than Aretha and Maddy. I'd forced myself to stay home in the morning and finish some history coursework, meaning I'd had to decline their invitation to travel up with them the previous night and spend all day getting ready together. Aretha and I were sharing a room and Maddy and Seb were going to be next door.

When I eventually navigated my way through the musty corridors filled with portraits of earls and dukes in gilt frames and found our plush (if spooky) bedroom, it looked like a bomb had gone off in it. There were piles of clothes, make-up and half-drunk glasses of champagne everywhere. As I took in the scene, I began to wish like anything I could just turn away and go home.

'BAAAAAAAAAAAAABES!' Maddy spotted me first and threw her arms around me. It was a crushingly tight hug, more like one a close family member would give if you'd just come back from war than suitable for a casual acquaintance.

'Hi' I laughed nervously, trying to extract myself. 'Hey, Aretha.' I waved to my friend, who was sitting on a windowsill on the opposite side of the room, overlooking the vast grounds. 'Happy birthday! Where should I put my stuff?'

'Left-hand bed' she said, without turning her head. 'Oh my god, I think it's actually going to rain. Can you believe it? That *never* happens on my birthday.'

'Still, we're going to be inside all evening, aren't we?' I asked, confused.

'That's kind of not the point,' Aretha replied, crossly.

I heaved my suitcase on to the bed. It was stuffed with a fake fur bolero belonging to Mum, some T-bar heels I'd found in the sales and a string of pearls I'd managed to obtain for a fiver from a charity shop. I hoped that, when paired with my trusty jumpsuit, the overall aesthetic would be suitably 'twenties'.

There was also Aretha's gift. Giving presents was one of my favourite things. I loved the whole process – spending ages searching for the perfect item, wrapping it beautifully using oodles of curling ribbon and, most of all, seeing the recipient's face when they opened it. I carefully extracted the signed, framed print of Aretha Franklin I'd found on eBay and handed it to my Aretha with reverence.

'Thanks babe. I'll open it later,' she said, tossing it on top of the debris on her bed. 'I'm kind of stressed right now.

My brother is running late. I just spoke to him on the phone. It won't be a proper birthday without him.'

'Oh, no. But he's on his way?' I asked.

'Yes. Driving from Bristol.'

'Who else is coming?'

Aretha sighed impatiently. She really was in a peculiar mood.

'My parents and Steph are already here. A whole bunch of my cousins. I have a zillion of them. Then there's Maddy and Seb, obviously. Oli, Ava, Cassy, Henry and Riley from college. Oh, and Grace and Sam.'

'From St Edith's?' I asked, aghast.

'Yeah. Why, is that a problem?'

'No. I'm just surprised. I didn't think you were friends'

'You don't own me, Loo. I do occasionally have interactions with people in sixth form who aren't you,' she retorted, rolling her shoulders back and flicking her wig, a jet-black crimped bob, haughtily.

'Anyway,' Maddy exclaimed brightly. 'Have a glass of champs, Loo. You have some catching up to do!'

'That rhymes. You're rapping!' I made a pathetic joke, hoping to lighten the mood and dispel the palpable grey cloud which had settled around Aretha.

Maddy and I both forced out a chuckle.

'Oh, by the way,' Aretha said. 'I wanted to talk to you about Oli. So there's no . . . misunderstandings tonight'.

'Oli? Your friend from college?' I asked, suddenly remembering that we'd sent him that selfie, months ago now, during our first night out together. Aretha had never heard back as far as I knew and with everything else going on I'd forgotten to ask.

'Yeah, uhm. I told him how excited you were that he thought you were pretty . . . And he said to tell you he hadn't really meant to start anything. It was just a casual comment. Okay?'

'Oh. Right. Okay,' I said, feeling a bit deflated but not really understanding why. I remembered looking at Oli's Instagram the night after Giuseppe's and thinking he was cute, but it wasn't like I was in love with him.

'Also, when he saw the shoot photos he said you looked like . . . you'd eat him alive!' Aretha continued, laughing.

'What, the one of me with the red lipstick?'

'Yeah . . .' Aretha confirmed, 'and that slutty dress Crystal knocked up. You did look *quite* the femme fatale!' She put on a silly voice. 'I tried to explain that you don't really look like that but . . . Look, can I be honest with you?'

I nodded.

'I actually have thought for a while now that Oli has a crush on me . . . and I'm so sorry, babe, I never would have put you in that position if I'd realised earlier, but I think he was using you to get closer to me.'

'Boys! They're all wild for Aretha. It's best not even to try and compete,' said Maddy, refilling the flute of champagne I'd somehow downed without noticing. 'Hey, do you want a little livener?' she asked.

'A what?'

'You know.' She put one finger on the side of her nose and sniffed. She was asking me if I wanted drugs, I realised abruptly.

'Actually,' I replied, half my mind still focused on trying to make sense of the conversation about Oli. 'I'm really anti-drugs. I did do some poppers, once, but I regret it. I watched this documentary, actually, about the drug trade—'

'Ha! Babe! You are hilarious!' Maddy interrupted. 'Isn't she hilarious, Reeth?'

'Oh my god. Babe.' Aretha's tone was sharp. 'Don't try and pretend you didn't know. Maddy would never have put angel dust in your drink if you hadn't consented. She isn't like that.'

I reeled, as the reality of what I was being told dawned on me. That Angel Dust cocktail, the one that had made me feel so serene and full of love for Aretha, wasn't just alcohol. There were all kinds of implications to this and I didn't have the bandwidth to deal with them right now. So, I just gulped down some more champagne, sure that the lump in my throat must now be visible, like a bullfrog's, from all the emotion I was swallowing down with it.

An hour later, I was in my half-arsed twenties cosplay. I'd had to put a bulldog clip at the back of the jumpsuit to pull it in at the waist and avoid looking like I was drowning in it.

I'd drunk three glasses of champagne on an empty stomach and the world was blurry around the edges. We'd moved downstairs, and were sitting beneath a brass chandelier around several oak dining tables. I was chatting to Henry (who was sat to my right) while studiously avoiding Oli (sitting to Henry's right).

'It's weird seeing you in real life after seeing you on your blog. I feel like I know you already,' Henry was saying.

'Oh . . . yeah! Well . . .' How did you answer that? 'It's lovely to meet you in person!' I finished, somewhat lamely.

Ziek still hadn't arrived, but the rest of us were waiting for our starters to be served. There were about forty of us in total – Aretha really did have a spectacular amount of cousins – and the air was filled with the buzz of chatter and laughter. The birthday girl didn't seem to be able to get into the party vibe, though. She was bellowing orders at the waiting staff, circling the tables prodding people and asking if they were having a good time (but in a shouty way which suggested she might kill you and serve you as the main course if you said no).

After a while, she came over to her seat next to mine, but remained standing behind it, craning her neck and scanning the room while standing on tiptoe. Even once our soups had been served, she kept leaping up, running to the side of the room to look out of the window for Ziek's car, leaving hers virtually untouched.

Ziek arrived just as our bowls were being taken away. There followed a brief interlude where it transpired a place hadn't been set for him and one of the waiters was sent to find him a chair.

'They're just so incompetent! I'm having such a shit birthday,' Aretha huffed.

I looked around at her assembled friends and family, some of whom had travelled miles and paid hundreds of pounds to be here to celebrate with her and hoped they hadn't overheard. Then Delroy gently tapped the side of his wine glass with a spoon and everyone, including Aretha, was silent.

'Thank you all for being here to celebrate my little girl's eighteenth,' he said. 'I don't know where the time has gone. It seems like only a few days ago I was teaching her to ride her little pink bike with stabilisers—'

'That was a few days ago!' Maddy, who was now very drunk, heckled.

Delroy made a single 'ha' sound, before continuing.

'I'm very proud of the young woman you have become,' he said, looking directly at Aretha. 'You are strong, determined and talented and I know you are destined for great things.'

He raised his glass, inviting us all to do the same. It was such a tender moment and Delroy's eyes were filled with pride and affection. I felt like I was going to cry. I hastily wiped the beginnings of my tears away, not wanting to do anything which might draw attention to myself and evoke Aretha's ire.

'I'm sure Aretha has a few things she'd like to say herself...' Delroy continued, gesturing at her to stand.

Aretha leapt up like a jack-in-the-box, champagne flute held aloft.

'Thanks, Daddy,' she began. 'You know, you're right. I can be so focused on what I want to achieve. It means sometimes I don't take a minute to smell the roses and appreciate what I have. I'm so excited to be recording an EP with the brilliant Stuart Simpson, from Simpson Productions.' She raised her glass in the direction of a table in the far corner of the room, where Stu the Birdman, who I hadn't realised was there, stood up and took a bow.

'As you all know, music is everything to me, so I hope you'll all look out for updates and promote the EP when it lands. But I'm also thankful for so much more. My wonderful family and brilliant friends...'

Did she think she was at the Grammys? I was cringing on her behalf, but as I looked around the room everyone else was either genuinely rapt or doing a great job of pretending they were. It was only me who seemed to find the speech embarrassing.

Obviously it was me, not Aretha, that was the odd one, here. I tuned back in, hoping I looked interested and supportive.

' . . . particularly, I'm grateful for my best friend. You've only been properly in my life for a while, but I already can't imagine being without you.'

Dear God, I know I never pray because I technically don't believe in you, but if you do happen to exist and are listening, please don't let her make me stand up, I thought. I shrank down into my fake-fur shrug, hoping I'd discover a Narnia inside it I could crawl into.

'Thanks for always being there for me and being the best mate a gal could ever ask for . . .' Aretha turned towards me and I thought if it was possible to die of humiliation I might very well expire there and then. Still, it was nice to have our best-friend status reaffirmed. And publicly, too. Perhaps we would be OK.

' . . . here's to Maddy,' she finished.

I felt all the energy drain from my body in an instant, like I was a balloon that had just been popped. Maddy, who was sitting a few seats to my left and dressed top-to-toe in fabulous, authentic vintage got to her feet, mouthing *I love you*.

I was stunned, yet found myself joining in with the applause as Aretha sat down. Waiters re-emerged bearing plates of roast beef. I knew somehow that Aretha wouldn't have bothered to request something pescetarian for me.

'Wow,' said Henry, 'that must have stung.'

'What?' I feigned ignorance.

'Well, you have, like, literally a business together and you didn't even get a mention.' He gestured with a nod of his head towards Aretha.

'It's OK, I wasn't expecting one.' Only half of this was true –

I hadn't been expecting anything, but what had just happened was very far from okay.

I eyed my plate forlornly as it was placed in front of me. The juices from the meat had seeped over everything, meaning I couldn't even eat the vegetables. I was so hungry. And so tired. I'd been hungry and tired for a while, I realised. And I was tired of being hungry and tired.

'So, what are you into, other than fashion and feminism?' Bless Henry, still trying to make a conversation happen, despite my obvious reluctance.

'I'm not really into fashion, if I'm honest. That's Aretha's thing,' I replied, making an effort to focus. 'I ...' I paused. What was I passionate about? For a moment, I couldn't remember. 'I'm a writer, really,' I said, at last. 'Although I like acting, too.'

'That's cool,' Henry replied.

'What about you?' I deflected, thinking he might ask me what productions I'd been in and desperate to avoid thinking about *Merchant*.

'Well, you know Aretha and I met at music college?' I nodded. 'I play piano and keys. I'm in a band. We sort of have a Muse-meets-Queens of the Stone Age sound going on.'

'Nice,' I said, although I didn't really know what that would sound like.

'Yeah, we're hoping to get out there and do more gigs. Maybe some festivals. Hey, did Aretha tell you about when she won a competition to go on stage with Brass Traps at Glastonbury last year?'

She had and she hadn't. But now was not the time to try and unravel the discrepancy.

'No, she didn't,' I lied, hoping Henry would tell me more.

'Ah, man, it was sweet,' Henry said. 'Brass Traps sent one of their unfinished tracks and the singers in the year had a competition to come up with the backing vocal. Whoever's composition was their favourite got to go and perform it with them. They do it every year, with different bands.'

'So . . . just the one performance?'

Henry looked at me quizzically. 'Well, yeah . . . but it's a pretty big deal, you know, performing at Glastonbury.'

'I know.'

'I'm really surprised Aretha didn't mention it. I thought you guys were really tight?'

'Me too,' I replied, miserably.

Chapter 27

'So, what's the problem?' Linda asked, leaning forward in her squishy armchair and surveying me over the rim of her glasses.

It was the same question I'd been asking myself for weeks now, as I viewed Aretha's behaviour through a post-birthday lens.

I couldn't be in this friendship any more, of that I was certain. I couldn't give Aretha the support she needed while I was struggling with my own mental health. I couldn't just gloss over her lies while every perceived misdemeanour of mine was used against me. I couldn't keep investing when the status of best friend was only granted when she needed me for something. I knew getting out of this toxic dynamic would ultimately be worth sacrificing the time and money I'd put into Aretha and Loo. I felt like I was suffocating under the weight of it all.

Yet, somehow, I just couldn't bring myself to end it.

'I . . . don't know . . .' I replied, resisting the urge to add, 'if I did know I wouldn't need a therapist to help me work it out, would I?' It wasn't Linda's fault I'd got myself into such a mess. 'I guess there's a part of me that wonders whether we can salvage it? Go back to how we were?'

'We've discussed in quite a bit of depth why that's very unlikely to happen.' Linda could be very cutting if she thought I wasn't trying hard enough. 'Aside from that, are there any other reasons?'

There were, but I knew they were illogical, which made them too embarrassing to say out loud. I was aware of Aretha's ability to rewrite history. I knew she'd package up our story in a different way, so it seemed like her behaviour was flawless and she was beyond reproach. I was worried about what she would tell her parents, Ziek, Steph, the other people at school.

Aretha's self-diagnosis had changed everything. Now, if I 'dumped' her, I'd be the heartless bitch who abandoned a friend when she was struggling with her mental health . . . A friend who really ought to know better, having gone through mental illness herself.

'You can say whatever it is you're thinking, you know,' Linda said gently, after we'd sat in silence for a moment or two.

I took a deep breath and told her half the truth. 'I don't want to desert Aretha when she's going through a tough time with her mental health. Lots of people distanced themselves from me when I was diagnosed and it really hurt. I . . . I don't want to be that person.'

Linda considered this for a moment. 'You know the difference between a reason and an excuse, right?'

'Of course.' A child could tell you that.

'Does the possible reason for Aretha's bad behaviour towards you mean it's OK, then?' Linda asked.

'I don't know, if I'm honest. I read on all these websites that the best way to support someone with bipolar is not to question their view of the world. But it's ended up with . . . only *I* ever say sorry. And I know it's petty but it just seems so unfair. But then I think, if I force her to try and see things from my perspective, will I make her illness worse?'

'Let me ask you a question. If you were walking down a road and you saw someone in a big hole, crying for help, what would you do?'

'Uhm . . . I'd talk to them first. Let them know I'd seen them and I wasn't going to just leave them there,' I replied, thinking about how much I had wanted someone to do that for me when I was languishing in my own deep hole of anxiety. 'And then . . . I'd call the emergency services, maybe?'

'Great.' Linda nodded her approval. 'And what do you think would be the least helpful thing you could do, in that situation?'

It was a weird question, but she was obviously going somewhere with it.

'Uhm. I'm not sure. I suppose it would be to ignore them and carry on walking down the road?'

'That would be quite an unhelpful response, from the point of view of the person in the hole, but it's not actually the least helpful thing you could do.'

I frowned, trying to think of a less helpful course of action than refusing to acknowledge a human in dire need. 'The least helpful thing you could do would be to jump down into the hole with them. Then, there would be two of you in a hole. All you would have done is double the problem.' She sat back with her fingers intertwined, hands resting on her belly – her equivalent of a mic drop – while I attempted to absorb the ramifications of her words.

'When you first came to see me back in Year Ten, we discussed how there were some unresolved issues which might crop up unexpectedly in the future,' Linda continued, using

233

a strangely formal, almost legal tone as she read her notes from our earlier sessions. She always did this when she was 'recapping'. 'Then, at Christmas, you told me you had several episodes of relapse into anxiety. We later talked about how that was at least in part due to your friendship with Aretha, as well as the online brand you started together, which has increased your work load and left you unable to focus on your studies during a crucial year in your education. It has also meant you giving up other activities which are very important to you.'

It sounded pretty bad when she put it like that.

'Since then, Aretha has claimed to have mental health issues herself. Right now, you're both in a hole together. You've established that you can't support her whilst you're struggling and she certainly can't support you. The only thing you can do is concentrate on getting yourself out of the hole. And, unfortunately, if you're going to climb out it will involve distancing yourself from Aretha. At least for a while. You might feel differently when you're in a better head space.'

There was no arguing with what she was saying. But that didn't make the prospect of confronting Aretha any more appealing.

'I don't know how to talk to her about it,' I confessed, feeling the sudden and familiar urge to get it over with.

'Why don't you frame it the way I just have?' Linda meant well, but I wasn't sure Aretha had the patience for convoluted metaphors involving holes. 'If she is a true friend, she will understand.'

And, with that last statement, Linda had accidentally, yet neatly summarized my dilemma.

I knew it wasn't ideal to do it over the phone, but nonetheless found myself immediately reaching for mine as I left Linda's office. I had a missed call from Olivia. This had happened a couple of times in recent weeks, after I'd avoided her attempts to catch my eye in the common room. I didn't know whether Olivia wanted to make up, or to revisit the argument we'd had about Aretha. I did know I didn't have the brain space for whatever it was. I swiped the notification away.

I held the phone up to my face, wondering at what point I had become the type of person who walks along the pavement FaceTiming – the kind of dickhead I used to ridicule for their self-inflicted lack of spatial awareness. I wasn't sure whether or not I actually wanted Aretha to answer. Just as I had decided that, on balance, I'd rather she didn't, she picked up.

'Hey,' she said, more warmly than I'd expected. 'I was just about to call you. Where are you?'

'Just leaving therapy,' I admitted, shuddering at how small my voice sounded.

'Oh, that reminds me.' Aretha's face was suddenly serious. 'I was just reading a post on Reddit about how psychology is a conspiracy. We're meant to experience our feelings and psychologists teach us to numb them.' She stopped just short of adding, 'just to confirm why I'm not seeking professional help myself even though I'm definitely as sick as, if not more than, you.' We both understood the implication.

'Right,' was all I trusted myself to say.

'Anyway, the reason I wanted to talk to you' – Aretha papered over the tension, behaving as though it was she who had called

235

me and not the other way around – 'is I was chatting to Maddy and she said why don't I come with you next week when you do the live telly thing? You know, for moral support?'

This threw me totally. I wracked my brain, trying to think of a good, non-harsh-sounding excuse to refuse her offer. My stupid brain, however, fatigued from therapy and not expecting to be having this conversation, gave me absolutely nothing to work with.

'Ok, sure,' it instructed my mouth to say, instead.

Chapter 28

Three days later, Aretha and I were headed to the *English Breakfast!* studios.

When I phoned her from Wales, Jess had been delighted I'd changed my mind. We'd negotiated a schedule which would mean I'd film four reviews the first Saturday of every month, with one airing every Monday. This meant I didn't have to miss any sixth form. If the segment proved popular, we could talk about increasing it to a daily feature, but that would be much further down the line.

Jess seemed worried Mum might object. She told me parents often intervened when they thought a shot at fame might interfere with their children's education. She had clearly never spoken to a parent like Cerys. Mum gave her permission freely and joyfully, just like I knew she would.

I signed a complicated legal agreement, which Mum had looked over by her solicitor. While I owned the 'intellectual property' associated with Loo Reviews (i.e. it had been my idea), *English Breakfast!* owned the televised format and could use it in any way they wished, including selling clips on to other TV shows and putting them out on social media.

The most important part of the contract, the solicitor had emphasised, related to confidentiality. I wasn't allowed to tell anyone about what happened behind the scenes on *English Breakfast!* If I said or did anything which brought the show into disrepute, they could sue me for reputational damage. I wondered how I could possibly conduct myself in a way which would be deemed worse than Cyrus Peyton, who was regularly getting into social media spats with celebrities and was widely rumoured to be, as the tabloids put it, 'handsy' with female colleagues. I supposed it was all a question of power. I, as a newcomer, had none, so had to tow the line. Cyrus was a brand in and of himself, with an army of slavish fans who found a way to excuse and defend every offensive remark or action. Anything he did, no matter how outrageous, was therefore considered good publicity.

We were due to film the first Loo Review segment the following day and it would air on Monday. Before that, they wanted me to do a live interview with Cyrus and Jemima, to introduce me to their audience. It meant missing lessons, but as it was a one-off, Aretha and I pleaded extenuating circumstances and were granted permission by Ms Trebor, so long as we 'didn't make a habit of it'.

'You don't look very nervous,' Aretha said, side-eyeing me.

'Oh. I'm not really,' I replied, wondering if I should be.

Aretha crinkled her nose, studying me for a moment. 'You know you're likely to get shit from people after this, right?'

'Why?' I was alarmed. It wasn't like I was there to say or do anything particularly controversial.

'Goes with the territory.' Aretha responded casually, running her hands over her pleated mini skirt, as though to smooth it out. 'I looked it up. *English Breakfast!* has 1.3 million viewers on average, you're bound to say something which will piss off at least a couple of thousand of them. And people can find out all kinds of stuff about you – they dig up anything dodgy from your past, publish your address. Jemima gets death threats – she had to get extra security at her house and everything.'

And just like that, I was nervous as hell.

'Hello, ladies!' Kiara exclaimed when we collided with her in the cold grey stairwell leading up to the *English Breakfast!* make-up room. 'How are you, darling?'

'Great, thanks, how are you, lovely?' Aretha responded, as though the question had been aimed at her and she was taking the opportunity of catching up with an old mate. I recognised her smile as the one she used when she wanted to charm, the one I'd been spellbound by back in September.

'Big day for you, Llewella.' Kiara ignored the question, causing Aretha to look momentarily put out. 'Are you excited?'

I gulped. 'Yeah. I am excited. Also a bit nervous.' As though to emphasise my point, my voice came out as a squeak on the final syllable.

'Come here, bab.' Kiara wrapped me in another one of her comforting hugs. 'Listen, I heard the big cheeses loved your tape. They said you had "star quality".' Out of the corner of my eye, I saw Aretha shudder and turn her head to look pointedly out of the see-through pane in the centre of the door we'd just come through. 'You will smash it. And remember, it will fly by, so work out what you want to say in advance and just say it, whatever Cyrus and Jemima ask you. It's easy to get side-tracked and then before you know it, the interview's over and all you've done is have an argument.' She released me from her grip and I stepped back, reluctantly.

'Thank you so much. Were you on your way up?' I gestured at the staircase, indicating that she should go first.

'Oh, you go on and don't wait for me, duck,' Kiara insisted. 'I'm trying to shift some of this' – she gestured to her plus-size form, which was today clad in a rather fabulous embroidered magenta wrap dress – 'and get fitter, but I have to keep stopping on the stairs.'

I wasn't sure how to respond to this, but Kiara saved me the trouble by leaning towards me conspiratorially. 'You know when you're in a really hot bath and you stand up too soon? When you feel all light-headed and get those little spots in your vision? That's what it's like for me climbing stairs. It won't be forever, though. I'm working on it.' She winked.

'But you always seem so confident?' This from Aretha, who was now staring at Kiara with wide eyes.

'Oh, I am!' She chuckled, batting at something invisible in the air between us. 'Don't get me wrong, I'll never be a Skinny Minnie. I have polycystic ovaries, you see, which means I gain weight like that.' She snapped her fingers. 'But just because I'll never look like Cheryl Tweedy doesn't mean I shouldn't look after myself.'

'Well . . . good luck,' was all I could think to say in reply.

'Bless you, lovely. Now off you go and do your thing.' Kiara wiggled in a little 'good luck' dance.

As Aretha and I headed up the stairs, I smiled, thinking how much I liked Kiara and how she seemed to have a magic ability to make me feel better. But as soon as we were out of earshot, Aretha gripped the top of my arm.

'That was bollocks, you know,' she said.

'What was?' I asked, confused.

'What she said about having polycystic ovaries. That's just

the sort of excuse fat people always make, when everyone knows it's a simple question of eating locally sourced, plant-based produce and exercising regularly. There's no excuse to get yourself into that state.'

I blinked, aghast. Aretha didn't seem to notice. Before I could reply, one of the Britney-mic-ed, black-legging crew I was now so familiar with burst out into the corridor from one of the many doors on either side, saw us, put her finger to the speaker wedged into her ear and said, 'Ah, found her.'

'So, I'll just run through some of the questions Cyrus and Jemima will ask you, but remember it's a casual conversation, so try to forget the cameras are there and have fun.'

Jess was briefing me in the make-up room, where I was perched in front of the wall of mirrors, wearing a protective gown in shiny leopard print. An extravagantly made-up man with flame-orange hair, incongruously called Bernard, was applying winged eyeliner to my lids. A woman whose name I'd forgotten was simultaneously straightening my hair, while another kept running up to show me potential outfit choices (much to Bernard's annoyance, since I had to open my eyes in order to evaluate them).

'Hi, I'm Aretha, Llewella's best friend.' She'd emerged from where she had been flicking through newspapers at the side of the room and had her hand stuck out aggressively towards a startled looking Jess.

'How lovely . . .' Jess shook Aretha's hand politely. ' . . . for you to come along for moral support. Now—'

'Actually,' Aretha interrupted, 'Llewella and I started Loo

Reviews together.' If I hadn't been instructed to avoid moving my head on pain of death, I would have turned to gawp at her in disbelief. 'And I know you said you only wanted Llewella for the segment, but I wondered if we could do this interview together? You know, just from a branding point of view it would be good if we could be seen as a pair.'

I tried to project the idea that I really didn't want this to happen using telepathy. Fortunately, Jess made it very obvious she wasn't keen.

'I think,' she said, kindly but firmly, 'that since Llewella will be the one presenting the segment, it would be confusing to have the two of you do the interview today.'

Aretha had obviously been prepared for this response. 'Could I just sit on the sofa next to her and not say anything, then? I just think, even if it's only from a visual perspective, it would be good for everyone to know there are two of us involved in the blog.'

'I'll ask the producers,' Jess replied, to my horror. Aretha grinned, triumphant.

Mercifully, it transpired that 'asking the producers' was simply a stalling tactic. Jess finished her brief with me then left for a while, before returning to tell Aretha she was very sorry, but there was really no way she could come on set for the interview. She was, however, welcome to hang out in the green room after the show and meet some of its stars. I exhaled in relief.

Aretha, who had sat in surly silence with her arms folded ever since, was obviously unhappy about the situation but reconciled to defeat. I resolved to address that situation later and focus on the task ahead.

Sitting in front of the familiar glass table, the scene of the Quality Street altercation with Cyrus, I considered Kiara's earlier advice, writing the key points I wanted to get across during the interview in the notes app on my phone.

> • Toilets are a big thing for people with OCD and anxiety.
> • If they aren't clean or spacious it can ruin an otherwise great experience.
> • The poshness of a venue isn't always indicative of the quality of its loo.

I gazed up at the vast silver vending machine taking up most of the wall in front of where we were seated, as though it might provide me with additional inspiration. The woman I recognised as being in charge of microphones came in, looked at both of us and said, 'which one of you is Llewella?' I swear, for a moment, Aretha looked as though she was about to claim it was her.

I stood up, allowing a mic wire to be threaded down the collar of the yellow-and-black polka-dot mini-dress the stylist and I had eventually settled upon and the woman to clip the pack on to the back of my tights.

'Excuse me, darling,' she said, as she lifted up my dress to get to my tights' waistband. 'Nothing I haven't seen before!' Then, 'Just wait here and the floor manager will take you on in a minute.'

I stood awkwardly by the door, suddenly very aware of my hands and feet, just as Aretha said, 'You know, a dress with buttons was a very strange choice for someone as busty as you.'

I looked down, wondering if the buttons would gape and expose my bra to the nation as soon as I sat on the sofa and, if so, whether there was time to change.

There wasn't. A man emerged from a door to our right marked 'STUDIO' just then, his fingers pressed to his lips.

'Llewella?' I nodded. 'I'm Brian the floor manager. I'm going to take you in now, OK?'

Chapter 29

I tiptoed through the door, which led to a health and safety nightmare of wires and cables – the studio's 'backstage' area. There were small screens which showed the view through various cameras: Cyrus and Jemima from several angles; the weatherman, Darryl, poised for his turn; the show as seen by the audience at home on their television screens; as well as the autocue.

'Be careful of the wires and follow the arrows!' Brian whispered, pointing to various pieces of luminous white tape fashioned into crude arrows and pointing at two plastic chairs to the side of the set. I did as I was told, perching myself on one of the chairs, marvelling once again at how much smaller the *English Breakfast!* set seemed now I was actually in it. I could have lunged and caught the side of Cyrus's smirking cheek with my fingers.

'After the break,' Jemima was saying, 'has feminism gone too far?'

'YES!' shouted Cyrus, at which Jemima, her long blonde hair falling in perfectly sculpted waves, let out a 'what's he like?' titter. My hackles rose.

'We talk to a young chap who says he is scared to even *speak* to modern women and has set up an online community for men who want to reclaim their masculinity.'

'Plus,' Cyrus chimed in, 'has a substandard toilet ever ruined your night out at a restaurant, bar or club? We'll introduce the latest addition to the *English Breakfast!* team, our Toilet Investigator Llewella "Loo" Williams. Stay tuned.'

'OK, we've cut to commercials. Three minutes, everyone,' said a disembodied voice from somewhere behind a black curtain.

Brian reappeared at my shoulder. 'Follow me, Llewella, let's get you on set.'

He guided me to the famous red sofa, the scene of so many viral arguments and humiliations, just to the right of where Cyrus and Jemima usually sat at their glass desk.

'OK, if I can have you here, Llewella' – Brian thumped a cushion on one side of the sofa – 'then Cyrus and Jemima, can you sit over this side.'

'Two minutes!' came the disembodied voice again.

Jemima obediently trotted over to the sofa, teetering precariously in a skin-tight pencil skirt with a frill at the bottom and some pointed, nude patent pumps with high, slender heels. Cyrus continued to bellow orders at the production staff, ignoring Brian's instructions completely. Jemima sat down in a strange, stiff way, back poker-straight, legs pressed together.

'Control underwear,' she said by way of explanation, when she caught me staring. Yet another make-up person materialised from the wings and sprang into action, pulling brushes out of a black pinny which was tied around her waist and applying powder to Jemima's nose and forehead.

'You must be Loo.' She smiled, leaning forward with difficulty and offering her hand. 'Lovely to meet you.'

'One minute!' The voice was urgent and shrill, now.

I smiled thinly, a little overwhelmed by all the noise and

bustle, not to mentioned blinded by the bright studio lights which had been pointed directly at my face.

'You get used to it,' Jemima said kindly. 'Try to relax. It'll be over before you know it!'

'TWENTY SECONDS! Cyrus, we really need you on the sofa!' said the voice.

I heard Cyrus sigh, then felt the sofa groan as he plonked himself down.

'Hello again, Llewella,' he said, imperiously. 'Ready for the fray?'

A bald man wearing thick glasses stepped in front of the curtain and began a countdown. 'Ten, nine, eight, seven, six.' And then he fell silent, holding up his hand to indicate 'five' and losing a finger with each second that passed.

The time had come. I had no choice but to be ready for whatever Cyrus meant when he'd said 'the fray'.

'Welcome back.' Jemima was looking directly into camera three as she spoke and I followed her words on the autocue, hoping it would help me to relax.

'Now. Have you ever been to a lovely restaurant, bar or perhaps a museum and been disappointed by the state of their toilets? Did it take the shine off your experience? Well, we're joined by latest addition to the *English Breakfast!* team, eighteen-year-old Llewella Williams, who everyone calls "Loo" – I know! Isn't her name a happy coincidence!' [LAUGH]. She laughed. (It actually said that on the autocue.)

'Loo has created the hugely successful blog "Loo Reviews". Starting Monday, she'll be going undercover to investigate the toilets of some of London's most famous and poshest landmarks and reporting back to us. Those eating their breakfasts might want to look away! Welcome, Loo.'

'Thank you,' I replied, forcing the sides of my mouth up into what I hoped came across as a genuine smile.

'Can you explain to us how Loo Reviews got started and why you think toilets are so important?' Jemima asked.

I let go of the breath I'd been holding throughout her entire introduction, relieved she had started off with such an easy question.

'Well, I have an anxiety disorder, so for me and lots of other people things like whether a toilet is clean, or if there is enough space to not feel claustrophobic, are really important. Feeling trapped, especially around germs, is one of the most popular triggers for panic attacks.'

I cursed myself for using the phrase 'most popular', thinking I might have unwittingly trivialised the issue. I didn't have too long to dwell on it, however, before Cyrus jumped in.

'So, what would you say to those of us, and there are lots out there, who think this whole "mental health" thing has gone too far? I mean, previous generations have lived through wars without complaining and yet here you are moaning about having to go to the toilet somewhere that doesn't quite meet your standards. Isn't that just a sign that you're a snowflake who needs to grow up?'

I could hear my heartbeat thundering in my ears. My right knee began to tremble violently. I glanced down at it, hoping it wasn't shaking enough to be seen by the cameras. Both presenters seemed to sense the change in my demeanour. Cyrus raised his eyebrows expectantly. Jemima decided to rescue me.

'Well.' She chuckled. 'Loo's blog has had hundreds of thousands of views, so clearly there are just as many people in this country who feel the same way as her and of course we're delighted to be able to represent their concerns on *English Breakfast!*. Can you tell us, Loo, what kinds of things you'll be looking for in your investigations for us? What makes the perfect toilet?'

It took a tremendous effort, but I managed to swallow down my anger and focus my energy on answering Jemima's question.

'Aside from the obvious things, like they should be clean and smell nice, there are also little touches which make all the difference, like having relaxing music playing, or nice toiletries,' I answered, relieved to be back on familiar ground but wishing all descriptive words other than 'nice' hadn't fallen out of my brain. 'But I think the main thing for me is space. There are so many toilets I can barely squeeze myself into and it makes me feel really trapped. And I always think "what would I do if I was larger?"'

'Ha!' Cyrus interrupted, slapping his knee as though I'd just told a hilarious joke. 'I think the majority of sensible people who watch this programme would agree that if you're OBESE' – he spat the word, sending spittle flying to the corners of his mouth – 'you shouldn't be eating in a restaurant anyway. I mean, I've said it for a long time – if a barmaid can turn you away from a pub for being visibly drunk, why can't waiters refuse to serve food to fat people?'

I thought immediately of lovely Kiara, with her polycystic ovaries, who would no doubt be watching on the tiny screen in the corner of the make-up room. And then I thought about all the people watching at home who might be fat because they're poorly, or sad, or have an eating disorder, or just because they're built like that and don't give a fuck about society's stupid beauty standards.

Then I thought about myself, just under a year ago, not technically obese but chunkier than I had believed was ideal. So much had happened since September. Was I any happier, or healthier now I was a few sizes smaller?

No, I realised, abruptly. I wasn't. I'd been carrying around so many unfounded beliefs about what would make my life better – being thinner; changing my blog; forging a friendship with someone who didn't conform to the Chiddy archetypes. Yet, in reality, gaining the things I thought I'd wanted had meant sacrificing the things that made me, me. I'd started the school year full of feminist determination and, somewhere along the line, I'd become a person who put a chocolate back in its bowl and ignored the protests of her grumbling stomach because a man told her to. The same man who was now sneering in my direction, thinking he was too clever for me to clap back.

And just like that, I wasn't in control any more . . .

CYRUS PEYTON FINALLY PUT IN HIS PLACE BY TEEN TOILET INSPECTOR

CYRUS PEYTON CLASHES WITH OUTSPOKEN SCHOOLGIRL OVER 'FATPHOBIC' COMMENTS

OUCH! SIXTH-FORMER LOO WILLIAMS DELIVERS KILLER BLOW AFTER CYRUS PEYTON TAKES A 'CHEAP SHOT' AT FAT PEOPLE

Those were the more positive headlines, which had begun to pop up online just minutes after my TV debut. Also in the mix were:

ENOUGH! CYRUS PEYTON SPEAKS FOR THE NATION WHEN HE SAYS IT'S TIME TO STOP PANDERING TO FAT PEOPLE

HAS CYRUS PEYTON UNCOVERED THE ULTIMATE CURE FOR THE OBESITY CRISIS?

And, perhaps most distressingly:

NOT ANOTHER ONE! LLEWELLA WILLIAMS, LATEST GENERATION Z SNOWFLAKE TO BE GIVEN UNDESERVED AIRTIME
When will the Woke Brigade give us all a break?
asks our columnist Peter Sullivan

This last one was, of course, the article I felt compelled to click on. It was strange, I reflected, how we are drawn to criticism more than praise. For all the hundreds of people on social media applauding me for 'sticking it' to Cyrus, it was the comments from trolls who told me I was a fat, ugly, woke feminazi which I read again and again until it was like they were etched on to the backs of my eyelids.

An unflattering picture of me on the *English Breakfast!* sofa, mid-sentence, mouth agape, eyes blazing furiously filled the screen. Underneath:

As *English Breakfast!* introduced its latest attempt to portray itself as 'down with the kids' – a gobby, self-entitled teen named Llewella Williams – I shook my head in despair. When will this mollycoddling of young people, this glorifying of the offence they feel towards the rest of us simply for existing end, I asked myself?

Apparently not any time soon. Llewella Williams is a privately educated, mixed-race, feminist 'blogger' (heaven help us) who has somehow managed to amass a following amounting to hundreds of thousands by writing about the state of the nation's toilets. The A Level student, who claims to suffer from 'anxiety' (who doesn't, these days?) deems British public loos to be below her exacting standards, something she says contributes to her 'symptoms'.

Her 'anxiety' didn't stop her from giving Cyrus Peyton (just about the only TV commentator brave enough to say what we're all thinking, these days) a piece of her mind in front of *English Breakfast!*'s 1.5 million viewers this morning. Williams didn't hold back, firing a selection of Gen Z clichés at the presenter, accusing him of being everything from 'fatphobic' (whatever that means) to deliberately contributing to the stigma which apparently surrounds mental health issues. Evidence of this 'stigma' is, incidentally, scant, since everyone from royalty to Z-list celebrities have been bleating about their dull-as-dishwater 'struggles' for the past decade.

***

I slammed my laptop shut, thumping my mattress for wont of a better way to express my frustration.

After my 'outburst', in which I'd told Cyrus in no uncertain terms what I thought about his views on mental illness and body image, he'd grinned. I understood why – I'd done exactly what he'd wanted me to do and what Kiara had tried to warn me about in the stairwell: I'd taken the bait.

Jemima had intercepted his reply, claiming that was all they had time for but that she was sure I would be invited back for 'round two' soon. Then she and Cyrus were moving seamlessly over to the desk to interview the guy who thought feminism had gone too far via Zoom.

When they cut to the ad break, Brian the Floor Manager had assured me I'd done 'really well'.

As we passed the desk, Jemima gave me her kind and, I now recognised, kind-of defeated smile and mouthed 'see you soon'. Cyrus had stood up, done a military style salute and said, 'it's all pantomime, you know. No hard feelings.'

Aretha had seemed intent on getting back home to Surrey as quickly as possible, despite Jess's offer for us to stay and mingle after the show. She was quiet in the car, which I didn't have the energy to try and interpret.

I hadn't been able to face going back to St Edith's for the afternoon. Our school's no-phones policy was no match for anything which went viral on TikTok, like my 'spat' with Cyrus had. I didn't feel up to answering the inevitable questions. Instead, I'd come home, defiantly grabbed some Pringles from the kitchen and munched them on

253

my bed while flicking through the fall-out on social media.

My followers had jumped up by almost 3,000. I had several DMs from journalists asking if they could interview me and allow me to 'expand the thoughts' I'd expressed on air. None of this was inherently bad, as such. In fact, there was part of me that was proud of myself.

In many ways, I was simply being true to form – no one who knew me well would describe me as backwards in coming forwards with an opinion. At least not prior to the past nine months, when hunger and anxiety had rendered me a lot less spirited. So why did I have this niggling sense of doubt? Why, instead of exhilarated, did I feel tired and deflated?

I was turning over this question while absent-mindedly drawing a sketch of an eye on one of my notepads when I heard the front door slam. This was followed by various *thunk*s as Hugh went through his daily routine of dropping his school bag, whipping off his smelly shoes, chucking them vaguely in the direction of the shoe cupboard and making his way to the kitchen in search of sustenance.

After a few minutes, I heard his footsteps thundering up the stairs. Considering he weighed about nine stone wet-through, Hugh really made a racket just walking around. To my surprise, he didn't charge past my bedroom door to slam his own and only emerge from his XBox-centric boy-cave to eat or use the bathroom like usual, but instead knocked on my door.

'Yeah.' I sighed, steeling myself for the piss-taking session which would inevitably follow.

Hugh cautiously poked his head around the door, as if not quite sure what to expect. When he saw me sitting alone on the bed, his face broke into an impish grin.

'All right?' he asked.

'Sure. You?' I replied, reflexively.

'Everyone was talking about you at school today.'

'Look, Hugh—' I began, wondering if I could somehow delay this until I was feeling better.

'You're a HERO!' Hugh interrupted.

'Wait. What?' I was genuinely shocked. Hugh took a few tentative steps into the room.

'Mia said everyone at St Edith's is stanning you. Even the boys at my school are, like, "respect, your sister's all right."' I stared at him with wide, disbelieving eyes. He, in turn, took a few more steps towards me, reached the bed and perched on the edge, with his back to me.

'It's true, you know,' his back said.

'What's true?' I asked. He twisted round and looked at me, if not exactly in the eye, at least somewhere around my earlobe.

'Look, don't make me say it again, OK?' He blushed. 'Just . . . I'm proud of you. For standing up for yourself. What that Cyrus guy said, it wasn't right. And the way you went for him, you were so, I dunno . . . calm and eloquent.'

'Really?' This was news to me. I'd felt anything but calm and eloquent at the time.

'You know you were! I told Mia you're only so good at arguing because of all the practising on me.'

'Oh, so you're taking credit for me now, are you?' We grinned at each other.

'Yeah, well. Maybe I don't say it enough. Or, you know, like, at all. But I'm glad you're my sister.'

I couldn't help myself, then. Even though he protested, his cries of 'geddoff!' muffled by my sweatshirt, I leapt on my brother and gave him the most enormous hug.

Chapter 30

'You've really come on leaps and bounds since Christmas.' Linda smiled, indicating the open notebook on her lap. 'You were having two, sometimes three panic attacks a day when you first came back here and now you say you're down to one a week. You seem much happier in yourself. Do you feel that way?'

'I do, actually,' I replied. 'Thank you for all your help.'

'Don't thank me. You were the one who did it. Thank yourself,' said Linda and I rolled my eyes, but gave myself a little internal high-five all the same. 'Now, considering the progress you've made, I think it's time to revisit the conversation we had about your father three years ago.'

Her words were like being slapped with a wet fish. There was a sudden ringing in my ears and the room seemed to shrink. *Anything,* my brain protested. *Get her talking about anything but that.*

'Well, actually,' I tried, and failed, to keep my tone light, 'I still haven't talked to Aretha so maybe we can focus on that today?'

'You know what you have to say to Aretha,' Linda insisted, firmly. 'You've written it down. I feel confident we've prepared you for that as much as we can. Now, to stop you relapsing, it's important we address the root cause of your anxiety.'

'But—' I began to protest.

Linda held up a hand. 'I know you don't want to talk about it, but unless we get it out, it will stay inside you, Llewella. We discussed this before, remember? Our traumas are like little bags of poison we carry inside us and when you talk about them in therapy, it's like sticking a needle in them and draining the toxicity—'

'But if you ignore them, they burst anyway, when you least expect it,' I finished for her.

'Exactly. I promise I won't push you too far, but we're going to need to go outside of your comfort zone, OK?'

I nodded, already feeling a pressure at the back of my eyes, a sure sign tears would follow.

'Now, make sure you're sitting comfortably. You're safe here, OK?'

'OK.'

'Tell me again what your mother said and how it made you feel.'

Mum had come home from work late. I think she might have been slightly drunk, but not enough for me to register anything unusual – she often had a few glasses of wine at the gallery while entertaining potential buyers.

She'd called me down to the kitchen. She'd made hot chocolate and Kate Bush was playing softly from the record player in the next room. The French windows were open and the night beyond was vast and starless.

'Llewella,' she'd said, sitting at the kitchen table and motioning at the chair opposite her. 'I've been meaning to talk to you about something.'

God knows why she picked that particular night. There was

nothing extraordinary about it, that I can remember. It had been a normal sort of day at school in Year 10. Nothing out of the ordinary had occurred. It wasn't, as far as I knew, a significant anniversary.

'I feel that you are old enough now to know the truth,' she'd continued as I, sensing that this was going to be more serious than one of Mum's more regular conversational whims, stared at the tiny marshmallows floating on top of my hot chocolate. Three pink. Two white.

'I'm not going to lie to you, I was expecting you would have tried to get in touch with your father before now.'

'I don't want to,' I'd reassured her, like I had on so many occasions before.

'I know you say you feel that way now,' Mum replied calmly, in a way that I'd remembered thinking was quite patronising. Why couldn't she just take my word for it? 'But if you do change your mind, there is something you should know.'

Mum took a deep breath, blowing on her own hot chocolate, making to take a sip and then changing her mind.

'I know I told you that he didn't know I was pregnant when he disappeared but . . . that isn't quite true.'

My head had snapped up, even though I don't remember telling it to. 'He knew about me?'

'He did.'

It was Mum's turn to have her head down, her chin wobbling slightly, looking as though she was battling some internal demons. 'Well, he didn't ever meet you. You know, on the outside of my tummy. But he did know I was expecting.'

'Oh,' was all I could think of to say in response.

'And, for a long time I really didn't know where he disappeared to. I assumed he'd gone back to wherever he was originally from.'

'You really can't remember that?' I'd asked this question a hundred times before.

'I really can't, carriad. I'm sorry. Like I said, somewhere in Asia.'

'It's a massive continent, Mum.'

'I know. It must have been South Asia. He was brown. And so beautiful . . . Anyway' – she shook her head from side to side as though to clear it – 'we've been over this already.' A beat of silence. 'I never slagged your dad off in front of you. Never hid the truth, either. You do understand that?'

'I understand, Mum. You did the right thing.'

She nodded once, sucking in my reassurance like it was a shot of vodka, fortifying her for what she had to say next.

'You were so sure, even when you were little, you wanted nothing to do with him. So, when I found out he had come back, I didn't tell you.'

'What do you mean, came back?' I asked.

'He moved back to the UK when you were ten. He wrote to me. Asked if he could see you. I told him no.'

I stood up, scraping my chair. I made for the kitchen door, my escape route back to the safety of my room, but Mum blocked my path, gripping my shoulders.

'I did it for all the right reasons,' she insisted. 'He wasn't here, all that time we were struggling, on our own, you and I. I did everything by myself. Then he wanted to be a part of your life, this wonderful human I had brought up alone and I thought "he doesn't deserve you."'

Mum had got it wrong, though. She thought I was angry with her for telling my dad he couldn't see me. I wasn't. I wasn't even particularly bothered that she hadn't told me, or given me the option to decide for myself, at the time.

It was something else entirely which made me shake Mum's hands away, push past her and run up the stairs. It was for a different reason we had never discussed since, but instead attempted, by unspoken agreement, to continue our lives as though that conversation had never happened.

I'd spent my whole life thinking my dad didn't know I existed. It was a blissful ignorance I'd worn like a warm winter coat.And now it had been ripped away from me and I was shivering in the harshness of the realisation that for ten whole years my father knew he had a child and hadn't even tried to get in touch. And when he had, all it took was one rejection from my mum to send him scuttling back into denial.

It wasn't that he didn't know about me. He didn't *want* me.

And suddenly, everything I'd ever felt about being alien and different – of being darker than the other girls at school but not dark enough to legitimately call myself a person of colour, of not being part of a normal family, of being toweringly tall and plump and awkward and not like other teenagers; a misfit who belonged nowhere – came rushing to the surface, engulfing me like a wave until I was gasping for breath.

That was the day I'd had my very first panic attack.

'You are allowed to be angry with your mother.' Linda's gentle voice jolted me back to the present.

'I love my mum,' I replied, snatching a handful of tissues from the table ledge and blowing my nose.

'We can be angry at the people we love. It doesn't mean we love them any less.'

I wiped away the mascara which had snaked its way down my face, carried by my tears.

'I'm angry at the situation.'

'OK,' Linda said softly. 'And what is it about the situation in particular that makes you angry?'

I tried to speak, but the words got stuck. Instead, a strange, strangled wail emerged and I collapsed forward, hugging myself, my nose almost colliding with my knees.

The sentiment remained unspoken, locked away in my chest:

'I am angry with myself. I'm angry because I push people who care about me away. I'm angry because the one person I let in was toxic and for a long time I couldn't admit my mistake. I'm angry for all the time and energy and money and self-esteem I lost trying to make it work because I had to prove that the problem wasn't me. I'm angry because I'm the only teenage girl in the world who doesn't have a best friend.

'I'm angry, and the only thing I can do with that anger is put it into campaigns and try to make the world a bit better because there's nowhere else for it to go. The people at school don't want me. My dad didn't want me.

'I'm angry because I wasted so much time believing I was impossible to love.'

Chapter 31

As I opened my locker, a piece of card fell out and fluttered to the floor. I bent to scoop it up. It was covered in hand-drawn stars, decorated with multi-coloured glitter. I turned it over and read:

> Loo
> I know we haven't been talking and it's weird between us, but I wanted to tell you how proud I am of everything you've achieved with Loo Reviews and English Breakfast!
> Also, I miss you. I'm sorry we had that fight. Please call or text me.
> Love
> Olivia

It dawned on me, in that instant, why the new school motto, 'actions speak louder than words', had seemed so significant to me. Because while Aretha had always soothed and fussed and pretended to understand when anxiety had rendered me incapable of functioning, when things had gone well for me she'd become cold and distant. Or worse, thrown a jealous tantrum.

We're always taught a 'friend in need is a friend indeed', but what about when you're celebrating a win? Real friends, I now understood, were the ones who could be happy for you in the good times, rather than seeing your successes as a reflection of their own inadequacies. In one simple gesture, Olivia had shown what my relationship with Aretha had been missing.

Checking no teachers were nearby, I furtively pulled out my phone and fired off two texts. One was to Olivia. I thanked her for the card, told her I was so sorry for how I'd spoken to her, I missed her too and asked if we could meet up soon.

The other, to Aretha, read:

We need to talk. I'll come to yours after class.

I lifted my hand to knock on Aretha's bedroom door, then lowered it again. Could I do this? I knew already, somewhere deep down, that nothing I said would change Aretha's perspective. I was never going to get a sorry, or a moment of realisation. Self-reflection wasn't her style. But this wasn't about her. I had things I needed to say.

It was as though I could hear Kiara in my ear as I remembered her words: *work out what you want to say in advance and just say it . . . It's easy to get side-tracked and then before you know it, it's over and all you've done is have an argument.*

I patted the piece of paper in my pocket, took a deep breath and knocked.

Aretha opened the door, face like thunder, nodded once and turned and walked into the house without saying anything. She spun round to face me once she was a couple of metres away, one hand on her hip and chin jutting out. She was waiting for me to apologise. I almost laughed.

'I've come to say I don't think we should carry on with Aretha and Loo,' I announced. 'I think what we want from the brand are very different things. I'm sorry it hasn't worked out.'

She hadn't been expecting that. She stared at me for a moment, looking wrong-footed.

'Look, this is what's called a "creative difference" in my industry,' she eventually replied. 'They happen all the time. I'm sure we can work through it. I'm not comfortable with just abandoning Aretha and Loo. After all, I could be going on tour again this summer but I chose not to. I chose to dedicate time to our brand. You have to think about it from my perspective.'

It would be so easy to give in. Unexpectedly, an image of Jemima popped into my head, her tiny body bent at strange angles as it was pummelled into submission by the painfully restrictive garments she wore every day. The way she glazed over whenever Cyrus said something hideous, or made a sexist 'joke', forcing herself to sweep aside any offence or indignation and smile in the name of 'entertainment'. *You get used to it,* she had told me. How many small sacrifices had she made to end up with that daily horror as her normal? If I let Aretha talk me around now, one day I'd wake up and not recognise myself.

'That's the problem, Aretha!' I shouted, startling both her and myself. 'All I have done since we met is try to see things from your perspective! And it's made me feel like shit!'

'Well, yes.' Aretha remained calm, making to put her hand on mine and looking confused when I snatched it away. 'I don't think this situation – you getting lucky with *English Breakfast!* – has bought out the best in either of us, if I'm honest.'

Wendy was stood before me in my mind's eye now; the memory of her saying *if anyone should be on telly, it's you.*

Wendy had known me since I was five. She knew I deserved this chance. I drew on her certainty.

'It wasn't just luck, though,' I retorted. Aretha started to shake her head, but I put my hand on her shoulder, forcing her to look me in the eye. 'I need you to understand this. I'm not saying luck and privilege don't exist or that I haven't benefitted from them.'

'Right!' Aretha nodded, as though I was a dog who had just mastered the 'fetch' command.

'BUT, privilege takes lots of forms.' Wow. I didn't even know where that came from as soon as I said it, I knew just how true it was. 'It's not like because my mum has money I've never struggled with anything. I've also worked really hard. And I'm talented.'

'I'm just as good as you.'

I thought back to how Aretha had been in the toilets in that bar in Hoxton, showing me a glimpse of what was behind her arrogant mask. She didn't really believe what she just said. She didn't think she was clever or deserved her place at St Edith's. I reminded myself to be kind.

'At loads of things, yes,' I replied. 'In fact, you're better at quite a few things than I am. But not at writing and not at presenting. And that's what this opportunity is. That's what it's always been all about. I deserve this.'

'You wouldn't even have this opportunity without me!' Aretha's eyes were blazing. She was furious.

'I . . . I don't know how you reached that conclusion.' I could feel my heart hammering in my chest.

'You really think *English Breakfast!* would have wanted the version of you I met in September? The fat one with shit clothes who could barely speak?'

Mum was with me, now. I could almost feel her arms around my shoulders. What was it she had said . . .? *The losing weight, the accessories, fashion, make-up – it's just icing on a cake. You're the sponge. And you've always been a beautiful sponge.*

'That's the thing, Aretha. I could speak. I could. Just not in front of you. You never met the real me. I was a bit fat and I didn't care how I dressed but . . . I was happier than after you changed me.'

Aretha actually gasped.

'I deserve this,' I repeated, 'and I'm going to go for it and I'm not going to feel bad.'

'Right.' I noticed Aretha's expression shift. It was as though there was suddenly a glass wall between us. 'So all that stuff you say about wanting to change the world is bollocks, then? You're giving up on your so-called principles the first time someone offers you a TV gig? Good to know who you really are, Loo.'

I'd actually believed this myself, for a while. But then I remembered what Ms Tidwell had said to me, back when she was telling me off for coming by her office with a new petition virtually every week. Narrowing my focus wasn't the same as 'giving up'.

Aretha, sneering now, carried on. 'You're so selfish. All that talk about this TV thing being an opportunity for us both, then you have a go at the presenter! I will never get invited back to *English Breakfast!*, now!'

All the masks she'd worn were gone, now. This was the real Aretha Jones in front of me and every word she spoke just served

267

to show me how right it was that I was here, officially ending whatever the relationship between us had been.

'This was never really a friendship,' I said. 'I'm going to go now.'

'So, you're just going to abandon me when you know I have bipolar? After everything I did to support you? Nice.'

I still didn't know whether Aretha was faking mental illness, but I was sure she was capable of it. Either way, it wasn't a reason to keep putting up with her bullshit. When I opened my mouth to reply, Linda's words came out. 'You might be in a hole right now, but if I jump in with you it doesn't help either of us.'

'What the hell are you talking about?'

'Think about it,' I said, knowing she wouldn't. I turned to leave. As I reached the threshold, I couldn't resist adding, 'I know, by the way, that you didn't go on tour last summer.'

Aretha launched herself at me then, making an anguished noise. 'Get out!' she yelled. 'I never want to see you again!'

And with that, she slammed the door in my face.

It was like I floated down the stairs, out of Aretha's house and down the street. It felt so surreal to have done it. I reached the corner and leaned against a lamppost, inhaling huge lungfuls of air and waiting for my heart to stop pounding. I reached into my pocket and took out the piece of paper. It was starting to get a bit greasy and floppy where I'd opened and refolded it so many times.

It was Nain's words written there and kept close.

That's the sign of a good relationship – you know it's right if you can be yourself.

I could feel Nain's approval, radiating across the miles.

I squared my shoulders and carried on walking towards home. I wasn't alone. Mum, Nain, Linda, Kiara, Wendy, Crystal, Ms Tidwell and Olivia were all with me in spirit. I imagined them giving me a round of applause, this army of supportive women who had each, in their own way, helped me out of the hole.

I was free.

Results Day

'For in companions that do converse and waste the time together,
Whose souls do bear the equal yoke of love,
There must needs be a like proportion
Of lineaments, of manners and of spirit.'

The Merchant of Venice
Act 3, Scene 4

Chapter 32

'Oh my GOD, will you SHUT UP and let me go to SLEEEEEEEEEP!'

I'd been trying all night to reason with my brain silently, inside my head, but had eventually given up and resorted to talking to myself aloud. Like you do.

I glanced at Mrs Potts. It was 3 a.m. Reconciled to the idea I wasn't going to drift off, no matter how many guided meditations I tried on YouTube, I heaved myself out of bed. I opened the curtains and surveyed the back garden, which was bathed in moonlight. Fiona managed to frighten the absolute crap out of me by creeping into my bedroom in ninja-like silence and leaping up on to the window sill. I recovered myself and stroked her silky-smooth head as she too looked down at the garden, no doubt seeing all manner of wildlife goings-on invisible to me with my rubbish human eyes.

I'd got a conditional offer from my first-choice university – Durham – to study English. I needed two As and a B. I'd been predicted three A*s, but that was before the 'dip' in my academic performance. Still, I'd tried my hardest and I knew, logically, that was all I could do.

Yet, my ridiculous brain, which had miraculously managed to remain calm during the actual taking of the exams, was now freaking out totally. What if I had failed? What if I couldn't go to university? What if that set off a chain of catastrophic events which ruined the whole of my life and I died full of bitterness and regret?

I shook my hands, which had gone numb, and looked at Fiona for inspiration.

'Distraction! You're right, Fiona. That's what I need,' I said, wondering if talking to your cat in full sentences was one of the indicators of a breakdown.

I opened my laptop and scrolled through my inbox, searching for anything to take my mind off . . . well, my mind. There was the email from Jess, explaining that we could record all my Loo Review segments for the autumn term of university during the summer holidays, meaning I wouldn't have to travel back from (hopefully) Durham once a month. There was also confirmation of the agreed fee, an amount which would mean, when coupled with my student loan, I wouldn't have to get a part time job at university and could focus totally on my studies. Result.

I clicked on Spotify. Our school had an account and the cast of *Merchant* had made a playlist of songs whose themes vaguely matched those of the play. *Might as well prod that wound,* I thought, masochistically, as I plugged in my headphones. It would at least give me something other than exam results to feel stressed about.

I pressed 'shuffle'. The track selected was called 'Tokyo I'm Yours' by a band called Fire&Lights. I laid back and closed my eyes, my foot starting to tap involuntarily along with the beat. It had a pleasing, cheerful melody full of keyboard and synth. I could have happily bopped along unthinkingly for a while, were it not for the lyrics:

I pull my collar up, I got my hair in my face
So no one can see.
Feel like I'm choking up, I never knew
How broken my heart could be ...
... I'll give you my heart
I'll give you my soul
I'll leave them in the city streets
Every time I close my eyes, I'm losing control
Don't you hear my cold heart beat?
I don't wanna feel like this

I could see why the *Merchant* cast had chosen it. The lyrics perfectly summed up Antonio's relationship with Bassanio, a person he literally puts his life on the line for and is rewarded by finding himself the unwanted point in an awkward love triangle. But the resonance of the words went deeper than that, for me. They also seemed to articulate how anxiety made me feel on the bad days and how I'd once felt about Aretha.

It was the sort of song you know you're going to immediately play again the second it finishes. The sort of lyrics you could see yourself idly doodling on lever-arch files and notepads in moments of lapsed concentration in class. I let it wash over me, the piano becoming more dramatic, the singer's voice becoming stronger, building to a crescendo. And then, the words which made my eyes spring open as I sat bolt upright, grabbing at my own throat as though to stem the tide of emotion they inspired:

When I lose myself
In the dark and rain
I turn toward the lights
And I am found again

It was like he was singing directly to me. For a minute there, I really did lose my grip on everything – my school work, my passions, my sense of who I was. When you're lost, it feels like you can flail around forever trying to make it right and only ever find yourself in perpetual darkness. But really you're just under a cloud.

The thing about clouds is, they pass. And, if you're very lucky, you have some lights to guide you home.

The *Merchant* playlist was about an hour long in total and I played it twice, occasionally jumping from foot-to-foot in an approximation of dancing to try and burn off some of my nervous energy, before padding downstairs to forage for something to eat. I didn't really feel like food, but all my experience of anxiety told me skipping breakfast made it worse. Mum had, in an unprecedented move, taken the morning off work to come with me to collect my results.

'Big day for you, carriad,' she said, opening cupboard doors and taking out coffee, mugs and the other complicated bits of machinery she used to make herself a fancy cappuccino every morning.

'Yeah,' I replied, noncommittally.

Mum stopped what she was doing and pulled me into a hug so fierce it caught me off guard.

'Whatever happens today, know that I am so proud of you. I never could have imagined I'd make such a brilliant daughter.'

'Thanks, Mum,' I murmured into her hair. 'And thank you. You know. For everything.'

She pulled back and looked at me. We stood there, in a half-embrace, a thousand unspoken words passing between us. I knew she understood that I'd made peace with what she'd told me about my father and that one day I'd be ready to hear her side of the story. It was enough, for now.

Mum insisted on driving me the mile or so to St Edith's, even though I'd walked there every day for the past seven years.

When we arrived, Mum waited in the car so as not to 'cramp my style' (as though such a thing were even theoretically possible, from either point of view).

Grace, Sam and a few of their gang were sitting on the front steps clutching ripped envelopes in one hand and their expensive handbags in the other. Some of them looked jubilant, others crushed.

'Hey, Loo.' Grace waved. She'd been incredibly nice to me, since Cyrus-gate. Hugh hadn't been wrong about it increasing my popularity and I now had the sort of social currency which she found appealing. Unfortunately for her, she wasn't selling anything I wanted to buy.

'Hi.' I smiled, waving back as I passed because why not?

As I approached the entrance, I saw a familiar mass of soft, silver-blonde curls. I hovered by the revolving door, unsure of what to do. The last time I'd spoken to Aretha, she'd told me she never wanted to see me again. We'd managed this just fine. We were on study leave, after all, so it was easy to avoid one another.

Even during the English exam, I'd only caught the back of her head as she, with her surname far ahead of mine in the alphabet, had been ushered into the hall in single-filed silence in front of me.

As Aretha emerged, I wondered if I had time to make a run for it. Even if I'd wanted to, my feet seemed to be glued to the floor. And then it was too late. Aretha was there and neither of us had anywhere to hide. She caught my eye.

'Hi, babe,' she said, almost in a whisper. Then she looked over at Dawn, who was waiting by the roadside, and shook her head sadly. I understood what that gesture meant – her results weren't good.

I looked down at her, so much smaller in reality, somehow, than she had become in my mind.

You have no power over me. I thought, once again summoning the line from *Labyrinth* I'd chanted to myself back in Year 10, when I was trying to convince Linda I didn't need any help. This time, though, it was true.

The world isn't divided into heroes and villains like it is in films, though. It's just full of flawed people, trying their best to get by. And while I knew there was no chance of salvaging the ruins of our friendship, if I carried an Aretha-shaped grudge with me into the next phase of my life, that was just another bag of poison I'd have to deal with one day.

'Good luck. With everything,' I said to her, as she clomped away on her chunky heels. And I surprised myself by meaning it.

'Loo!' I turned to see Olivia running up the steps, late as usual, half-tripping over the hem of her maxi dress. 'WHAT DID YOU GET?'

I laughed, thinking, not for the first time, that she was the human equivalent of a Labrador puppy.

'I haven't been in yet.'

'Oh, cool! We can get ours together! And then some of us from drama are going to the pub. You'll come, won't you? Say you will!' Olivia broke into an impromptu kind of twerk which made me burst out laughing. I nodded.

All this time, Olivia had been right there showing me what true friendship is. I'd just been too self-absorbed to notice her properly. I'd be appreciating the hell out of her from now on.

Linking arms, we each used our free hand to push the door. I saw it, then – the blazer on a mannequin in the entrance hall, the new motto stitched defiantly on its left breast.

Facta non verba.

I'd done it. I'd finally fixed an injustice.

OK, so it was a team effort . . . In fact, if it had been left to me it never would have happened at all. But it wasn't who got the glory that was important.

I blinked away a happy tear as I thought of generations of St Edith's pupils to come, who'd have 'Actions Speak Louder than Words' on their pockets as they marched up the hill at the beginning of the day, or sat in assembly, or listened to a teacher drone on about Henry the sodding VIII. All because of our student council. It was a victory we would forever share and could be proud of. Maybe teamwork wasn't so terrible.

And I knew, then, that whatever was waiting for me on the other side, whatever letters were inside the envelope with my name on it, I was going to be OK.

A note from the author

If reading this book has made you want to get yourself acquainted with Shakespeare's *The Merchant of Venice*, then that makes me really happy. However, I should warn you that some of the characters in it are incredibly anti-Semitic, so it's not an easy read.

I played Antonio in a school production of Merchant when I was Llewella's age and we had a brilliant director, a teacher called Dr Cochran. He explained that there were two ways of interpreting the play. A straightforward reading is that Portia and Bassanio are the heroes and Shylock gets what he deserves. However, Dr Cochran argued that Shylock behaves as he does because of all the racism he has faced (and that Jews living in Venice at that time would have experienced) and that his hatred of Antonio is understandable in that context.

Ultimately, Merchant is a play about the importance of being kind to others because, as my mum would say, 'you meet the same people going up as you do coming down.'

Further Support and Advice

If, like Llewella, you struggle with anxiety, panic attacks, or your relationship with food and your body, please know you are not alone. Also, please don't Google it. (There are three billion people on the internet and, unsurprisingly, not all of them know what they're talking about when it comes to mental health.) Below are some organisations I recommend who can give you safe, confidential support and evidence-based information:

The Mix (themix.org.uk)
A free, confidential service for 13–25 year olds, covering everything from homelessness to finding a job, from money to mental health, from break-ups to drugs.

Young Minds (youngminds.org.uk)
The UK's leading charity fighting for children and young people's mental health.

Student Space (studentspace.org.uk)
Advice, information and support for anyone in higher education.

Beat (beatingeatingdisorders.org.uk)
The UK's leading eating disorder charity.

Help for England
Helpline: 0808 801 0677
Email: help@beateatingdisorders.org.uk

Help for Scotland
Helpline: 0808 801 0432
Email: Scotlandhelp@beateatingdisorders.org.uk

Help for Wales
Helpline: 0808 801 0433
Email: Waleshelp@beateatingdisorders.org.uk

Help for Northern Ireland
Helpline: 0808 801 0434
Email: NIhelp@beateatingdisorders.org.uk

Acknowledgments

When I present to parents or schools on mental health, I make the point that we often discuss 'resilience' as though it's a character trait when in fact it's a by-product of being well supported. Llewella couldn't have overcome the challenges she faces were it not for the fact that she is surrounded by incredible women (and the occasional man – shout out to Taid!) who guide and look out for her. So, it's fitting that Toxic would never have existed were it not for the fact that I have been supported by some exceptionally brilliant women:

First of all, the young women in my mental-health focus groups who said they wished they'd been taught about how to negotiate toxic friendships at school – you're where the idea for this novel came from.

My agent (and legend) Anna Pallai, who was the first person I spoke to when I knew I wanted to write a work of fiction and who believed in and advised on Toxic from day one.

Claire Eastham, who was the first person I gave the manuscript to read before sending it to publishers and who said, 'F*ck yeah! This is the best thing you have ever done!' Thank you for giving me confidence.

Hazel Holmes and the team at UCLAN Publishing, who took on Toxic during 'the great acquisition freeze' (basically meaning that no one who wasn't already a really well-known author was getting a book deal because of COVID) – thank you for believing this was a good enough novel to cut through in difficult times.

Emma Roberts, the editor who made the words I originally wrote (much) better. Thank you for diving headfirst into Llewella's world and immediately understanding who she is and why I wanted to tell her story.

And finally, my mum, the wisest woman I know. There's a little bit of you in Cerys, in Nain and in Linda.

Thanks also to Chris Russell, for lending me some of his lyrics and giving fans of his Songs About a Girl trilogy a Toxic Easter egg!

About the Author

Natasha Devon MBE is an activist, writer and presenter. She tours schools, universities and events throughout the world, delivering talks as well as conducting research on mental health, body image, gender & equality. She has a show on LBC and writes regularly for Grazia Magazine.

Photo by Alex Cameron.

Natasha is a trustee for the charity Student Minds, an ambassador for the Reading Agency and a patron for No Panic, which helps people experiencing anxiety. She is also an ambassador for Glitch; a charity which promotes digital citizenship, helping marginalised communities stay emotionally safe online. She is a certified instructor for

Mental Health First Aid England and eating disorder charity Beat.

In 2018, Natasha co-founded 'Where's Your Head At', a campaign aimed at improving the mental health of British workers through education and law change. She is also founder of the Mental Health Media Charter, which scrutinises media reporting on mental health with the aim of reducing stigma.

Her book *A Beginner's Guide to Being Mental: An A-Z* was published by Bluebird in 2018, followed by *Yes You Can: Ace Your Exams Without Losing Your Mind in 2020*. This is Natasha's first novel.

Find out more at www.natashadevon.com

HAVE YOU EVER WONDERED HOW BOOKS ARE MADE?

UCLan Publishing is an award winning independent publisher specialising in Children's and Young Adult books. Based at The University of Central Lancashire, this Preston-based publisher teaches MA Publishing students how to become industry professionals using the content and resources from its business; students are included at every stage of the publishing process and credited for the work that they contribute.

The business doesn't just help publishing students though. UCLan Publishing has supported the employability and real-life work skills for the University's Illustration, Acting, Translation, Animation, Photography, Film & TV students and many more. This is the beauty of books and stories; they fuel many other creative industries! The MA Publishing students are able to get involved from day one with the business and they acquire a behind the scenes experience of what it is like to work for a such a reputable independent.

The MA course was awarded a Times Higher Award (2018) for Innovation in the Arts and the business, UCLan Publishing, was awarded Best Newcomer at the Independent Publishing Guild (2019) for the ethos of teaching publishing using a commercial publishing house. As the business continues to grow, so too does the student experience upon entering this dynamic Masters course.

www.uclanpublishing.com
www.uclanpublishing.com/courses/
uclanpublishing@uclan.ac.uk